BREACH OF PRIVILEGE

BREACH OF PRIVILEGE

A Brock and Poole Mystery

Graham Ison

This first world edition published 2009
in Great Britain and in the USA by
SEVERN HOUSE PUBLISHERS LTD of
9–15 High Street, Sutton, Surrey, England, SM1 1DF.
Trade paperback edition published
in Great Britain and the USA 2010 by
SEVERN HOUSE PUBLISHERS LTD

British Library Cataloguing in Publication Data

Ison, Graham.
Breach of Privilege.
1. Brock, Detective Chief Inspector (Fictitious character)–
Fiction. 2. Poole, Detective Sergeant (Fictitious
character)–Fiction. 3. Police–England–London–Fiction.
4. Politicians–Crimes against–England–London–Fiction.
5. Detective and mystery stories.
I. Title
823.9'14-dc22

ISBN-13: 978-0-7278-6799-5 (cased)
ISBN-13: 978-1-84751-168-3 (trade paper)

All Severn House titles are printed on acid-free paper.

Typeset by Palimpsest Book Production Ltd.,
Grangemouth, Stirlingshire, Scotland.
Printed and bound in Great Britain by
MPG Books Ltd., Bodmin, Cornwall.

ONE

There is a popular myth that prevails among producers of fictional police programmes on television. They imagine that the officer best qualified to investigate a murder is always the one who gets assigned to the case. In most of these dramas, one detective chief inspector investigates all the murders that take place in his force area. Usually, this heroic individual is aided by a none-too-bright detective sergeant. Well, I can tell you, it ain't necessarily so.

My name is Harry Brock, and I know about these things because I'm a detective chief inspector in the Homicide and Serious Crime Command (West). Our offices are in Curtis Green, a building that is virtually unknown to most people – including the police – that was once a part of New Scotland Yard. But that was before politicians, who wanted the building for themselves, forced the whole of New Scotland Yard to move to an unappealing glass and concrete pile in Broadway, Westminster. Outside this grey building is a gimmicky revolving sign proclaiming, on two sides of this magic roundabout, that it is New Scotland Yard. Surprise, surprise. On the third side it says that the Metropolitan Police is 'Working together for a safer London'. Working with whom, one may well ask.

It is in Curtis Green that a list is kept showing which officers are available for the next serious crime to be committed in our area. That area stretches from Westminster to Hillingdon in the west, and includes such places as Barnet, Chelsea, Hammersmith, Heathrow Airport, Kensington and Richmond. And all the other insalubrious hotbeds of crime and general mayhem that lie in between.

I was sitting in my office one pleasant July Tuesday morning, struggling with yet another report for the Crown Prosecution Service, when Detective Sergeant Colin Wilberforce, the incident room manager, appeared in the doorway. Colin is an administrative genius, and under his supervision the incident room runs like a well-oiled machine. It will be a sad day for us if he ever gets posted elsewhere.

'Good morning, sir.' Colin was clutching a piece of paper.

'Good morning, Colin,' I said, glancing apprehensively at the piece of paper.

'There's been a shooting, sir. A drive-by shooting, by the looks of it.'

'And I'm next on the list, I suppose.'

'Indeed, sir. The commander directs that you investigate.'

A positive direction from the commander is rare. He usually charges confidently into indecision.

'How nice of him. Where is it, Colin?'

'Fulham Road, sir. Near the bus stop at the junction with Old Church Street.'

'What's the SP?' I asked, culling a useful bit of shorthand from the racing fraternity. It actually means 'starting price', but when policemen use it, it means 'What's the story?'

'Bit confused, sir,' said Colin, glancing at his piece of paper. 'Apparently, two guys on a motorcycle pulled up just as the victim was approaching the bus stop, and blasted him with a handgun of some sort. They then made good their escape. Local police are on scene and dealing.'

'Where's Dave?' I asked.

'Here, sir.' As if by magic my bag-carrier, Detective Sergeant Dave Poole, my most valuable asset, appeared in the doorway. Of Caribbean descent, his grandfather arrived from Jamaica in the 1950s and set up practice as a doctor in Bethnal Green. His son, Dave's father, is an accountant, but Dave, having graduated in English from London University, decided to become a policeman. He often describes himself as the black sheep of the family, a comment that always manages to discomfit those among our ranks to whom 'diversity' is the most cherished word in the English language.

Dave also has a very attractive wife, Madeleine, who is a principal dancer with the Royal Ballet. She, by the way, is white. There is a rumour circulating that Madeleine sometimes attacks Dave physically. But given that she is five foot two, and Dave is six foot, that particular story is put down to canteen gossip.

'We have a shooting in the Fulham Road, Dave,' I said.

'Really, guv? Someone making a film?'

'Not that kind of shooting,' I said with a sigh. Dave is a great wind-up merchant. 'This one is apparently a shooting with real bullets.'

Dave laughed. 'Yeah, I know. There's a traffic car waiting for us.'

I greeted this information with some misgivings. Traffic officers of the Metropolitan Police are the finest drivers in the world, but I always get a sinking feeling whenever I'm conveyed anywhere by one of them. In fact, despite being a detective, I frequently feel that I am most at danger when travelling in a Traffic Division car. Actually, it's now called a Traffic Operational Command Unit. Personally, I couldn't see what was wrong with 'Traffic Division', but the boy superintendents at Scotland Yard – they of the funny names and total confusion squad – thought differently.

I saw one of the aforesaid boy superintendents emerging from Scotland Yard the other day, a rarity in itself. I knew he was a boy superintendent: he was blinking in the strong and – to him – unaccustomed daylight.

I emerged from the traffic car somewhat shakily. It had taken six minutes to get from Curtis Green to Fulham Road and, by some miracle of advanced driving, I was still alive.

The scene of my latest investigation was shrouded in a small tent, and the immediate area cordoned off with the customary blue and white tape. Fulham Road had been closed, thus causing the maximum disruption to traffic. It is this sort of disruption that the aforementioned Traffic OCU delights in attributing to 'sheer weight of traffic', rather than doing anything about it.

An inspector with a clipboard homed in on me. 'And you are?' he enquired, waggling his government-issue ballpoint pen.

'DCI Brock, HSCC.'

'Thank you, sir.' The inspector wrote it down, and glanced at Dave. 'And you?'

'Colour Sergeant Poole, ditto,' said Dave, with a grin on his black face. It was a comment that caused the inspector to suck briefly through his teeth, but Dave is a great one for disconcerting pompous uniformed inspectors. Especially those who have achieved their exalted rank via the accelerated promotion course held at Bramshill Police College.

'What do we know?' I asked.

'There's a DI from Chelsea over there, sir,' said the inspector, swiftly abdicating any responsibility in the matter of briefing me.

The Chelsea DI ambled across, hands in pockets. 'You copped this one, then, guv?' he asked.

'Yes. What's the score?'

'At eleven thirteen a solo motorcycle stopped long enough to allow the pillion passenger to pull out a gun and fire at the victim.' The DI waved at the tent.

'I don't suppose anyone noted the number of this motorcycle,' I said.

'You suppose wrong, guv,' said the DI. 'A vigilant passer-by took a note of it.'

'Excellent,' I said. But, in the event, my joy at this revelation proved to be premature.

'However, the motorcycle's been found abandoned. Not that the number would have helped much. It's got bent plates on it that go out to a milk float in Exeter.' I got the impression that the DI was rather enjoying this, secure in the knowledge that he would shortly walk away from this particular crime, and have nothing more to do with it.

'Where was it found?'

'In Belgrave Square.'

'That's a strange place for it to have finished up,' I said thoughtfully. 'Isn't Belgrave Square full of bloody embassies?'

'Yes, guv. There's about seven of them.' The DI knew what was coming next.

'And embassies have policemen standing outside them,' I continued. 'Are you going to tell me that none of these officers saw anything?'

'Nothing of consequence, guv. Within about ten minutes of the shooting the motorcycle was driven into Belgrave Square. Two officers, one outside the German Embassy, the other outside the Syrian, saw the rider and the pillion passenger alight and run towards a car. The engine was running and there was a third bloke already behind the wheel. It was about then that the call came out over the air, just as the car took off at high speed. They'd noticed its arrival only minutes before, but hadn't thought anything of it.'

Unfortunately, I couldn't find fault with that. 'They're armed, aren't they, these Diplomatic Protection blokes?' I asked, just for the fun of it.

Beside me, Dave laughed. 'Well, they couldn't fire at fleeing felons, guv, could they? Might get done for murder, and the victims' families would get legal aid to sue the Job for pain and suffering, or whatever. Then they'd appear on television muttering about justice and closure.'

'Did they at least get the number of the bloody car then?'

The Chelsea DI nodded. 'Yes, but it's the mixture as before. Duff. Seems to belong to an invalid carriage in Dyfed Powys.'

'Terrific,' I said. 'What about ID? Do we know who the victim is?'

'According to documents found on his person, his name is Hugh Blakemore with an address at seven, Carfax Street. It's a turning off Old Church Street, so the guy wasn't far from home when he was topped.'

'Anyone informed the family?'

'Yes, guv,' said the Chelsea DI. 'It's a Mrs Anne Blakemore. He paused before delivering his punch-line. 'And Hugh Blakemore was a Member of Parliament.'

'Wonderful,' I said. 'Just what I needed.'

'Morning, Harry.' The Home Office pathologist, Henry Mortlock, emerged from the tent clutching his bag of ghoulish instruments, and joined our little group.

'What can you tell me, Henry?' I asked. Mortlock is a master of witticisms and black humour to rival any CID officer. He didn't disappoint me.

'He's dead,' said Mortlock. 'If you want to know what killed him, you'll have to wait for Part Two, and that comes after the postmortem.'

'Thanks,' I said. I shouldn't have asked really. Henry Mortlock is never one to commit himself. He left us, whistling a snatch of Beethoven's Fifth Symphony.

It was nearly three o'clock by the time the first of the witness statements had been typed and filed, and I began to read them. As usual the witnesses gave widely differing descriptions of both the event and the suspects, and – also as usual – they were pretty useless.

'The car's been found abandoned, sir,' said Colin Wilberforce, entering my office with a sheaf of papers in his hand.

'Where?' Despite all the legislation prohibiting smoking

just about everywhere, I lit a cigarette. It's my way of making a protest.

'Richmond Park. Just near the Richmond Gate.'

'Richmond Park! How the hell did it get from Belgrave Square to Richmond Park without anyone spotting it? I presume the embassy PCs put the number up the moment it took off.'

'Yes, they did, sir,' said Colin.

'Well, why wasn't it seen?' I couldn't believe that it hadn't been spotted by a police officer somewhere along the route.

'There's a simple answer to that, guv,' said Dave. 'Probably because there aren't any coppers on the streets any more. They're all indoors writing up reports for the Crown Prosecution Service, I expect.' His comment was larded with the usual sort of cynicism I'd come to expect from him.

'Has it been examined yet, Colin?' I asked, ignoring Dave's aside.

'It's been removed to Lambeth and the forensic practitioners have made a start, sir,' said Colin. 'Forensic practitioner' is a recent title visited upon those who, for many years, we knew as scenes-of-crime officers. I wondered why they'd changed it, but I knew. 'The crash helmets and two sets of leathers were in the boot, and the lab guys are working on those and on the interior of the vehicle.' He paused to give his next statement added emphasis. 'And there was an American passport in one of the pockets of the leathers.'

'Was there really?' This sounded too good to be true. 'What sort of murderer leaves his bloody passport for us to find, Colin?'

Colin shrugged. 'I suppose everyone has to make a mistake at some time or another, sir,' he said. 'But it could have been the passport of the guy they stole the leathers from. I don't suppose they went out and bought them.'

'What's the name in the passport?'

'Vincent Rosso, born in Delaware, Ohio, thirty years ago. I've lodged an enquiry with Joe Daly.' Daly was the euphemistically styled legal attaché at the American Embassy. In reality, he was the most senior FBI agent in London.

'And the motorcycle, Colin? Any joy on that?' I asked.

'They've gone over it with a fine-tooth comb, sir. The engine and frame numbers had been filed off, but the lab is confident of bringing them up. Until we know where it came from there's not much we can do about it.'

'Fingerprints?' I asked hopefully.

Colin laughed. 'We should be so lucky, sir,' he said. 'However, there is something in General Registry about Hugh Blakemore.'

I never had to tell Colin Wilberforce to do anything. He just leaped into action doing all the things that needed to be done.

'And what's that?' I asked.

'There was an incident at Melbury prison some months ago, sir. Blakemore was on a sort of fact-finding tour of the prison when a prisoner went for him with a knife.'

'How the hell does a prisoner come to possess a knife, Colin?'

Colin just smiled. He knew the answer and so did I. 'Unfortunately for the prisoner, Blakemore was an Oxford boxing blue, and before the screws could intervene, Blakemore chinned the guy.'

'Good for him,' I said.

'Not really,' said Colin, referring once again to the file. 'The prisoner fell backwards down a flight of stairs, fractured his skull and died.'

'Sounds like my sort of MP,' I said.

'The file contains a number of threatening letters, sir, but they're the usual sort of crank rubbish that most people in the public eye receive from time to time. There were a few referring specifically to the Melbury incident, but they ceased after a while.'

I took the file and glanced through it. It contained a collection of the type of letter that most MPs got, often from harmless lunatics, the crabbed writing filling the entire page – a common feature of the crazed letter-writer – some even written in red ink as if to suggest blood. It seemed that there had been an increase in the number of such letters at the time of the death of the prisoner in Melbury, not all of them hostile, but for the police to have interviewed the few who identified themselves would merely have inflated their ego.

'Leave the file on my desk, Colin, and I'll have a thorough look at it later. In the meantime, assemble as many of the

team as you can lay hands on. I have a feeling that this is
going to be one of those awkward enquiries.' I knew from
previous experience that any enquiry involving politicians would
present not only difficulties, but a measure of obstruction also.
Politicians don't like being put under the spotlight.

'Dr Mortlock called, sir,' said Colin, as he was leaving
the room. 'The postmortem is scheduled for nine o'clock
tomorrow morning.'

It took only a matter of minutes for Colin to round up those
members of the team who were in the building. In theory, I'm
supposed to have three detective inspectors, and twenty-six
assorted sergeants and constables at my disposal. But when
you take away those on leave, those who are sick, those who
are at the Old Bailey giving evidence, and those who have
been filched by another DCI, there aren't many left.

In fact, I had about fifteen officers to assist me in discovering the murderer of Hugh Blakemore, deceased Member
of Parliament.

I outlined what we knew so far, and then got down to details.
'Charlie,' I said, looking round the crowded incident room for
DS Charles Flynn, late of the Fraud Squad.

'Yes, sir?'

'I want you to follow up the enquiry that was made of Joe
Daly at the American Embassy. But knowing our luck, the
Vincent Rosso of Delaware, Ohio, whose passport was found
in the getaway vehicle had nothing to do with the shooting.'

I turned next to Detective Sergeant Tom Challis who had
previously served on the Stolen Car Squad. 'Tom, follow up
on the getaway car and the motorcycle. See if you can find
out anything about them. They've obviously been nicked, but
we shan't know for sure until the laboratory comes up with
something.'

I decided that I would visit Blakemore's widow immediately, it being an axiom of criminal investigation that enquiries
start at the centre and work outwards, and that they begin at
the earliest possible moment. Speaking to the relatives of
someone who had just been brutally gunned down in the street
was not a task I welcomed. But it had to be done. In most
cases of murder, victims have been killed by someone they
know, and where better to start than their family? 'What was
that address for Anne Blakemore, Colin?'

Colin thumbed quickly through his daybook and read off a Chelsea address. 'Seven, Carfax Street, sir.'

I glanced at DI Kate Ebdon. 'You and I, Kate, will visit the grieving widow. See what she's got to say about it all.'

Kate was an Australian who usually dressed in jeans and a man's white shirt. Her flame-coloured hair, invariably tied back in a pony-tail, matched her character, and she was extremely useful when it came to putting the bite on villains. The commander did not approve of her mode of attire, but hadn't got the bottle to tell her. Our esteemed commander believes that everyone promoted to the rank of inspector automatically becomes a gentleman. Or lady, as applicable.

Kate had begun her CID career in the East End of London before gravitating to the Flying Squad as a detective sergeant. It was rumoured that she had given pleasure to a number of male officers on the Squad. Whether that is true or not, I don't know, but she could certainly charm the pants off recalcitrant witnesses when the necessity arose.

I glanced at my watch. 'Let's go, Kate.'

TWO

Kate and I drove to Chelsea. Accompanying her driving with a continuous flow of Australian invective, Kate eventually found her way through the maze of one-way and dead-end streets between King's Road and the Embankment, and stopped outside the town house that the late Hugh Blakemore had shared with his wife.

'Now that, Kate, is a *real* town house,' I said, looking with envy at Anne Blakemore's property. 'None of your neo-Georgian three-storied terraced about that.'

Kate made a pretence of being mystified. 'But it *is* a three-storied terraced house, guv,' she said.

Kate mounted steps ahead of me to be confronted by a uniformed constable who was guarding the door.

'And which newspaper are you from, then, darling?' asked the PC, his arms folded across his chest.

For a moment or two, Kate gazed at the young policeman. 'If you were doing your job properly, *sonny*,' she said caustically, 'by now you would have checked the index mark of our car on the Police National Computer and you would have found that it belonged to the Receiver to the Metropolitan Police District.' After a suitable pause, she added, 'Detective Inspector Ebdon, HSCC West.'

'Sorry, ma'am.' The PC gulped and turned to ring the bell.

Kate put a restraining hand on the policeman's arm. 'How d'you know that's true?' she asked, and waved her warrant card under the unfortunate constable's nose. 'Now you can ring the bell,' she said. It doesn't pay to cross Kate Ebdon.

The woman who answered the door was in her late thirties or early forties. Her hair was light blonde, and she was a little on the plump side, but attractively so. I would have expected a widow of less than twenty-four hours to be attired all in black, but she was wearing a pink, summery dress. Perhaps I'm old-fashioned.

'Can I help you?' she asked, her unfriendly gaze appraising the two of us. Her tone implied that that was the last thing she had in mind.

'We're police officers, madam,' I said, showing her my warrant card. 'Are you Mrs Blakemore?'

'Yes, I am.' Anne Blakemore's haughtiness slowly ebbed. She smiled weakly and held the door open. 'You'd better come in,' she said, and led us into the sitting room at the front of the house.

'What a charming room,' I said smoothly as I gazed around.

'Thank you,' said Anne Blakemore. 'We like it very much.' She faltered and her voice broke slightly. 'That is to say, we did like it. I mean, I—'

'I quite understand, Mrs Blakemore,' I said. 'And may I offer my condolences on your loss. A terrible thing. A tragedy.'

Kate Ebdon raised her eyes to the ceiling, not that she had any particular interest in it, or in the magnificent rose. It was more likely that she was already suspecting the dead man's widow of some involvement in her late husband's death.

Anne Blakemore recovered herself sufficiently to offer us coffee, and left the room briefly to arrange it. She returned and sat down opposite us.

'I presume that you're investigating the murder of my husband,' she said.

'Yes, I am,' I said. 'I'm Detective Chief Inspector Brock of New Scotland Yard.' I couldn't be bothered with all this Homicide and Serious Crime Command stuff every time I introduced myself. After all, it was technically correct. 'And this is Detective Inspector Ebdon.'

'I know that the Prime Minister is taking a close personal interest in Hugh's murder,' said Mrs Blakemore in a vain attempt to impress me with her influence, 'but so far I've heard none of the details. Sir Charles Austen, your Commissioner, telephoned me this morning, shortly after it happened, but he wasn't able to tell me any more than the officer who'd called earlier.'

I was surprised that the Commissioner knew even that much, but I outlined, as briefly as possible, what we knew, which, in fact, added very little to what she knew already. 'I have to ask you, Mrs Blakemore,' I continued, 'whether your husband had any enemies.' It sounded stupid, but it was the question that policemen always asked.

Anne Blakemore gave a short, bitter laugh. 'I should think so,' she said, 'especially after that business at Melbury. You know that a prisoner was killed there, I suppose?'

'Yes, I do,' I said. I was amused at the way in which the woman avoided attributing blame to her late husband. 'But the man who died was not a habitual criminal. You probably know that he was serving a sentence for the murder of his wife.'

'So I believe,' said Anne Blakemore dismissively, her tone implying that the reason for the man's imprisonment was unimportant, and that anyone who attacked her late husband got what he deserved. 'It was a terrible accident, of course, but the gutter press tried to make something out of it.'

A woman – the Blakemores' housekeeper, I presumed – appeared with a tray of coffee. The coffee pot was of Georgian silver and the cups were bone china, and I knew instinctively that it would not be instant coffee that was served.

'Do you think there might be some connection with that rather unsavoury business?' Anne posed the question lightly, as though she was not really interested in knowing the answer.

'I don't know,' I said candidly, 'but it's obviously something I'll be looking into.' I glanced at a silver-framed photograph on a sofa table. It was of an attractive young woman striking a theatrical pose.

'Your daughter?'

'Yes, that's Caroline,' said Anne Blakemore as she handed round the coffee. 'She's an actress.'

'Is she working?' My girlfriend Gail Sutton is a 'resting' actress, and I was familiar with the insecurity of the acting profession. In Gail's case, her insecurity was because she'd come home early one day from the theatre and found her husband, Gerald Andrews, in bed with a naked dancer. In fact, they were both naked, but it spelt the end of the marriage, and Gail reverted to using her maiden name. Gail was always convinced that, out of sheer spite, her ex, who was a theatrical director, had blocked any attempts by her to secure other parts. At one stage, she was reduced to working in a chorus line. Which was where I'd met her. It was at the Granville Theatre, and at the time I was investigating the murder of one of her colleagues, Patricia Hunter, an actress and occasional shoplifter.

'I believe she's in rep somewhere in London at the moment. To be perfectly honest, I can't keep track of her.' Anne Blakemore spoke as though she was not really interested in her daughter's career. 'But I understand that she's hoping to get a part in television.'

'She's not here, then?' I queried.

'Why should she be? She doesn't live here.' The woman raised her eyebrows. 'Anyway, she's always busy in the theatre, so she tells me.'

It appeared as though there was an element of coolness – what Dave would call *froideur*; he likes words like that – between mother and daughter. 'I just thought she might have come home to stay with you, following her father's death.'

'Hugh was not her father,' said Anne Blakemore curtly. 'I divorced my first husband eight years ago.'

'I see. What is her name, then?'

'She's Caroline Simpson.' There was a certain reserve about the way in which Mrs Blakemore answered, as though divorce was something not quite socially acceptable.

'Tell me, Mrs Blakemore, were you aware of any threats made against your late husband?' I asked. 'Strange telephone calls, anonymous letters, that sort of thing?'

Blakemore's widow appeared to weigh her answer carefully. 'Not that I know of,' she said eventually. 'At least, nothing of any importance. All MPs get communications of that sort from time to time. Usually the secretaries destroy them, but if they're serious they're sent to the police.' She gazed at me as though I should have known that. And I did. I'd seen the file of threatening letters that had been sent to Blakemore over the years.

'What was your husband's reaction to that incident at Melbury prison, Mrs Blakemore?'

'One of remorse, naturally, but the man did attempt to stab him. He would much rather that it hadn't happened, of course. But what could he do? He had to defend himself.' Anne Blakemore looked distantly at the empty fireplace. 'Unfortunately, it may have harmed his parliamentary career,' she added wistfully, as though that was the most important aspect of the whole affair. 'Not that that matters now.'

I waited to see if she would modify that statement, to soften it in some way, but it was obvious that the possible endangerment to her husband's career was the only feature of the prisoner's death that had concerned her. 'Forgive me for asking what may seem an indelicate question, Mrs Blakemore,' I continued, 'but was your divorce from Mr Simpson an acrimonious one?'

The woman, clearly puzzled, stared at me, and for a moment

I thought that she was going to refuse to answer. 'It wasn't exactly amicable,' she said quietly. 'I was working for Hugh as a parliamentary researcher and we had an affair. It happens quite often, you know.'

'Was Mr Blakemore married at the time?'

'Yes. We both were.' The woman made the admission quite openly, as though there was nothing wrong in it. It was an attitude entirely different from her earlier pronouncements, and I rapidly concluded that she was something of an enigma.

'And presumably the first Mrs Blakemore wasn't too pleased about it.'

'No. Particularly when she came back here one night and found us in bed together. She was supposed to be in France.' Anne Blakemore laughed, but there was no humour in it. 'And as for my mother-in-law, well, she was openly abusive about the whole business.'

I was surprised at her frankness, but I had found over the years that women of her type were surprisingly candid about their private lives. They didn't seem to worry who knew what they were doing. 'Your mother-in-law?' I queried.

'Yes, Hugh's mother. She's still alive. Lives in Henley somewhere, I believe.'

'You believe?'

'Yes. We haven't kept in touch. She can't stand the sight of me. And it's mutual,' Anne added before reverting to her original train of thought. 'Of course, the newspapers made a big thing out of the Melbury prison incident.' She seemed very concerned about the press, but that was a common enough paranoia in politicians and their wives. 'However, it all blew over very quickly and was soon forgotten about. I seem to recall that there was some tragedy – a train crash or something of the sort – that wiped it off the front pages.' She still had a distant expression on her face and it was some time since she had looked directly at me.

'Do you happen to know where Mr Blakemore's ex-wife lives now or, for that matter, where your ex-husband is?' But I didn't think that she would have been interested in what had happened to either of them, or would have bothered to find out. I sensed that, even if she had, she was unlikely to tell me.

'Is that relevant? I mean, why do you want to know?'

'I need to interview everyone who knew your late husband, Mrs Blakemore,' I said. 'Who knew him closely, that is.'

Anne Blakemore scoffed. 'Charles and Dorothy—'

'Would that be Charles Simpson and Dorothy Blakemore?' asked Kate, glancing up from the notes she was making in her pocketbook.

'Yes, of course. They were pretty angry at the time, but they're not the sort of people to commit murder.'

'I'm not suggesting they did,' I said.

'Well, there you are, then. But to answer your question, no, I don't know where they are.'

'What was your daughter's reaction to the divorce?'

'Upset, naturally. I think any child would be when its parents split up. But she was only twelve years old at the time and she soon settled down. Children of that age are very adaptable. Anyway, she was away at school for most of the time.'

I had come rapidly to the conclusion that Anne Blakemore was a very selfish woman. 'Is Caroline your only child?' I asked.

'Yes, but I hope you're not going to bother her.'

'I don't think that'll be necessary.' I had every intention of interviewing Caroline Simpson, but I was not going to give her advance warning. That said, though, I knew her mother would be on the phone to her daughter to tell her that the wicked police had been bothering her. I stood up. 'Thank you for your time, Mrs Blakemore, and for the coffee,' I said. 'I may have to see you again and, rest assured, I shall keep you fully informed of any developments.' But I had no intention of doing so. At least, not until my enquiries had progressed much further than they had at present.

'Well, what did you think of her, guv?' asked Kate as we were returning to Curtis Green.

'In my opinion, she's one selfish bitch,' I said, 'and I wouldn't mind betting that even now she's having an affair with someone else, and has been for some time. She certainly didn't seem too cut up about darling Hugh's demise. However, I don't think she'd have resorted to having him murdered. Frankly, I don't think she's intelligent enough to have planned something like that.'

Henry Mortlock had already started his postmortem examination by the time that Dave and I arrived at his carvery on

Wednesday morning, even though we were there at five minutes to nine. But then he was always an impatient man.

'Those are what you're looking for, Harry.' Mortlock pointed at a kidney-shaped bowl in which there were three rounds of ammunition. 'And they're what killed him.'

'Look like nine-millimetre, guv,' said Dave as he bagged the rounds, and did the necessary paperwork to ensure that continuity of evidence was fully catered for. Defence counsel will get extremely sniffy if they think they can find a break in that chain.

We were back at Curtis Green by ten o'clock, and I decided it was time to find out a bit more about the incident in which Blakemore had snuffed out a prisoner. Somewhat optimistically, I thought that therein might lie the answer. I was wrong.

'Colin,' I said, 'make an appointment for me to see the governor of Melbury prison as soon as is humanly possible. It's in Wiltshire,' I added, unnecessarily as it happened.

'Yes, sir, I know.' Colin flicked over a page in the internal telephone directory and seized the phone.

'In the meantime, Kate,' I continued, turning to DI Ebdon, 'I want Charles Simpson and Dorothy Blakemore located as a matter of urgency.'

'D'you think they might have some connection with this job, guv?'

'Shan't know until we talk to them, shall we, Kate?' I said. 'And get someone to make some discreet enquiries about Caroline Simpson. Oh, and see if you can track down Eleanor Blakemore. Anne Blakemore said she lived in Henley, didn't she? If you find her, make an appointment for me to see her.'

The governor of Melbury prison was a tall and painfully thin man in his fifties with a stooped and scholarly appearance. His suit hung about his gaunt frame, and he reminded me of a schoolmaster of yesteryear.

'It happened three months ago, Mr Brock, just before I came to this prison,' he said when Dave and I were seated in his office, 'but Principal Officer Watkins here was on duty at the time.' He indicated a grey-haired man with a broken nose who was sitting to one side of his desk. 'He'll be able to tell you all about it.' He turned to the principal officer. 'Mr Watkins.'

'You've seen the report, I suppose, Mr Brock,' said Watkins.

'Yes, but was there more to it than that? In my experience

reports are more interesting for what they leave out than for what they include.'

'Well, I don't think that was the case here.' There was an element of hostility in Watkins's voice, as though his professionalism had been impugned. 'Blakemore was on some self-propelled fact-finding mission, looking into conditions at prisons.' He glanced at the governor. 'To be frank, we get too many of these do-gooders swanning around, trying to tell us that all our inmates are capable of being reformed. They just get in the way. However, Blakemore was being escorted round the first floor landing in C Block when Johnson suddenly went for him with a knife. The escorting officers moved in very quickly, but not as quickly as Blakemore. I heard afterwards that he'd been a useful middleweight when he was up at Oxford. Anyway, Blakemore chinned Johnson and knocked him backwards down a flight of iron stairs. When he reached the bottom he cracked his head on the stone-flagged floor and that was that. One of the escorting officers examined Johnson, but it was quite obvious that he was dead. And our own medical officer confirmed it.'

'Was there any trouble after that?' I asked.

'There would have been,' said Watkins, 'but the governor ordered an immediate lock-down. The prisoners were sent back to their cells to cool off.'

'Was that it, Mr Watkins?' asked Dave.

'Not really. There was a simmering undercurrent of resentment, and there were one or two minor scuffles, mainly in the mess hall. But it quietened down after a few days.' Watkins gave a dry, throaty chuckle. 'Mind you, a few harsh words were spoken about Members of Parliament going round prisons and murdering inmates.'

'What was Johnson in for?' I asked, wishing to confirm what was contained in our file on the matter.

'He murdered his wife about four years ago, and he'd been sent down for life with a tariff of fifteen years before he could apply for parole. He'd never been any trouble previously, and I don't know what possessed him to have a go at Blakemore. Mind you, he reckoned he'd been wrongly convicted, but there again, all of them in here think that. I don't believe there was any personal animosity; it was just that Blakemore represented the Establishment. And that, I suppose, made him a legitimate target, at least in Johnson's eyes.'

'Was there anyone in here who was particularly vocal about the incident?' I asked.

Watkins gave that some thought before replying. 'There was one prisoner, name of Peter Crowley, in for robbery with violence, doing a twelve. He was a mate of Johnson's and seemed particularly incensed about it all.'

'Is he still in?' asked Dave.

'Yes, but not here,' said Watkins. 'Because he was seen as a troublemaker, Crowley was transferred to Wormwood Scrubs almost immediately. He's only done half of his twelve years, but knowing what our lily-livered government is like, he's probably been paroled by now.'

'How did Johnson get hold of a knife?' asked Dave, more out of devilment than curiosity.

'He'd been working in the machine shop – he was a trusty, you see – and we think he probably fashioned it out of a piece of metal. Obviously we have officers in there supervising, but they can't be everywhere at once, and we're short-staffed.'

'Crowley was the only one who was a real mate of Johnson's, then?'

'No, there was one other. Mickey Lever, doing seven for robbery.'

'Is he still in?' I asked.

'No. Released last month. But he, Johnson and Crowley used to gather in Johnson's cell and listen to Radio Three or Classic FM. Reckoned they were keen on that sort of stuff. Personally, I think it was only a ruse to get in with the good-looking bird who came in once a month to hold discussion circles about classical music.' Watkins shrugged, probably in wonderment at the naivety of those who sanctioned such visits.

The only piece of information that had come out of a largely pointless interview at Melbury prison was that a prisoner named Peter Crowley harboured a great resentment against Blakemore, but if he was still in stir it was doubtful that he had played any part in the MP's murder. But career villains do have friends on the outside.

I decided to look more closely at Peter Crowley and Mickey Lever, but they could wait.

THREE

Kate Ebdon had not only tracked down Eleanor Blakemore in Henley-on-Thames, but had arranged for me to see her at eleven o'clock the following morning. Dave and I drove to the small town and eventually found the cottage overlooking the river where, the elder Mrs Blakemore told us, she had lived for the past forty years.

She was an elegant woman in her early seventies, expensively dressed, and charming. But I noticed that she limped heavily and supported herself with a walking-stick.

'Do come in, gentlemen,' she said, 'and take a seat.'

The sitting room was small but comfortably furnished with several armchairs and a sofa with flowery loose covers. There was bric-a-brac everywhere, the sort of ornaments my mother would have condemned as dust traps.

'I'm Detective Chief Inspector Brock of Scotland Yard, and this is Detective Sergeant Poole,' I said, by way of introduction, 'and I'm investigating the death of your son.'

Eleanor Blakemore looked momentarily sad. 'A bad business, Chief Inspector,' she said, glancing through a window at the river beyond, 'but I can't say I'm surprised.'

'Oh?' I wondered if I was about to discover something that had, so far, eluded us, but I was wrong.

'You must have heard about that business at the prison.'

'Yes, of course. As a matter of fact, Sergeant Poole and I were there yesterday.'

'It must have been one of those prisoners who killed him,' continued Mrs Blakemore. 'One that had been released, I mean. I told him he ought not to have poked his nose into such things. It was none of his business. And another thing: he had this obsession with the vice trade. He would visit nightclubs and those tawdry little dives in Soho where they have naked women dancing on tables, and then make rambling speeches about it in the House. I would have thought that he had enough to do looking after his constituents. It's a very poor area, you know, Millingham.'

'I've been to see your daughter-in-law, of course, and she's—' I began, but didn't get to finish the sentence.

'I presume you're talking about Anne?' There was an element of disdain in Mrs Blakemore's voice.

'Yes.'

'That woman trapped my Hugh into leaving Dorothy so that she could marry him. It was all very calculated, you know, Mr Brock. She even arranged to be in bed with Hugh when she knew Dorothy would find them.'

'But Anne Blakemore said that she thought Dorothy was in France on that occasion.'

'Pah!' Eleanor Blakemore waved a dismissive hand. 'It was nothing of the sort. She knew perfectly well that Dorothy wasn't away, and was pretty certain that she would come home and find them. I wouldn't be surprised if she hadn't set it up. It was deliberate, Chief Inspector. And she hasn't finished yet.'

'What d'you mean by that, Mrs Blakemore?' asked Dave.

'She's been having affairs from almost the first day she married my Hugh. And very likely before, when she was married to that Charles Simpson person.'

'Have you met Mr Simpson, Mrs Blakemore?'

'No, and I have no desire to do so.'

'D'you know who Anne was having affairs with?' I asked. Out of the corner of my eye, I noticed Dave wince. It must've been my sentence construction that pained him.

Mrs Blakemore scoffed. 'Several,' she said, 'but as far as I know the latest one is a man called Geoffrey Strang, and I've no doubt she will continue seeing him. I think you'll find she plays the field.' She paused, and put a hand to her mouth. 'Oh, how remiss of me. I haven't offered you gentlemen any tea.' Before we had time to decline, she picked up her stick from the floor, and rose from her chair with some difficulty. 'I shan't be a moment.'

While Mrs Blakemore was making tea, I glanced around the room. There was a gallery of framed photographs on a table between the two windows. One of them was a wedding photograph of Hugh Blakemore and a bride I presumed was his first wife Dorothy. There was another print of Hugh standing on a platform apparently making a political speech. Significantly there were no photographs of Hugh's second wife, or of Hugh's stepdaughter Caroline.

'I wonder if one of you gentlemen would carry in the tray for me.' Mrs Blakemore looked round the door from the kitchen. 'I've an arthritic hip, I'm sorry to say, and I can't manage a tray and a walking stick.'

Dave leaped into action and brought in the tea. Ever courteous – when it suited him – he put the tray on an occasional table that he then moved within reach of Mrs Blakemore's chair.

'Thank you, young man. That's very kind of you.'

Once we were settled, and drinking tea, I determined to find out more about Anne Blakemore's latest lover.

'What can you tell me about this Geoffrey Strang whom you mentioned just now, Mrs Blakemore?'

'Nothing I'm afraid.'

'Then how—?'

'Hugh told me. Whatever else he may have lacked, he was always a loyal son, and came to see me as often as his parliamentary duties would allow. He mentioned on one occasion that he was sure Anne was having an affair with this man Strang, and it had been going on for some time. I think he was a bit riled because he said that Strang was about ten years younger than Anne. He described him as her toy boy. I didn't press him on the matter, but it was obvious that he was worried about it, probably because of the effect it would have on his career. There's nothing the tabloid press likes better than to catch an MP's wife who's playing away, so to speak. And following that awful business at the prison, the gutter press would have had a field day. I merely confined myself to saying that he hadn't hesitated to have an affair when he was married to Dorothy, and what was good for the goose was also good for the gander.' Mrs Blakemore gave a crooked little smile. 'Or is it the other way round? I never can remember.'

We had learned a little more, but not much. We thanked Mrs Blakemore for the tea, and left.

A uniformed constable had been stationed permanently at Anne Blakemore's front door, mainly to prevent her from being pestered by a prurient tabloid press.

I instructed Kate Ebdon to speak to the operations chief inspector at Chelsea nick, and ask him to brief the PCs on that duty to make a note of any visitors, and to telephone the result to the incident room without delay.

The response came quicker than I had hoped for. On the morning following our interview with Mrs Eleanor Blakemore, Colin Wilberforce appeared in my office.

'A PC from Chelsea phoned in last night with a car number, sir. Said you wanted to know. It turned up at about seven in the evening and was still there when he went off duty at ten.'

'That was quick, Colin,' I said. 'Who does it go out to?'

'A Geoffrey Strang, sir.' Colin placed a message form on my desk. 'Address in Fulham.'

'How very convenient,' I said. 'Thank you, Colin. Ask Tom Challis to see me.'

When Challis arrived I briefed him about Anne Blakemore's paramour, and asked him to find out what he could about the man.

I decided next to interview Peter Crowley, one of the two prisoners who had befriended Kenneth Johnson in Melbury prison, and who had already served six years of a twelve-year sentence for armed robbery. He entered the interview room at Wormwood Scrubs with a surly expression on his face.

'I'm Detective Chief Inspector Brock of Scotland Yard. And this is Detective Sergeant Poole.'

'So?' Crowley, in common with most top-class villains, knew that the sudden arrival of the police at the Scrubs did nothing to reinforce his hope that he might be nearing parole. 'I've got nothing to say.'

'Then why did you agree to be interviewed?' I asked. Prisoners serving a sentence were under no obligation to speak to the police.

'Makes a break, don't it?' Crowley crossed his legs and leaned back in his chair, a picture of churlish non-cooperation.

'You were a mate of Kenneth Johnson's in Melbury.'

'So what?'

'You were there when he fell downstairs and killed himself.'

'He didn't fall, he was pushed. By a bloody MP called Blakemore who, I was pleased to see, got his comeuppance a few days ago.'

'What d'you know about Blakemore's murder?' I asked.

'What I read in the papers and what I saw on telly. And if you think I had anything to do with it, well, I've got the perfect alibi, ain't I?'

'Why should I think you'd got anything to do with it?'

'You tell me. You're the copper. But I ain't surprised that someone had a pop at him. Had it coming, didn't he.'

'Oh? And why was that?'

Crowley scoffed. 'Why not? He knocks a prisoner down an iron staircase and kills him, and you ask why someone topped the bastard. Bloody obvious, ain't it?'

'Did you hear anything afterwards that suggested that someone might have a go at Blakemore?' I sensed that I was not going to get very far with Crowley.

'Nope.'

'Perhaps I ought to explain the law of conspiracy to you,' I said, contriving a sort of conversational tone.

'What's that supposed to mean?' Crowley recognized the implied threat immediately and moved his position slightly.

'I mean that it is possible for a prisoner who's banged up in a nice comfortable nick like this still to be done for conspiring to commit murder. Particularly these days when a beneficent government gives you phone cards.'

'Don't worry me,' said Crowley nonchalantly. 'I never had nothing to do with it. Anyway, I'm up for parole soon and I wouldn't do nothing to risk that.'

'Up for parole are you? Really?' I raised my eyebrows. 'Well, I wish you luck.'

'Look,' said Crowley. He sat up, leaned forward and folded his arms on the table. 'There was a lot of chat round the nick after it happened, but no one in their right mind is going to take an MP out, is he? All right, what he did was well out of order, but you'd have to be bloody crazy to have had a go at him. I mean, that's why *you're* here, ain't it. They never sent none of the filth from the Yard when Ken Johnson got his. Not bleeding likely. Had to make do with some swede-bashing DI from the local nick in Wiltshire. And nothing happened to Blakemore, did it? 'Course not. Might have put the kibosh on the chief constable's knighthood, that might. All pals together, that lot.'

'What about Lever? Did he have anything to say about it?' I lit a cigarette and laid the case on the table. Crowley eyed it hungrily and I nodded.

'Who's Lever?' asked Crowley, taking one of my cigarettes.

'Mickey Lever, as you well know, was a robber doing seven at Melbury. You, he and Johnson used to hold hands and listen to Radio Three, according to the principal officer.'

'Pah! Bloody Watkins,' said Crowley, and made a pretence of spitting on the floor.

'Well?' I was getting impatient but I knew that the only way in which I could coerce a prisoner already serving a substantial sentence was with subtlety, and so I continued to give the impression of amused tolerance. 'What did Lever think about Johnson getting killed?'

'You'll have to ask him yourself, won't you?'

'Well, I won't hold you up any longer, Peter.' I paused, knowing that Crowley was wondering if he was about to be fitted up for conspiracy to murder.

'You ready to go, Mr Brock?' asked the prison officer who had been waiting outside.

'Very nearly,' I said, pausing once more to glance back at Crowley, still lounging thoughtfully in his chair.

The prison officer pointed a finger at the prisoner. 'On your feet, Crowley,' he said.

I was almost out of the door before Crowley spoke again. 'Mr Brock.'

'What?'

'There was something.'

'Well?'

'I ain't no grass, Mr Brock, but I'd have a word with that Mickey Lever if I was you. He's a bad bastard, that one.'

I walked back across the room and sat down again. 'Well, is that it, then?' I asked. 'I know Lever's a bad bastard, and I'm going to have a word with him anyway. Now, what else have you got to tell me?'

'Well, when it happened, like, Mickey said as how it was diabolical, and that something ought to be done about it.'

'Like what? Did our Mr Lever mention his plans to you? Did he tell you what he had in mind?'

'Nah! 'Course not. But he was bloody angry about it. Went on forever about someone ought to do something.' Crowley lowered his voice. 'You've got to remember, Mr Brock, that Mickey Lever got out about a fortnight after Ken Johnson was killed. And he was still pretty angry when he went. Between you and me, I wouldn't put nothing past him.'

'Well, thanks for that,' I said.

'There's one other thing,' said Crowley.

'Surprise me,' I said.

'Post Office van job at Dartford, about a month ago. If I was you, I'd ask Lever some questions about it.'

I smiled. 'Not bad for a bloke who's not a grass,' I said.

Tom Challis reported back next day. 'I followed Strang from his address in Fulham this morning, guv. He went to Golden Square in Soho, parked his car, and went into a film studio. Stayed a couple of hours and then went home.'

'Good. It'll be better to interview him there, rather than at Anne Blakemore's address, and there's no time like the present.' I summoned Dave and we set off.

Strang lived in a basement flat off the Fulham end of King's Road. Not very far from where Blakemore was murdered. His old Ford Sierra was parked nearby.

'Mr Strang?' I introduced Dave and me. 'Could we have a word?'

Geoffrey Strang, about twenty-six or so, was stockily built, and a little under six foot tall. He was dressed in jeans and a denim shirt, and had the sort of chiselled good looks that many women find attractive. 'Don't tell me,' he said, running a hand through his shock of blond hair, 'you want me to make a film about the police.'

'I think there's been quite enough of those already, don't you, Mr Strang?' I said.

'Oh, well, I live in hope,' said Strang. 'You'd better come in. You'll have to excuse the mess the place is in.'

Strang had not exaggerated the chaos. The living room was cluttered with books and newspapers, dirty glasses and cups and saucers. There was an ironing board in one corner and a pile of washing draped over the back of an armchair.

'Hang on a moment and I'll make some space. Just trying to catch up on my ironing, as a matter of fact.'

'Don't worry,' I said. I was surprised that Strang ironed anything. From his appearance, he seemed to manage without too much in the way of clothes care. And if dry-cleaners depended on him, they'd go bankrupt.

Strang moved the pile of laundry and put it on the ironing board. 'Take a pew,' he said, and sat down opposite us. 'So, what's the problem?'

'You went to Golden Square this morning,' I said. 'At least, that's where your car was parked.'

'How the hell did you know that?' Strang looked surprised but then laughed. 'Oh, come on, fellahs, I know enough about the CID to know that they don't do people for parking. Anyway, the meter was out of order. I put a note on the windscreen.'

'Your car doesn't interest me, Mr Strang,' I said, 'but there was a robbery near there this morning. A snatch from a security van.' There had been no such robbery, but I'd invented the whole story just to get close to the man Eleanor Blakemore had described as her daughter-in-law's toy boy.

'There was?' A brief expression of alarm crossed Strang's face. 'Nothing to do with me,' he said, and laughed nervously.

I laughed too, but wondered why Strang should so quickly have protested his innocence. 'We're not suggesting there was, Mr Strang,' I said, and continued with my fictional tale, 'but officers at the scene took details of all the vehicles in the vicinity in the hope that the drivers might have seen something that would assist us in our enquiries.'

'Oh, right.' Strang appeared relieved at that. 'Well, I'm sorry,' he said, 'but I didn't see a thing.'

I shrugged. 'Nobody ever does,' I said, 'but sometimes we get lucky. As a matter of interest, between what times were you in the area?' It was a pointless question, but I was going through the routine of investigating my fictitious crime.

Strang pursed his lips. 'Got there about ten, I suppose. Left at about a quarter to one. Something like that.'

'And you saw nothing.'

''Fraid not.'

'Oh, well, sorry to have bothered you.' I paused in the act of leaving. 'So, you're in the film business, then.'

'Yeah, sort of.'

'Sort of?'

'I make trade films, adverts, documentaries, all that sort of stuff. In fact, anything that's going. When I can. It's a cut-throat business and everyone wants to get in on it. They seem to think it's glamorous but, frankly, it's a hand-to-mouth existence. To be honest, I'm thinking of packing it in and trying something else, or going to the States and having a go there. If I can get enough money together.' Strang paused. 'Mind you,' he said, 'it's worse over there than it is here.'

'Have you been to America before?' asked Dave.

'Only the once. I was working for a bloke who was making

a documentary about the New York harbour master. Fortunately he'd already bought me my return ticket. The producer, I mean, not the harbour master,' he added.

'Why fortunately?'

Strang laughed. 'Went bust, didn't he. Never finished the bloody film. Not that it mattered. I think most of it would have ended up on the cutting room floor anyway. Story of my life,' he added cynically. 'It was a spec thing that he was hoping to sell.'

'When was it that you were in New York, Mr Strang?' Dave always persisted in getting all the details.

'End of last year. Why?'

'Just interested,' said Dave. 'I've never been to the States. It was something I'd always wanted to do.'

'I shouldn't bother,' said Strang. 'It's not all it's cracked up to be, believe me. I'd only been there a day and I got mugged.'

'It happens,' said Dave nonchalantly.

'Nothing seems to be going right just lately.' Strang looked decidedly gloomy. 'Then Mr Blakemore was murdered.'

'Why should that affect you?' For a moment I wondered if Strang knew that we were aware of his liaison with Blakemore's widow.

'I was hoping to get alongside him.'

'Really? What for?'

'See if I could get him to talk to the people in the National Lottery and squeeze some money out of them. The government's supposed to help struggling British businessmen, or so I've heard.'

'But why an MP?' I asked. 'Backbenchers don't have anything to do with the National Lottery, surely?'

'I'm a friend of his stepdaughter, Caroline,' said Strang. 'I met her when we were working on a TV ad.'

'And did you get to meet him?'

'No, unfortunately. Caroline introduced me to her mother and she listened sympathetically and promised to speak to her husband, but I never heard any more. The next thing I know is that he's been murdered.' Strang shrugged. 'Some you win . . .'

'When was this?' asked Dave.

Strang looked across the room, at a picture of a man poling a punt. 'About four months ago, I suppose,' he said.

*   *   *

'What did you make of all that, then, Dave?' I asked, on our way back to Curtis Green.

'I don't think he'd got anything to hide, guv. He seemed quite open, and if he'd had anything to do with Blakemore's death, I think he'd've been decidedly more cagey. In fact, I doubt that he would have mentioned him at all. But, as far as I could tell, he regarded the incident as another door closing on his business hopes. It certainly didn't appear that he was well off. I think that when he said his was a hand-to-mouth existence, he was telling the truth. Frankly, I don't think the poor bastard's got two ha'pennies to bless himself with. Not if his car and his flat are anything to go by.' And that, for Dave, was a remarkably charitable observation.

'Ah, but don't forget he's in the film business, Dave,' I said. 'It's all fiction, you see. Very good at making things up, those fellows.'

FOUR

Mickey Lever, the robber who had been at Melbury with Johnson and Crowley, proved to be much more difficult to track down than Geoffrey Strang. He was no longer at the address he had given the prison authorities when he was released – if, in fact, he had ever been there – and everyone in the area to whom the police spoke denied all knowledge of him. But that was not unusual. The villains of Catford were not noted for helping the police.

Detective Sergeants Poole and Challis searched the bogus address that, unsurprisingly, proved to be the home of another villain, but one who was of no interest to us. Poole and Challis were, therefore, reduced to more primitive methods: debts owed by informants were called in; landlords of dubious pubs were leaned on; and petty criminals who frequented that particular tranche of south London were talked to in less than kindly tones.

The two detectives did not, however, bother to extend their enquiries north of the river; Mickey Lever was a south London villain and would never cross the Thames. Not if he valued his life.

But it was Detective Inspector Kate Ebdon who eventually found Lever. She had persuaded a small-time criminal that he owed her a favour, although he could not for the life of him recall what it was, and he had 'surrendered' the robber whom I was anxious to interview. And there was a bonus: Mickey Lever, said Kate's informant, had been involved in last month's robbery of a Post Office van in Dartford. Peter Crowley had told us this when we visited him in Wormwood Scrubs but, from our enquiries, it appeared that Lever's involvement was, so far, unknown to the detectives of the Kent County Constabulary. They were interested to lay hands on him.

'How very interesting,' I said, when I received this crumb of information. But rather than delight me, this confirmation of Lever's alleged participation in the Dartford Post Office van job left me wondering. Wondering whether it was a smokescreen

put up by Lever to divert our attention from his possible involvement in the Blakemore murder.

The address where Kate Ebdon's informant said that Lever
would be found proved to be a seedy terraced house in Forest
Hill. Ironically, it was less than two miles from Catford.

Living with Lever was a stripper and part-time prostitute
called Melanie Gabb who described herself as an artiste.

Not wishing to disappoint our target by varying our business practices, I took a small team – Kate Ebdon, Dave Poole
and Tom Challis – and hit the Lever household at five o'clock
the next morning. Dave knocked lightly, whispered 'police',
and then waited while a PC from the local nick opened the
door with a rammer; he called it a seven-pound key. We were
met with the usual depressing scene of disorder and an over-
powering stench of decay and dirt.

Lever was dragged from his bed while Melanie Gabb,
unwilling to display her undraped female form in the absence
of adequate remuneration, cowered under the bedclothes.

'What the bleedin' hell's this all about?' demanded the naked
Lever, faced with the difficult task of attempting to pull on
his jeans while wearing handcuffs. 'It's a bleedin' liberty,
that's what. Just because I've done time—'

'Save it, Mickey,' I said. 'Post Office van job. Dartford, last
month. Down to you. You're nicked,' I added, fulfilling the
spirit of the law, if not the letter, in advising the prisoner why
he was being arrested. 'Anything you say will be taken down
and if you don't say anything, that'll be taken down as well.'
I'd never managed to memorize the intricacies of the Judges'
Rules caution, and had lost the little card with it on.

'It's a bloody liberty,' said Lever again. Verbal communi-
cation was, it seemed, not one of his strong points.

'Where d'you keep your personal papers, Mickey?' asked
Dave.

'I ain't saying nothing,' said Lever.

Dave turned to Melanie. 'Where does Mickey keep his
personal papers, love?' he asked.

'Search me,' said Melanie, without looking at him.

Dave laughed. 'I'd rather not,' he said.

'OK, take the place apart,' I said.

The search, under Kate's directions, took the best part of
an hour, but she was a thorough officer.

Finally, it was Tom Challis who came up trumps. He returned to the bedroom and handed me a chequebook relating to a numbered Swiss bank account in Lever's name, together with a statement showing that the petty villain had deposited some £25,000 a few weeks ago, but had paid out £20,000 a matter of days later.

'What's this all about, Mickey?' Challis asked Lever.

'I ain't saying nothing,' said Lever.

I took the chequebook and statement from Challis and showed them to Melanie. 'What d'you know about this?' I asked.

Melanie's eyes opened wide when she read that Lever appeared to be worth £5,000. 'You double-dealing little sod,' she exclaimed, staring malevolently at Lever. 'You never told me nothing about this. And me scraping and screwing, trying to make ends meet.' She was obviously infuriated at the extent of Lever's wealth. 'He must've won the bleedin' lottery,' she said.

'We can soon check that,' said Dave, 'but somehow I doubt it. Your Mickey's never been that lucky.' He took back the papers relating to the account. 'He didn't say anything about it, then?'

'Did he hell, the bastard,' yelled Melanie.

I sat down opposite the sprawling figure of Lever in the interview room at Lewisham police station. 'Peter Crowley told me that you were a bad bastard, Mickey, and that I ought to have a word with you,' I said, not believing in reinforcing the fallacy that there was honour among thieves.

But Lever had been interviewed by police many times in his professional career, and was not going to be persuaded to talk that easily.

'I've got nothing to say. You've nicked me for the Dartford job, what I never done, and you ain't s'posed to ask no questions about that. And I want a brief.'

'Given your apparent in-depth knowledge of the Police and Criminal Evidence Act and related legislation, you don't seem to need one,' I said. 'In any case, I have no intention of talking to you about the Dartford job. That's a matter for the Kent police.'

'Oh!' said Lever.

'No, Mickey, it's far more serious than that.'

Lever did not like the sound of that. 'What, then?' he asked apprehensively.

'The contract that was put out on a certain Hugh Blakemore,' I said.

''Ere, bloody hold on,' said Lever, sitting up sharply in alarm. 'That's not down to me.'

'My information is that you took grave exception to Kenny Johnson falling downstairs and doing his head, so you determined to even the score.'

'Did bloody Crowley tell you that?' asked Lever, now clearly very angry.

'You should know that the police never divulge their sources of information,' I said, 'but the word is that you were very cross about it.'

''Course I bloody was. Some bleeding MP comes in the nick and thumps Kenny. Poor sod falls down the stairs and that's his lot. And what happened? Nothing, that's what happened. Bloody walked away from it, didn't he? Blakemore, I mean.'

'Yes, I assumed that's who you meant,' I said. 'Who gave Johnson the knife?' I knew that Johnson had, in fact, fashioned the weapon himself while working in the machine shop. At least, that was Principal Officer Watkins's view.

'What knife?'

'Oh, come on, Mickey. We both know that Johnson went for Blakemore with a knife. Several witnesses testified to—'

'Yeah!' scoffed Lever. 'All bloody screws, wasn't they? Say anything, those bastards would. Swear your life away.' He paused. 'Just like your lot.'

'Where were you on the second of this month, Mickey?' I asked.

Lever's brow furrowed as he applied what passed for his mental processes. 'Nothing to say,' he said eventually.

'Riding a motorcycle along Fulham Road by any chance?'

Lever laughed loudly. 'You must be joking,' he said. 'Where would I get a BMW from?'

'Where you get most things from, I imagine, Mickey. By nicking them. Anyway, how did you know it was a BMW?'

'I read it in the *Sun*,' said Lever. 'What did bloody Crowley say about me, anyway?' He was determined to try and find out if Crowley had grassed on him.

'He suggested that you swore vengeance on Blakemore for killing Johnson, and you were going to top him,' said Dave. That was varnishing the truth somewhat, but Dave never shied away from putting a little pressure on a hardened villain.

'That's a bloody lie.' Lever's denial was so genuine that I was almost convinced that he was telling the truth. 'Chance'd be a fine thing.' A sudden frown crossed Lever's face. 'Did bleedin' Crowley really tell you that?'

'What is it between you two, Mickey?' asked Dave.

Lever shot a glance in my direction, hesitated and then said, 'Crowley was a bloody nonce.'

'He was in for armed robbery,' I said.

'Yeah, I know what he was in for, but he was a bloody perv. See, what you've got to understand is that Kenny Johnson wasn't no villain. He'd been sent down for topping his missus.'

'I know all that, too,' I said.

'Well, bloody Crowley was screwing Kenny's arse, and Kenny didn't like it.'

'I don't suppose he did.' I wondered why Principal Officer Watkins at Melbury had not told me this. But even principal prison officers do not know everything that goes on in the nick, despite imagining that they do. Although they do sometimes cast a blind eye out of spite.

'Well, Kenny come to me and asked what he ought to do about it. He wanted to know if he should go to the governor, see. So I told him not to waste his breath 'cos nothing'd get done, 'cept the screws'd take the piss out of him. So he fixed himself up with the knife what he'd made in the workshops, and said he was going to use it next time Crowley had a go at him. 'Course, the next thing as happens is Kenny's having a go at this Blakemore finger.'

I stood up and turned to Dave. 'Hand him over to Kent,' I said. 'They'll probably think he's quite important.'

'What d'you think, guv?' asked Dave, when we were discussing our interview with Lever.

'Lever's IQ is probably in single figures,' I said. 'I doubt that he's got what it takes to set up a job like that. But I'm still not prepared to dismiss him from our enquiries into Blakemore's death.'

'But he didn't want to tell you what he was doing on the second of July, the day that Blakemore got hit, did he?'

'We'll find out,' I said.

'What about this tale he told about Johnson having a go at Crowley for committing buggery?' Dave asked.

'Forget it, Dave,' I said. 'No caution, no case. Anyway, a scenario like that'd frighten the life out of the Crown Prosecution Service.'

It was then that another useful snippet of information came my way. It appeared that a certain PC Charles Hamilton, who had been posted to the Blakemore front door, had taken Caroline Simpson out for a meal. I realized that our disparity in rank would probably inhibit the young constable from telling me all that had happened, if indeed anything at all had happened. The interesting aspect of this was that Caroline Simpson now appeared to be living with her mother. I gave the job to Dave Poole who wasted no time in getting the story.

'I asked him if he'd got his leg over, guv,' said Dave with a grin when he returned from Chelsea police station an hour later. 'He puffed himself up with piss and importance and said no. He reckoned he'd taken her to a pub in the King's Road and they had a very pleasant evening. He also said that she was a very nice girl.'

'Well, he would say that. Anything else?' I asked. 'What did you find out about her?'

'She's twenty-one and she's an actress,' said Dave, 'but we knew that already. According to Hamilton she's a member of the Labour Party, and is very interested in the underprivileged.' He broke off to chuckle.

'But how come she can go out with him in the evening, Dave? I thought actresses did permanent late-turn.' I knew that when my girlfriend, Gail Sutton, was working, I never saw her in the evenings.

'Hamilton said she was resting at the moment.'

'He means she's unemployed,' I said. 'Is she living permanently at her mother's home, or was she just visiting?' I knew what Anne Blakemore had said, but I always liked to check.

'Yes. Hamilton mentioned that Caroline is staying there for a few days. But that was obvious. He wouldn't have met her otherwise,' said Dave, 'but she's got a pad somewhere in north London. That's where she usually lives.'

'Did you get the address?'

'Yes, sir,' said Dave pointedly. He always called me 'sir' rather than 'guv' when I'd made a stupid comment, or brought his professional reputation into question. 'She doesn't get on with her mother apparently.'

'Did Hamilton say why?'

'He dithered a bit at first, but I explained to him, rather forcefully, that we were conducting an enquiry into the murder of Caroline's stepfather, an MP, who was gunned down in the Fulham Road.'

I had witnessed some of Dave's 'forceful explanations' before, and I could imagine that it probably scared the living daylights out of the young star-struck Hamilton.

'I explained to him that Blakemore's murder might have been a professional hit, a terrorist maybe, or it might have been something far more mundane than that. I told him that his precious Caroline was a suspect along with everyone else, but whatever the motive, we'd got to get a result. I also mentioned that the Commissioner was taking an interest, and that he had the Prime Minister breathing down his neck.'

'What did he say to that, Dave?'

'He reckoned that Hugh Blakemore resented Caroline's presence, which was one of the reasons she left home at the earliest opportunity.'

'Did Hamilton mention rows, or anything like that?' I asked. 'Did he say, for example, whether her mother objected to her leaving home?'

'Hamilton didn't know, guv.'

'I suppose she's staying at home to give her mother some support until after the funeral,' I suggested. 'Do we know if Caroline's got a boyfriend? A regular boyfriend, I mean.'

Dave laughed. 'No, but Hamilton's not likely to admit that, is he, guv? Even if he knew. He's only about twenty, and to be honest he's a moonstruck little tosser. He said that Caroline was different, whatever the hell that means.'

'Did he know whether she'd had any arguments with her stepfather?' I asked.

'Only political ones, apparently. Caroline told Hamilton that she and her stepfather disagreed on just about everything, him being a Tory and her being a socialist.'

'Is he going to see her again, Dave?'

'He's taking her out to dinner tomorrow. I was in two minds whether to warn him off altogether, given that she's a suspect, but then I thought it might be handy to use him. I told him to chat her up about her mother some more. I also told him to find out from Caroline what he could about Geoffrey Strang, but not to mention Strang's name to the girl. I suggested to him that it was Anne Blakemore who might have a friend who called often.'

'Good work, Dave. But once that line of enquiry's exhausted tell Hamilton that under no circumstances is he to see Caroline again. I presume you've cautioned him against letting anything slip.'

'Yes, guv, I have,' said Dave. 'I told him that you would be very cross with him.' He paused and smiled. 'Or words to that effect.'

'In that case,' I said, 'I think we'll have to take a chance on him. Apart from anything else we may just need to use him to feed information in. Depends on how it goes.'

The relationship between Anne Blakemore and the much younger Geoffrey Strang interested me. The annals of crime are littered with eternal triangles where two of the parties decide that everlasting happiness will only be achieved by the removal of the third party.

I decided that an observation on Geoffrey Strang might yield some important information. On the other hand, maybe I was fooling myself. But, to be honest, we had little else to go on. I asked Kate Ebdon to arrange for a watch to be kept on Strang's comings and goings. She deputed DS Challis.

After two days, however, there was little to show for such a profligate use of manpower. I was in the incident room when Tom Challis reported back.

'All that Strang's done is to visit that same film studio in Soho, guv. Seems to spend a lot of time there.'

'What about this studio, Tom? Porn, is it?' asked Dave, who tended always to take the cynical view.

Challis shook his head. 'No, Dave. All kosher. They make television adverts mainly, a few short films and in-house training DVDs for large corporations. I haven't made any enquiries to see exactly what friend Strang does there. Didn't think it was worth the risk of showing out.'

'No, you're right,' I said. 'Has he been to see Anne again?'

'Yes, guv,' said Challis. 'Two nights in a row.'

'There must be more to that woman than we realized. Well, keep the obo going for a few days more, Tom. We've got damn all else.'

On my way back to my office, I looked in on Kate Ebdon. 'Any news on Mickey Lever, Kate?'

'Gave him to Kent Constabulary, as you said, guv. But they gave him back.'

'They *what*?'

'At the very time the hit on the Post Office van was taking place in Dartford, Master Lever was deep in conversation with an official at the local Jobcentre,' said Kate. 'It's what they used to call the labour exchange,' she explained. 'But that's not all. At exactly the time the Blakemore shooting took place, Lever was in Catford nick reporting the loss of his wallet. What you might call a copper-bottomed alibi.'

'The carney little bastard,' I said. 'I don't believe a word of it.'

'The station officer at Catford remembers him going in, guv,' said Kate, almost apologetically. 'He made a bit of a fuss apparently, banging on the counter and all that. And it's in the Property Lost book.'

'I'm sure it is, Kate,' I said. 'But I don't believe he lost his bloody wallet. I know he's a bit thick, but he's a cunning little bugger. And the trouble with thick, cunning little buggers is that they tend to take risks that no intelligent villain would.'

FIVE

The following day, however, DS Tom Challis made a discovery. He had been joined in his surveillance by DC John Appleby, the thinking being that Appleby would drive, and that Challis could bale out if the need arose to follow Strang on foot.

At the end of the day, Challis reported back. 'Geoffrey Strang left his flat in Fulham at about ten o'clock in the morning and drove to Soho, guv,' he said. 'After spending several hours in the film studios, he went to a McDonald's for a burger, called into a Waterstone's bookshop and purchased a paperback, and then went home to Fulham. On the way he stopped at a phone box and made a call.'

'I wonder why he did that,' I said. 'Strang's got a telephone in his flat.'

'And he's got a mobile, guv. I saw him using it outside McDonald's.'

'The bugger's up to something,' I said.

'I wonder if he thinks that we've got his phone tapped,' suggested Challis.

That amused me. 'Why should he think he's so important that we'd bother about putting an intercept on his line?'

'He's up to something,' said Challis, repeating what I'd just said. 'Anyway, Strang stayed in his flat all afternoon. At about seven o'clock he came out, looked up and down the street, and then got into his car. He drove to a pub near Buckingham Palace. I went in, and Strang ordered himself a gin and tonic and sat down. Ten minutes later, a young woman entered the pub. She was dressed in jeans and a shapeless sweater, and Strang stood up, kissed her, and bought her a drink. Then they both sat down and began to talk quietly: too quietly for me to hear what they were talking about.'

'Where did they go from there, Tom?'

'They spent about an hour in the pub, and then they drove back to Strang's flat at Fulham. When we knocked off at eleven, the young woman was still there. We took up the obo again this morning, and the woman left Strang's flat at eight o'clock, hailed a taxi and was taken to Anne Blakemore's house.'

'Well, well,' I said. 'That's bound to have been Caroline Simpson, Anne's daughter.'

'I managed to get a shot of her as she was getting into Strang's car,' said Challis, producing a digital camera from his pocket.

I took the camera and studied the photograph Challis had taken. 'Ask Colin Wilberforce to get that printed up. It does look a bit like the girl in the photograph at Anne Blakemore's house – the one she said was of her daughter.' I considered the implications of Strang not only taking Caroline – if, indeed, it was her – for a drink, but apparently bedding her at his flat. 'Either Eleanor Blakemore, Anne's mother-in-law, has got it wrong, or Strang's servicing both mother and daughter.'

'Unless he only befriended Anne to get to Caroline,' said Tom.

'That's not the information we got from Eleanor,' I said. 'But I suppose it could be that he's not giving Anne Blakemore a seeing-to after all,' I added thoughtfully, loath to give up on that crumb of gossip.

'But what about the phone call he made, guv? The one from a telephone box.'

'Probably fixing to see Anne,' I said, still hoping that Eleanor Blakemore might have been right about her daughter-in-law. 'Either Strang was being careful or his mobile had run out of battery. Anyway, we're not going to find out who he phoned just by following him around. Give it another day, Tom. Then we'll review the situation.'

'Right, guv.'

'And one other thing, Tom. Ask Miss Ebdon to speak to the guv'nor at Chelsea. I want Hamilton taken off that fixed point outside the Blakemore house. If Strang is having Caroline over, I don't want a bloody punch-up on the doorstep if Hamilton finds out. On your way out, ask Dave Poole to see me.'

Dave Poole entered my office with two cups of coffee. 'You wanted a word, guv?' he asked.

'I've directed that Hamilton be taken off the fixed post at the Blakemores' house, Dave, but have one last word with him. See if he's got anything useful.'

Dave reported back an hour later. 'Apparently PC Hamilton's date with Caroline Simpson didn't come off, guv.'

'What happened there?' I asked.

'He was very reluctant to tell me, guv, but apparently she told the lovelorn Hamilton that she'd already got a boyfriend.'

'Say who this boyfriend was, did she?' I asked.

'No, she didn't, but according to Hamilton someone phoned the boyfriend and told him that Caroline was going out with a copper. And Caroline told Hamilton that she'd had a terrible row with this bloke, whoever he is.'

'And Caroline didn't tell Hamilton who this phone call was from,' I said.

'No, she wouldn't tell him. But she then went on to tell Hamilton that said boyfriend had asked her to move in with him. Then came the crippler: apparently the boyfriend strongly objected to the idea of her going out with a copper. So, Hamilton got shirty and suggested that the boyfriend had got something to hide and asked if he was one of her little political friends, and perhaps he'd been done for assaulting the police on a demo or something. Seems it developed into a full-scale row. And that, I imagine, is the end of a beautiful relationship.'

'Thanks for that, Dave. I think we can forget Hamilton, and from what Tom Challis was saying, it looks as though Geoffrey Strang is the boyfriend. But if he has got something to hide, it might be interesting to find out exactly what it is.'

My thought that Strang might be the boyfriend referred to by Caroline was confirmed by a phone call at ten past ten the following morning.

'It's Tom Challis, guv. I thought you might be interested to know that the bird who met Geoffrey Strang yesterday moved in with him first thing this morning. She was with him in his car, and they unloaded a whole lot of gear.'

'That bears out what Dave Poole learned from the infatuated Hamilton, Tom.'

'What d'you want me to do now, guv?'

'Take the surveillance off, Tom. It's just a waste of time.'

I'd no sooner replaced the receiver than Kate Ebdon appeared. 'We've traced the owners of the motorcycle and the car, guv, and there are a few bits and pieces you ought to know about. The lab brought up the frame and engine numbers on the motorcycle, and the chassis and engine numbers on the car.'

'Good. So, what do we know, Kate?'

'According to the DVLA at Swansea, the solo was last registered to a Frederick Bolton who lives at Sydenham, and the car, a Ford Mondeo, went out to a Freda Atkinson of Battersea. The lab is still examining the crash helmets and leathers that were found in the boot of the Mondeo. But under the front passenger mat they found a parking ticket that relates to a car park in Surbiton. There were also traces of mud on the driver's mat which the lab are trying to analyse.'

'And both those vehicles had been stolen,' I said. 'But were they *reported* stolen?'

'Only the car had been reported, guv,' said Kate, 'a fortnight before the hit. But there's no report of the motorcycle having been nicked.'

'Which means,' I mused, 'that the car had probably been kept somewhere in the meantime. And possibly the motorcycle too. Get Tom Challis going on the vehicle enquiries, Kate, as soon as possible, but tell him to concentrate on the motorcycle.'

'I was going to suggest that we rigged up similar vehicles with the original number plates on them, and have them shown on television, guv,' said Kate. 'Might just jog someone's memory.'

'I think we'll mark time on that for the moment,' I said, 'unless we get desperate.' With something like half a million cars and motorcycles in the country, a substantial number of which are in London, there was little chance of anyone remembering having seen them.

'I'll get the results of the lab tests to you as soon as possible,' said Kate. 'By the way,' she continued, 'we've got a result from Joe Daly at the embassy about the American passport that was found in the pocket of the leathers used by these two guys. Name of Vincent Rosso of Delaware.'

'And?'

'Duff, guv. A pretty good forgery, by all accounts. According to State Department records only twenty-five passports were issued in the name of Vincent Rosso. And they've all still got them.'

'So why was it there? Either we're looking for someone using a false identity, or it was there deliberately to mislead us. And, talking of being misled, get on the phone to the station officer at Catford and ask him, or her, if they took a phone number from Mickey Lever when he reported the loss of his wallet on the second of July.'

A few minutes later, Kate laid the information on the table in front of me. 'There y'go, guv.'

'Good,' I said. 'I'm going to get someone to ring Lever and tell him his wallet's been found. That ought to blow his mind for him.'

'Why should it?' asked Kate.

'Because I don't think he lost it, Kate,' I said, 'and I'd love to know what the little bugger's up to.'

'Oh, right,' said Kate. 'Want me to do it?'

'Don't be silly, Kate,' I said. 'With that accent of yours, he'd never believe you were in the Job.'

The Jaguar drew up outside the strip club in that square mile of vice called Soho. A man alighted and moved swiftly across the pavement to be followed by the driver as soon as he had locked the car. The first man was called Barry Todd; the second, Kevin Fagan.

''Evening, gents,' said a blue-jowled bouncer in a tired and badly fitting dinner jacket. 'Looking for a bit of fun? Plenty of nude girls in here. Just the thing for weary businessmen.' He gave a false laugh, but his quick glance took in the flashy suits of the men, and something about the confident way in which they had approached made him feel uneasy. These were not the average punters. Neither were they the young executives who thought that to spend an hour watching women take off what little clothing they had on to start with was terribly daring. Nor was there the usual rush to get through the door with the shifty nervousness of men who hoped that they would not be seen by anyone who knew them. These were men with an air of menace about the way they carried themselves: they were either the Old Bill or villains. 'Er, that'll be twenty quid each, gents,' he added hopefully.

'Shut it,' said Fagan, who was clearly Todd's 'minder'. The two pushed passed the bouncer and then stopped. Fagan turned. 'And you'll keep your finger off that bell, if you know what's good for you,' he said.

The bouncer held up both his hands. 'You won't get no trouble from me, guv'nor,' he said. He knew overwhelming odds when faced with them.

The two men walked through the dimly lit main room of the club, stopping briefly to admire a pair of naked eighteen-year-old girls gyrating slowly on a microscopic stage. They looked jaded and utterly bored. 'Nice boobs, the one on the

left, Kev,' said Todd, and made his way to the staircase near
the bar. The audience, their eyes riveted on the girls, did not
notice the two newcomers.

''Ere,' said the swarthy-looking barman, 'that's private up
there.'

'Shut it,' said Fagan. It was one of his most favoured expres-
sions in a somewhat limited vocabulary. 'Unless you want your
lights punched out.' That was his other favourite expression.

Todd flicked his fingers irritably, but said nothing.

At the top of the stairs they passed another stripper making
her way down to the stage. She was attired in a garish, quick-
release costume and high-heeled shoes, and carried a bunch of
ostrich feathers. 'Hello, darling,' she said, and shifted her chewing
gum from one side of her mouth to the other.

Todd pushed open the door of an office marked 'Manager'.
In fact the so-called manager was the owner, and he knew
Todd, and he knew his accomplice, and their arrival did nothing
to maintain his equanimity. He began to stand up behind his
desk.

Todd signalled him to stay seated. 'You ain't going to take
up my boss's offer, then,' he said. He sounded like a disappointed
insurance salesman, which was how he saw himself. 'Bit silly,
that, after the little accident you had here last week.' The 'little
accident' to which he was referring was the wholesale destruction
of the bar area, an assault on the barman, and the rape of one
of the strippers. 'Pity that.' Slowly Todd withdrew a pistol from
a shoulder holster and casually affixed the silencer that he had
taken from his pocket.

The strip club owner's eyes opened wide and, once more,
he started to rise, but his cry of alarm was stillborn. With a
subdued noise, like corks coming out of bottles, two rounds
hit him in the chest, throwing him down again into his chair,
and he and the chair toppled over backwards.

Todd sighed, and shook his head as he removed the silencer
and put it back in his pocket. He replaced the weapon in its
holster. 'Some geezers never learn,' he said.

The two men went back downstairs, crossed the floor and
made for the door.

'You didn't stay long, gents,' said the bouncer. 'Not to your
liking?'

'Shut it,' said Fagan and seized hold of the bouncer by the

lapels of his dinner jacket. 'You ain't never seen us, pal. Got
it?' The bouncer nodded dumbly. ''Cos, if you say a word,
we'll be back for you.'

It was less than fifteen minutes later that one of the strippers, a girl who went by the professional name of Nikki, called
into the office for her money and discovered the body of the
club's owner. Despite being only twenty-three, she was a
mature woman who'd seen it all; working in the environment
she did tended to make one grow up very quickly. She did
not scream, and she did not panic. She closed the door of the
office and made her way quickly downstairs to Charlie Pearson,
the bouncer, who was still attempting to drum up trade
from the doorway of the club.

'Charlie,' Nikki whispered, 'someone's shot the guv'nor.'

'Christ!' said Pearson. 'Is he hurt bad?' He knew instinctively who had done the shooting.

'I think he's dead,' said Nikki.

'Better call the Old Bill, I s'pose,' said Pearson reluctantly.
The last thing he wanted was the police crawling all over the
place, but to attempt to dispose of the body illegally would
merely bring more problems than it solved. He turned to the
telephone and dialled 999.

The first police on the scene were the crew of the local
instant response car. Seconds later, a CID 'Q' car drew into
the kerb, to be followed within ten minutes by two Flying
Squad officers who happened to be passing through West
End Central's area on their way back to Scotland Yard.

When the initial activity had died down, Detective Chief
Inspector Mark Ledger of Homicide and Serious Crime
Command (West) arrived on the scene to take charge, and to
marshal the crime-scene teams that were an integral part of any
murder enquiry. And Pamela Hatcher, a Home Office pathologist, was called out.

I heard about the cold-blooded murder of Solly Goldman from
Colin Wilberforce, and shrugged at someone else's misfor-
tune. Murders like that of Solly Goldman were among the
most difficult to solve.

But it wasn't until two days later, when the enquiry was
transferred to me, that I found there was a connection between
the murders of Hugh Blakemore and Solly Goldman.

Detective Chief Inspector Mark Ledger swanned into my office with an expression of great satisfaction on his face.

'I've got good news for you, Harry,' he said, settling himself in my armchair.

'Which will doubtless not be to my advantage, Mark,' I said.

'Got it in one, pal. The murder of Solly Goldman, two nights ago.'

'What about it?'

'The commander directs that you take it over.'

'Bloody hell! As if I haven't got enough to do with this Blakemore topping. Why's he done that?'

'Because the two rounds taken from Goldman proved to have been fired from the same weapon that killed Hugh Blakemore,' Ledger said slowly, and sat back with a contented smile on his face. 'The guv'nor seems to think they're connected.'

That, of course, was the problem with our commander. After he'd spent a lifetime in the uniform branch, interfering with traffic, and fighting running battles with football hooligans, someone in Human Resources had made the monumental decision to translate him into a detective. The unfortunate aspect of this manoeuvre was that he actually thought he *was* a detective. Other senior officers finding themselves in that position had let the professionals get on with the job while they sat back and coasted slowly and leisurely towards their pension.

'What's the SP, then, Mark?' I asked, although I'd picked up most of the story on the grapevine.

'About ten o'clock the night before last, two guys strolled into Solly's dive, and blew him away. End of story.'

'Any word as to who these two guys were?'

'There's a rumour going round the village that two hoods called Barry Todd and Kevin Fagan were responsible.' In common with the inhabitants of Soho, Mark always referred to it as 'the village'. 'But there's nothing to back it up. So far. Anyway, Harry, it's all yours now.'

'Thanks a bundle.'

'In short,' Ledger continued, 'the bouncer, a geezer called Charlie Pearson, tried to stop them coming in, but stood aside when, he said, they indicated that they were tooled up. He claimed not to have recognized them, but I'd be inclined to take that with a pinch of salt. However, Pearson said that they were dressed in flashy suits, whatever that means, and were confident in their

approach, which probably means they scared the living daylights
out of him.'

'You're enjoying this, aren't you, Mark.'

Ledger just laughed. 'Pearson went on to say that they weren't
your average punter, but to be honest, Harry, I dismissed all
that he said. I reckon he knew them, but isn't going to grass.
Particularly when he found out what had happened to the boss.'

'Anything else?' I asked.

'The two killers had a brief one-sided exchange with the
barman, a Maltese called Michael Gonzo, when he saw them
making for Solly's office. He told them it was private, but was
told to "shut it", which he promptly did. He, too, claimed not
to know the pair. But I think he had a lapse of memory that
resulted directly from his overwhelming desire to stay healthy,
and denied that there had been any trouble, this evening or
previously. But he had fourteen stitches in his left arm that
looked like a knife slash, and that was probably enough to buy
his silence. I asked him how he did it, and he said it was an
"accident".' Ledger laughed cynically.

'I wonder how this topping ties up with Hugh Blakemore's,'
I said, 'apart from the two rounds that were found in Goldman's
body.'

'Might be able to help you there, Harry,' said Ledger. 'It's
not very much perhaps, but Blakemore had been taking an
interest in organized crime, particularly protection rackets, strip
joints and massage parlours. He'd had several meetings with
the Association of Chief Police Officers and, from what I've
heard, was anxious to start a clean-up campaign, especially in
the West End. There was a story that he'd been seen wandering
around the fleshpots late at night, and on his own.'

'God preserve us from reforming politicians,' I said. 'And,
for that matter, from ACPO.'

'He'd made one or two speeches in the House about
smashing the gangs,' continued Ledger. 'All the usual vote-
catching stuff about the right of citizens to go about the streets
unmolested. You know the sort of thing.'

'Why the hell can't these people leave it to the police?' I asked.

'It looks as though Blakemore might have trodden on one
or two toes,' said Ledger, as he stood up to leave. 'Pity really,
because he was probably just a voyeur.'

SIX

'Miss Freda Atkinson?'

'Yes?' The grey-haired woman looked to be about fifty, and wore a grey skirt and blouse, with a red scarf that lent colour to an otherwise dull outfit. She stared apprehensively through her spectacles, first at me, then at Dave Poole, and back again to me. Battersea was not the safest of places to live, and one heard such terrible stories of men forcing their way into houses and flats and raping the female occupant.

'We're police officers, Miss Atkinson.'

'Oh?' Miss Atkinson still seemed unconvinced.

'It's about your car.' I produced my warrant card.

The woman examined the document carefully. 'You'd better come in,' she said, but remained clearly ill at ease. Perhaps it was the sight of the black giant standing next to me.

'We have recovered the vehicle,' said Dave, as he and I accepted Miss Atkinson's invitation to sit down.

'Where?'

'Richmond Park.'

'When?'

There was something school-marmish about the way Freda Atkinson was asking questions. In fact, she reminded me of Miss Purvis, a form-mistress from my infants' school days.

'Last Tuesday,' said Dave. 'I understand that you reported it stolen on the eighteenth of last month.'

'That's correct.' Miss Atkinson frowned. 'Why has it taken you so long to find it?'

'We believe it to have been hidden in the meantime,' I said. 'It was used by the two men who murdered Mr Blakemore, the MP for Millingham.'

'Good heavens!' Miss Atkinson put a hand to her mouth. 'How dreadful. Have you caught them yet?'

'Not yet, but we shall.' I was by no means as confident as I sounded. 'Miss Atkinson,' I went on, 'we found a parking ticket under one of the front seat mats.' I held out a hand and

Dave gave me the ticket, now contained in a plastic bag. 'This ticket.'

Freda Atkinson studied the small piece of paper for some seconds. 'Yes,' she said eventually. 'That was the day I went to Surbiton, but I don't know how it got under the mat.' For the first time since we had arrived, she smiled, a little guiltily. 'I'm not very good at cleaning out my car.'

'I see,' I said, mildly disappointed, though not surprised, that this particular lead had come to nothing. 'Where do you usually park your car when you're at home?'

'Outside,' said Miss Atkinson. 'It's not very safe, but I don't have a garage. It was taken during the night on—'

'Yes,' said Dave, 'on the eighteenth of June. We know that from the report you filed at Battersea police station the same day. We also found a deposit of mud on the driver's mat. Could you explain that?'

'No, I'm afraid I can't. I sometimes take the dog for a walk in Battersea Park, but I don't use the car. I know I said that I'm not very good at cleaning it out, but I certainly wouldn't leave mud on the floor.'

'Thank you, Miss Atkinson.' Dave and I stood up.

'Er, when can I have my car back?' Miss Atkinson stood up also. 'It's very inconvenient, not having a car.'

'I'm sorry, but I'm afraid it may be some time yet, Miss Atkinson,' said Dave. 'We'll probably need to examine it further. You see,' he added, 'it played rather a significant part in our murder enquiry. But we'll return it as soon as possible.'

'Oh, very well.' But despite her rather forbidding attitude, Miss Atkinson seemed to have been impressed by the fact that her car had been involved in a murder. She smiled once more. 'It'll be something to tell my pupils,' she said.

'Your pupils?'

'Yes, I'm a schoolteacher.'

Which came as no surprise to me. Or to Dave.

Our enquiry at Sydenham was not, however, as straightforward. Frederick Bolton, the owner of the stolen motorcycle used in the murder, was about forty years of age, was dressed in dirty jeans and a singlet, and wore his hair in a pony-tail. Which looked rather silly, considering he was bald at the front. He was obviously unhappy at receiving a visit from the police.

'Yeah, sure I owned it,' said Bolton, 'but I flogged it, didn't I.' Reluctantly, he switched off *EastEnders* and turned to face us.

'When?' asked Dave.

Bolton ran a hand round his unshaven chin. 'Must have been about a month back, maybe six weeks.'

'Who is it, Fred?' A woman appeared in the doorway of Bolton's front room. She too was attired in a pair of dirty jeans, and seemed quite unconcerned to be seen wearing just a bra – a bra that had once been white.

'Nothing to worry about, Trace,' said Bolton. 'It's only the Old Bill, come about the bike.'

'Oh,' said the woman and promptly disappeared, presumably in response to a child's screams from somewhere else in the house.

'Who did you sell it to?' I asked.

'Ah, now you're asking,' said Bolton shiftily.

'Yes, I am.'

'I don't rightly know his name . . .' The man was clearly hedging.

'Did you send off the slip from the V5?' asked Dave.

Bolton switched his gaze to my detective sergeant. 'The what?'

'It's the slip at the bottom of the registration document,' Dave explained patiently. 'You're supposed to send it to the Driver and Vehicle Licensing Authority in Swansea when you dispose of the vehicle.'

'I must have forgotten,' said Bolton, but it was unconvincing.

'Have you still got the document?' Dave persisted.

'Nah! Give it to the geezer what I flogged the bike to, didn't I.'

I decided that the time had come to inject a little fear into my questioning. 'Mr Bolton,' I said quietly, 'we're investigating a murder; a murder in which your motorcycle played a material part.'

Bolton sat down, suddenly. 'Christ!' he said. He looked up at us. 'But, like I said, I flogged it.'

'So you say, Mr Bolton, but we've only got your word for that, haven't we? You say you can't remember who you sold it to, and you didn't send off the slip that I mentioned just now.' Dave paused meaningfully. 'Which makes us wonder whether you were involved in this murder.' He held out his hands. 'It does rather put you in the frame, doesn't it?'

''Ere, bloody hold on,' said the alarmed Bolton. 'I don't know nothing about no murder.'

'It was the murder of the MP, Hugh Blakemore, in Fulham Road, last Tuesday,' I said.

Bolton appeared stunned by that. ''Ere,' he said, 'you don't mean that—' He broke off, his brain racing furiously. 'D'you mean that was my bike what was used?'

'Precisely, Mr Bolton. So the next question is, where were you on Tuesday the second of July?'

'I was here, like, with the missus.'

'Not at work then?'

'Nah! Well, I'm out of work at the moment, see. One of the reasons I flogged the machine. I needed the cash.'

'Well, then, that rather gets us back to the original question. Who did you sell it to?'

'It was a geezer in the boozer—'

'Isn't it always,' said Dave quietly.

'No, honest, stand on me,' said Bolton.

'Which pub was this?' asked Dave.

'The one on the corner of the road. You must have passed it on the way here.'

'Depends which end we came in from,' observed Dave drily.

'But I never knew his name.' Bolton struggled on with his explanation. 'He paid in readies, see, and he never wanted no receipt or nothing like that.' He gave me a guilty glance. 'He said something about not bothering with the VAT.'

'Really? How interesting.' I didn't believe that for a moment. 'Well, we're not interested in tax evasion, Mr Bolton. At least, not at the moment. We're not tax collectors, we're murder squad detectives.'

'Yeah, I know,' said the worried Bolton, running a hand round his chin again.

'Had you seen this man before? The man you sold your motorcycle to.'

''Yeah, quite a few times. He was often in the boozer.'

'And have you seen him since?'

'Yeah.'

'When was the last occasion, Mr Bolton?' I was now debating whether or not to arrest Bolton on suspicion of murder, but thought that I would just wait to see what he said next.

'Last Saturday, I think.'

'You think?'

'Well, yeah, definitely.'

'Did he mention this motorcycle that you claim you sold to him? Did he, for example, say whether he still had it?'

'Nah! Well, I never spoke to him, like. Not then. He was with his mates and I was with mine.'

'But you don't know his name.' There was a deliberate note of scepticism in Dave's voice.

'I told you, no.'

'In that case,' I said, glancing at my watch, 'why don't we have a walk down there now? See if he's about.'

It was obvious that Bolton did not like the sound of that, but he was in the invidious position of not knowing what was going to happen next. Doubtless, he'd had one or two brushes with the law over the years, and sensed that, any minute now, I might just be tempted to arrest him. On the other hand, Bolton was well aware that the purchaser of his motorcycle might have been involved in the murder that we were investigating. And in Sydenham retribution for grassing was swift and very painful, if not fatal.

'Yeah, well, I s'pose we could.' Bolton paused. 'I'd better get me gear on then.'

'Right, let's go and have a pint,' I said. I held out no hope that Bolton would identify the purchaser, even if he was in the pub, but it would give me the chance to survey the interior. Because I had a plan.

While Bolton was upstairs getting his 'wad', as he called his money, I briefed Dave to make a call on the car radio once we arrived at the pub.

Bolton returned to the front room, a dirty T-shirt being the only addition to his clothing. He shouted to his wife that he was going out for a while.

It was a typical south London pub. Most of the clientele seemed to be local, and I somehow doubted it would attract the yuppies from the gentrified area of Sydenham.

I ordered three pints of bitter, and had just taken the head off mine when Dave joined me. 'Cheers, guv'nor,' he said, and nodded. And when Bolton's attention was distracted, he held up ten fingers, twice.

Exactly twenty minutes later, DS Tom Challis and DC John Appleby strolled into the bar, having raced from Curtis Green in an unbelievably short time. I learned later that they had requisitioned a traffic car, brave fellows. Ignoring Dave and me, they ordered a drink and stood at the far end of the bar, reading the evening paper.

'Is he here, then, Fred?' asked Dave.

Bolton made a pretence of looking slowly around at everyone in the bar. 'Nah! He's not here tonight. Just my bleedin' luck,' he added. 'But I did flog it to him, honest.'

We finished our drinks. 'Well, if you do see him, tell him we'd like a word,' said Dave, and gave Bolton one of his cards. 'It is important.' He glanced at his watch. 'Well, we must be on our way.'

'Yeah, right,' said Bolton, clearly relieved at getting us off his back. 'Sure.'

I instructed Dave to take the car to a quiet street some distance from both the pub and Bolton's house. There we waited for about fifteen minutes before I got a call on my mobile from Tom Challis.

'He's nicked, guv'nor. Dartmouth Road nick.'

Challis met us at the entrance to the police station. 'Piece of cake, guv,' he said. 'The moment you'd gone, Bolton's across the bar to this finger we've got banged up and told him you were looking for him about the bike.'

'Who is he, Tom?' I asked.

'Sid "Guts" Slater, guv'nor,' said Challis, and handed me a printout he had just taken from the Police National Computer. 'Quite a bit of form for blagging, but nothing recent.'

I scanned the printout, and followed Challis into the interview room where Guts Slater was being guarded by DC Appleby. Slater was about thirty-five and balding, and what little hair he did have was close-cropped. He wore an earring in his left ear, and a substantial beer gut hung over the straining waistband of his jeans, hence, presumably, his nickname.

'You in charge?' asked Slater aggressively, as soon as Dave and I entered the room.

'You could say that,' I said.

'Well, what the bloody hell have I been nicked for? These

two gorillas ain't told me nothing.' Slater waved a derisory hand in the direction of Challis and Appleby.

'So you're Guts Slater.' Although Slater was a well-known villain, I had not had dealings with him before.

'So?' Slater did not seem at all offended at the use of his uncomplimentary nickname. 'Who are you?'

'DCI Brock, Homicide and Serious Crime Command.'

Slater absorbed that piece of disturbing information without making it apparent that it had in any way unnerved him. 'I still ain't been told why I've been nicked.'

'You haven't been nicked,' I said.

'Eh?' Slater blinked and sat up slightly. 'Well, if this ain't being nicked, I don't want to know what it's like getting me collar felt.' He grinned, displaying a mouthful of irregular, nicotine-stained teeth.

'No, you're here to help us with our enquiries, Guts.'

'So I can go any time I feel like it. Right?'

'Sure,' I said. 'When you've answered our questions.'

'Fire away, then, squire,' said Slater.

'You bought a motorcycle from Frederick Bolton between four and six weeks ago.'

'Who says I did?'

'The same Frederick Bolton,' said Dave.

Slater shrugged. 'So what if I did?'

'Where is it now?' I asked, but I knew exactly where it was. It was at the Metropolitan Laboratory at Lambeth. In pieces.

'Haven't a clue, mate,' said Slater.

'You mean you sold it.'

'Yeah, sure I sold it.' Slater glanced at Dave. 'Haven't got a fag, mate, have you?'

'You're not allowed to smoke in here, Guts,' said Dave. 'It's against the law.'

'Who did you sell it to?' I was beginning to tire of repeating the very same questions I had asked Bolton an hour ago. 'And don't say a bloke you met in a pub.'

Slater laughed insolently. 'I sold it to me brother-in-law.'

I sighed. 'And who's got the registration document for the vehicle?'

'Well, he has, of course. That's the law, ain't it?'

'And did you advise the DVLA at Swansea of the transfer of this vehicle?'

'Nope. The brother-in-law said he'd do it.'

'Name?'

'Sid Slater.'

'Don't get clever with me, Slater.' Dave slammed his hand on the table so violently that Slater jumped. 'I know *your* bloody name, sunshine,' he said. 'It's your brother-in-law's name I want. And his address.'

'What's this all about?' asked Slater in an aggrieved tone, although I was certain that he'd been told by Bolton.

'Murder, that's what it's about, Guts.'

'Bloody hell,' said Slater, and promptly furnished me with the name and address of his brother-in-law.

After Sid Slater had been released on bail, and Challis and Appleby had gone on their way, Dave asked, 'But what about Guts Slater's brother-in-law, guv? Shouldn't we have held on to Guts until we'd seen him? I mean, Sid's probably on the trumpet right now, tipping him off.'

'We had nothing to hold him on, Dave,' I said. 'And, for all we know, his brother-in-law might be on holiday in Tenerife for a fortnight. If he exists at all. But if he doesn't we'll descend on Slater like a ton of bricks. He's not going anywhere.'

Dave was obviously unhappy with that, but saw the sense of it. 'Are we going to have a go at him tonight, guv, just in case?'

'What time is it, Dave?'

Dave glanced at his watch. 'Half ten, guv.'

I shook my head. 'He'll keep until tomorrow. As I said, if Slater's going to tip him off, he'll have done it already. Anyway, I'm not traipsing round the back streets of New Cross at this time of night.'

Dave nodded his head in agreement. 'Dead right, guv,' he said. 'Much too dangerous.'

SEVEN

In the end, I decided that none of my officers would be able convincingly to impersonate the station officer at Catford police station, so I imposed on the genuine article to make the telephone call to Mickey Lever about his lost wallet. I sent DS Flynn to Catford to monitor the conversation on an extension phone.

At first, Lever sounded mystified that the police at Catford should be telephoning him about a lost wallet. But then he recovered himself. 'Oh, yeah,' he said, 'I'd forgotten.'

'Forgotten that you'd lost your wallet, Mr Lever?' The Catford sergeant injected an element of surprise into his voice.

'Yeah, well I found it, didn't I?'

'So you hadn't lost it at all?'

'No.'

'I see. Well, I'll cancel the entry in my books.'

'Yeah, I s'pose so,' said Lever.

When Flynn recounted this conversation to me, I expressed no surprise whatever. 'How very interesting, Charlie.'

Dave Poole strolled into my office, hands in pockets. I really ought to speak to him about discipline, but he'd probably apply for a transfer. 'I've just had a call from Fat Danny, guv'nor. Wants a word about the Blakemore job. Reckons he's got something for us.'

Fat Danny was an odious creep and, as befitted such a character, was a crime reporter on one of Fleet Street's worst tabloids. Nevertheless, it was possible that he did have some interesting snippet for me, because he knew that if he ever crossed me, he'd never play a computer keyboard again.

'Where is he, Dave?'

'In the downstairs bar of the Red Lion, guv.' Dave spoke as though there was nowhere else Danny *could* be.

Sure enough, Fat Danny was at his usual place at the end of the bar.

'What have you got, Danny?' I did not believe in wasting time.

'What I haven't got is a full glass, Mr Brock,' said Danny with a lopsided grin. 'But have you got anything for *me*?' he asked hopefully.

'Nothing you don't know already,' I said, reluctantly buying Danny another pint. 'We've recovered the car and the motorcycle, but the villains'll know that. They left them in rather obvious places. They were both nicked, the vehicles I mean, but then they would've been, wouldn't they?'

'Does the name Tyler mean anything to you?' asked Danny. 'Paul Tyler?'

I shook my head. 'No, should it?'

'He was one of Anne Blakemore's fancy men.'

'*One* of them?' I was mildly surprised. I knew about Strang, although it was looking more and more likely that it was Caroline he was interested in, but that there could have been others was interesting. Certainly, Eleanor Blakemore had spoken of 'several' lovers.

'Believe me, Mr Brock, our Anne's a regular goer.' Danny extended his podgy little hands, and waved them about. 'I'm surprised you didn't know about it. Tyler is a Yank who was very friendly with Anne for at least eighteen months before Blakemore was killed. And I do mean *very* friendly. But about three months ago, round about the time that Blakemore topped Johnson in Melbury, Tyler disappeared from the scene. Probably went back to the States. It was common knowledge around Fleet Street that Tyler and Anne were having an affair, and we were just waiting to break the story when he upped and vanished. So I wondered whether he'd surfaced again, now that Blakemore's no longer with us.'

I shrugged. 'The name hasn't cropped up in our enquiries,' I said.

Danny gulped down the last of his beer. 'Of course, Blakemore wasn't all lily-white, but then you'd know that.'

'Are you talking about his affair with Anne, eight years ago, when he was still married to Dorothy?'

'Christ, no! Everyone knew about that, Mr Brock. And anyway, that's par for the course for politicians, isn't it?' Danny lowered his voice. 'No, I'm talking about dropsy.' He rubbed forefinger and thumb together.

'Bribes, you mean? You're joking.'

'It's no joke, Mr Brock.' The journalist pointed at our glasses. 'Same again?'

'About time,' muttered Dave.

'Would you care to expand on that, Danny?' I asked once he had paid for the next round. I was by no means convinced of the truth of what Danny was saying. I'd fallen for Fleet Street scuttlebutt in my younger days as a detective, and had no intention of doing so again.

'A little bit of encouragement here, a nod and a wink there, and suddenly someone's landed a great big contract that a better outfit should have got. Then Hugh gets a little present for his assistance. Surprise, surprise.'

'You got any proof of that?' asked Dave, the scepticism plain in his voice.

'If enough people say it, it's got to be true.' Danny gave a short, cynical laugh. 'But we don't need the same level of proof as you guys. We don't have the Crown Prosecution Service to worry about.'

'No,' said Dave. 'Just the libel laws.'

Danny laughed again. 'Worth it if it pushes the circulation up,' he said, 'and a nice little bonus for the reporter who dug it up. But I'll tell you this: Blakemore was in serious financial trouble. The settlement for his divorce from Dorothy cost him an arm and a leg, and he had to sell all his shares. But he still went on living the high life, with Anne spending most of what he'd got, so I heard. There was a whisper that the Tory party bailed him out, but I doubt that, although he does seem to have been what Wellington's army used to call a chosen man.'

'What's that mean?' Dave was obviously unsure what Danny was driving at.

'Blakemore was the member for Ferrington when the boundary changes were announced, and overnight his healthy majority was set to disappear. Word is that strings were pulled, possibly even a gong or two promised, and suddenly Blakemore finds himself selected for the neighbouring constituency of Millingham. With a majority of fifteen thousand.' Danny took another swig of beer. 'You know what I'm saying?'

'Bloody hell,' said Dave. 'Is that it?'

Danny laughed. 'Not quite,' he said. 'There was a rumour that Blakemore was having an affair with an actress.'

'Now *that* is interesting, Danny,' I said.

'Yeah? Why?'

'His stepdaughter's an actress.'

'Oh, that, yes, I know. Coincidence, isn't it?'

'D'you have a name for this actress?' I asked.

'Yeah, sure I do,' said Danny. 'Cost you a Scotch though.'

Back at Curtis Green, I was still mulling over what Fat Danny had told us, but I was unimpressed by his so-called information. 'I don't see that it helps at all, Dave,' I said. 'Sure as hell, we're not going to find anyone who'll hold up his hands to bribing a Member of Parliament. If it's true.'

'I think it's worth looking into, guv—' began Dave.

'In case he reneged on a deal and someone decided to top him, you mean?' I asked.

'Exactly, guv.'

'There must've been a lot of money involved, if that was the reason, Dave,' I said. 'And it might be as well to find out a bit more about this actress. Hell hath no fury, and all that.'

'If you're quoting Congreve, guv, it's, "Nor hell a fury like a woman scorned".'

'Thank you for that, Dave,' I said. 'But, moving on, have you got any informants in high places?'

'I've got a pal on the Protection Command, guv. It's surprising what these guys hear when they're sitting in the front of a minister's car.'

Two days after our interview with Sid Slater, Dave and I visited Reggie Manning who, Slater claimed, was his brother-in-law and the purchaser of the BMW motorcycle used in the murder of Hugh Blakemore.

Manning lived in a part of New Cross where villains were thick on the ground, and he proved to be one of them. When Dave had interrogated the Police National Computer, it had produced four Reginald Mannings; two of them were serving sentences of imprisonment, the third lived and operated in the Newcastle area, and the fourth in south London.

'It's got to be him, guv'nor,' said Dave. 'It's got to be.'

It was.

'I heard you was coming,' said Manning with the rare sort of confidence, for him anyway, of knowing that he was in the clear. At least, if his was the motorcycle in which the police were interested. For once, he found himself in the unusual position of being a victim rather than a criminal. 'Come in.'

'I suppose Sid Slater rang you,' said Dave as he and I followed Manning into his kitchen.

'Yeah, course. Families have got to stick together, ain't they? Want a cup of tea?'

I gazed round the kitchen, taking in the piles of dirty crockery and saucepans that seemed to cover every available surface, and a cooker top that appeared not to have been cleaned for months. 'No, thanks,' I said.

'Suit yourself,' said Manning, and poured tea into a grimy, chipped mug before sitting down at the stained, Formica-topped table.

'Your wife not here?' I asked.

'Nah!' Manning gave us a crooked grin. 'Doing six months up Holloway, ain't she? Got done for shoplifting. Seventh offence, silly cow,' he said. 'Least, the seventh they knew about. Have a pew, gents.' He waved a hand at a couple of chairs. 'Now, what can I do you for?'

'This BMW motorcycle, Mr Manning—'

'The one I bought from Guts, you mean?'

'Were there others then?' asked Dave.

A brief frown crossed Manning's face. 'No,' he said, his expression indicating that he thought Dave was a bit slow in grasping the situation.

'Oh, good. What happened to it?' I asked.

'Got nicked.'

'Did it really?' I was far from happy with Manning; his demeanour was too confident, his responses too bland. 'Then why didn't you report it to the police?'

'What's the point?'

'The point, Mr Manning, is that your insurance company will insist on your reporting it stolen. Otherwise they won't pay out.'

'Wasn't bloody insured, was it?' said Manning mournfully. 'Only had the bleedin' thing for twenty-four hours.'

I hoped that Dave wouldn't launch into a short lecture about the licensing and insuring of motor vehicles left on a public road.

Fortunately, he didn't.

'So what happened?' Dave had established that Bolton had sold the motorcycle to Slater on the sixth of June, and that Slater had sold it to his brother-in-law, Manning, on the twentieth of June. Now, Manning was claiming that it had been stolen less than twenty-four hours later.

'I left it outside, didn't I, and I put a bloody great chain round it. But when I come out the next morning, it had gone, chain an' all.'

'Even though it wasn't insured,' said Dave, 'did it not occur to you that the police might have recovered it, nevertheless?'

Manning shrugged. 'No chance,' he said. 'I know what happens to these things. Get chopped up for spares and then they're flogged.' He seemed resigned to the loss of his motorcycle.

'How did you get the bike here, to this address?'

'Rode it, of course, I—' Manning stopped abruptly.

'Using an uninsured motor vehicle on a public road is an offence,' said Dave mildly, but it was an empty victory; there was no proof other than Manning's statement. But that was irrelevant. Dave knew that we were going to get no further without much better evidence than our interviews with the recent owners of the BMW had provided so far.

Apart from anything else, uninsured motor vehicles were not really our concern, not when we had a murder to solve.

Manning knew it too. 'No, I forgot,' he said. 'I borrowed a trailer and brought it round here on that.'

'We shall undoubtedly have to see you again, Mr Manning,' I said, and silently vowed that if there was another interview, it would take place at a police station.

Dave Poole's friend in Protection Command had been at the Hendon Police Training School with him, and they had remained in touch ever since. And Dave's pal was now an inspector.

'I think I can help you out here, Dave,' he said. 'I know a particular MP who is very pro-police, and who takes a poor view of those of his fellow MPs who sail close to the wind. I'll arrange an interview with him.'

Dave and I entered the MP's office in the Norman Shaw Building in Bridge Street and accepted his invitation to take a seat and to have a cup of coffee.

'Well, Mr Brock, what can I do for you?'

Briefly I outlined what I had heard from Fat Danny, the journalist who had fed me the story of Blakemore's alleged venality, and waited.

The MP smiled. 'Yes, I've heard that,' he said, 'but quite frankly any MP who took a bribe would be wide open not only to severe censure – or even expulsion – by the House, based on the Nolan Rules, but doubtless to prosecution for corrupt practice as well.'

'Then how did such a story get about?' I asked.

The MP shrugged. 'Hugh Blakemore wasn't exactly having a love affair with the press,' he said. 'After that business at Melbury prison—' He broke off. 'You know about that, of course, Mr Brock?'

'Yes, I do.'

'Well, after that broke, the paparazzi hounded him, and journalists started poking about in his private life, which wasn't altogether above reproach.' The MP smiled archly at the prospect of another Member getting caught for what he had perhaps done himself in the past. 'And they generally made his life a misery. But you know what the tabloids are like. Once they get a sniff of scandal, they'll worry it to death. Some of them are even prepared to go out on a limb and risk an action for libel.' The MP took off his glasses and began to polish them with his handkerchief. 'But they know damned well that, in many cases, someone in public life won't risk a court case. They're always terrified at what else might come out.' He paused. 'And in Hugh's case, one never knew quite what that could be.'

'But surely,' I said, 'the prime minister would have known if there was even the slightest hint of scandal? And I understand that he got a safe seat when his own came under threat from the boundary changes.'

'You *have* done your homework, Mr Brock,' said the MP with a smile, 'but there is such a thing as loyalty, you know. I think the PM knew what was happening and was not going to have the media dictate to him who he should or should not appoint to government office. You've heard the phrase a dozen times: "The Honourable Member has the Prime Minister's full confidence." That's usually said just before the said Member resigns. But, that apart, the word was that Hugh Blakemore was in the running for a Minister of State's job.'

'I've also heard that Mr Blakemore had a bee in his bonnet about the vice trade. Strip clubs, massage parlours and that sort of thing.'

The MP laughed. 'I'll say he did. Whenever he could catch the Speaker's eye, he'd launch into some lengthy diatribe about it. He'd go on for ages. But he caught the Speaker's eye less and less and, apart from anything else, the moment poor old Hugh stood up, it signalled a rapid departure from the Chamber.' He paused to give emphasis to his next statement. 'Look, I think I know what you're getting at, and why you're getting at it. A promise that hadn't been honoured after payment had been made? That sort of thing?'

'Maybe,' I said cautiously.

'Mmm!' said the MP thoughtfully, and gazed out of the window. 'If I hear anything, Mr Brock, I'll let you know,' he said. 'Now that Hugh's dead, the tongues may start to wag a little more vigorously. Leave it with me.'

And I had to be satisfied with that. For the moment.

In the event, I never heard another word.

'So, Kate,' I said, 'tell me what you've learned about Mrs Blakemore.'

Kate Ebdon sat down and opened a file. 'Born forty-one years ago in Dagenham, guv,' she began. 'Her father was described on the birth certificate as a master baker and her mother was an usherette at a local cinema until the time of her confinement. The young Anne Croucher, as Mrs Blakemore then was, went to secretarial college and, at the age of seven-teen, got a job with a firm of wholesale fruiterers in Covent Garden. At the age of nineteen, she moved to a public relations company in the West End.' She turned over a page in the file and paused. 'It was there she met and married the boss, Charles Simpson, a year later. She was already pregnant and gave birth to her only child, Caroline.'

I laughed. 'She's certainly acquired a few airs and graces for a Dagenham usherette's daughter. Anything else?'

'It was the public relations business that gave her the entrée to parliament. She was engaged on some work for a political lobbyist and met Hugh Blakemore.

'Eventually he offered her a job as his researcher-cum-secretary and, parliament being what it is, he finished up spending more time with her than with his wife. Given that Anne was not averse to hopping into bed with him whenever he asked, and they were none too discreet about it, it was inevitable that the first Mrs Blakemore eventually found out, and there followed an acrimonious divorce.' Kate smiled. 'Anyway, Anne then divorced Simpson and married Blakemore.' She closed the file. 'That's about it, guv,' she said.

EIGHT

It was not very difficult to trace Charles Simpson, Anne Blakemore's first husband. Kate Ebdon had reported that he owned a public relations company in the West End of London, and a quick search on Google had taken her to a flash website, proving that it still existed.

The offices were typical of the more flamboyant PR businesses that charge a small fortune for providing very little in the way of public relations. There was a richly carpeted reception area with a profusion of large potted plants, expensive furnishings, and a languid blonde seated at a designer glass desk, chosen for its appearance rather than its practicality. All were of the highest quality, including the blonde. She looked up from behind a discreet flat computer screen.

'Mr Simpson, please,' I said. 'He is expecting us.'

'What name is it?' The receptionist glanced at her computer screen, her hands hovering expectantly over the keyboard.

'Brock and Poole.'

'Limited?' The receptionist looked up.

'Very,' said Dave.

The woman fed the details in, her fingers moving effortlessly over the keys. Without looking up, she asked, 'What's it in reference to?'

'If Mr Simpson wants you to know that, I dare say he'll tell you,' said Dave amiably, thereby arousing the woman's hostility.

'I'm supposed to put it all in.' The receptionist looked up, a plaintive expression on her face. 'We have to keep a record, you see.'

'It's a hard life,' said Dave.

With a resigned shrug at the unhelpful attitude of some of the agency's clients, the woman pressed a transmit key on her computer. Within seconds a reply appeared on the screen. 'Mr Simpson's secretary will be out shortly,' she said.

'Wouldn't the phone have been quicker?' asked Dave innocently.

'This computer embodies a telephone,' said the receptionist airily, and gave us another hostile glance.

A few minutes later, a woman, almost identical in appearance to the receptionist, emerged from a door at the rear. 'Would you come this way, please, gentlemen.'

Charles Simpson was a big man in his late forties, and was wearing a suit that must have cost at least a couple of thousand pounds. I guessed that, in his youth, he had been an enthusiastic sportsman, but since giving up, the muscle had turned to fat.

'Chief Inspector Brock?' With hand outstretched, Simpson advanced across his office, the beaming smile on his face a fixture designed to cultivate prospective clients and to put them at their ease. 'Do sit down, both of you.' He waved at a group of armchairs. 'What can I do for you?'

As we sat down, the secretary appeared with a tray of coffee.

'We're investigating the murder of Hugh Blakemore,' I said, once the secretary had left the office and the door had closed behind her.

Simpson nodded gravely. 'A dreadful thing to have happened,' he said, making it sound as though he had just lost a valuable account to a rival agency.

'You were married to Anne Blakemore at one time, I understand,' I said.

'Yes, I was. But we parted about eight years ago.'

'I gather that it was a rather acrimonious divorce,' said Dave.

Simpson frowned. 'How did you know that?' he asked.

'If the police disclosed their sources of information,' I said, 'people would be less inclined to talk to us. By which I mean that anything you tell us will be in confidence.'

'Yes, I see.' Simpson was obviously not too happy to find that someone else had been talking to the police about his marital affairs. He toyed briefly with a desk-tidy and then looked up, realizing that I was waiting for a reply. 'Yes, I suppose you could call it acrimonious,' he said, 'but, if you don't mind me asking, what has that to do with Hugh Blakemore's death?'

'I don't know that it has,' I said, 'but until I ask questions, I won't know, will I?'

Simpson sighed. 'Anne came to work for me, as a secretary

to start with, but she displayed a talent for the business and I moved her to the consultancy side.

'She was very good with clients and secured one or two quite profitable accounts. We got married and had Caroline.' He dismissed his marriage and the birth of his daughter in a single sentence. 'The problems arose when Anne moved into the field of political lobbying. She spent a lot of time at the House of Commons, and that's where she met Hugh Blakemore.' He gave a resigned shrug. 'The rest, as they say, is history.'

'Did you know that she was having an affair with Hugh Blakemore, Mr Simpson?' asked Dave.

'Not until it was too late. She came home one day and calmly announced that she was leaving me and was going to marry Blakemore.'

'And what was your reaction to that?'

For the first time, Simpson appeared to lose his urbanity. 'What the hell d'you think?' he demanded angrily, but immediately apologized. 'I'm sorry,' he said, 'but it still rankles, even after eight years.'

'I suppose so,' I said sympathetically.

I certainly knew all about divorce. I had met my German wife Helga Büchner when she was a staff physiotherapist at Westminster Hospital. As a uniformed PC, I'd been involved in a ruckus with a mob of youths in Whitehall and pulled some muscles in my shoulder. Helga was the physio who put it right. It was a whirlwind affair and a very quick marriage. The cynics at the nick asked if she was pregnant, and the wiseacres said it wouldn't last. But it did: for sixteen years. The crunch came when Helga insisted on continuing to work after Robert was born. One day she left him with a friend, and Robert, by then aged four, fell into the friend's pond and drowned.

I still remember that awful day. I was a detective sergeant on the Flying Squad at the time. My detective superintendent appeared in the doorway of the office, and crooked a finger in my direction. My immediate thought was that I was about to get a bollocking for something. But it was worse. He told me what had happened, and told me to take as much time off as I needed.

That was the beginning of the end. Affairs – on both sides – flourished, and divorce followed. The only lasting advantage of having been married to Helga was that I learned to speak fluent German, but, on balance, I'd've been better off going to night school.

I was about to dismiss the entire interview with Simpson as a waste of time when he spoke again.

'The trouble was that Blakemore was very useful to us.' Simpson lowered his voice. 'He was extremely sympathetic to some of the causes for which our clients were lobbying and . . .' He broke off, clearly wondering whether to commit himself, but two reasons prompted him to continue: one was that he had an old score to settle; the other that Blakemore was dead. 'He was not above accepting the occasional gift for, er, services rendered.'

'Are you suggesting he took bribes?' asked Dave crushingly.

Simpson, whose profession had made him a master of euphemism, winced. 'That's one way of putting it, I suppose,' he said hesitantly.

'Would you care to put it more specifically?' I asked, sensing that Simpson might be revealing a motive for Blakemore's murder. That interested me, and I had no intention of leaving the subject until I'd got as much as I could from him.

'It was nothing blatant, and I must emphasize that it was only what I'd heard. You must understand that I had no direct involvement,' said Simpson, hurriedly backtracking. 'If there was such an arrangement, it was between Blakemore and the company that wished to use his services. I don't think it amounted to asking questions in the House, or anything like that. More behind-the-scenes work really. It seems that he knew the right people to approach and, apparently, a client would pay for Blakemore to take a trip abroad if it was going to be helpful to their business. That sort of thing.' The PR man sighed. 'But it's only what I've heard,' he emphasized again.

'How often did this occur? Or, more to the point, how recently?' I noticed that Simpson was anxious to shift the responsibility for those payments on to his clients, thinking perhaps that he had committed some offence of corruption.

Simpson bridled at that. 'Our relations with our clients are confidential, Chief Inspector—' he began.

But I was having none of that. 'That sort of defence, Mr Simpson,' I said, deliberately using the word 'defence', 'can only be used by lawyers, medical practitioners and clergymen. And not always then.' Simpson looked decidedly unhappy and I drove home my advantage. 'We could always obtain a search warrant, of course,' I added. Secretly, I didn't think there was much chance of securing a warrant for what, so far, would be at best extremely tenuous evidence, and at worst a fishing expedition.

'This is in confidence, isn't it, Chief Inspector?' Simpson asked nervously.

'I've already said so, Mr Simpson.'

'I suppose it was about three months or so before he died.'

'So you continued to have business dealings with Blakemore long after your divorce.'

'Yes.' Simpson spread his hands. 'I wasn't going to ask too many questions,' he said, almost squirming at being forced to reveal his business practices.

'Well, I may have to,' I said.

Simpson looked gloomy at the prospect. 'Yes,' he said, 'I suppose you must.'

I'd come to the conclusion that if Blakemore had been accepting bribes for a period of eight years, the investigation was not only going to take some considerable time, but could well present the police with difficulties. Politicians tended to close ranks in the face of such enquiries. Oh boy, and how! 'You said that the most recent occasion that one of your clients made use of Mr Blakemore's assistance was about three months ago.'

'Yes, about then.' Simpson was clearly trying to keep things on an airy-fairy basis.

'And who were these clients?'

'It was a large British company seeking to secure a contract.' Simpson looked very uncomfortable at making the revelation.

'What sort of company?' asked Dave patiently. We both realized that it was not going to be easy to extract the relevant details from Simpson.

'Electronics. They were up against a Japanese company that, quite honestly, had a better deal on offer.'

'Go on,' prompted Dave.

'The British company approached us for assistance. We contacted Blakemore, and I gather that he spoke to certain people in the company that was placing the order. The next thing is that the company Blakemore had "assisted", so to speak, landed a multimillion-pound contract. And were very pleased.'

'And no doubt showed their appreciation in the usual way?' I said.

Simpson shrugged. 'Your guess is as good as mine, Chief Inspector,' he said. 'I, that is to say, my company, had nothing to do with that side of things. It would have been most improper.'

'Naturally,' I murmured. 'But presumably you told this company who it was who had been instrumental in their good fortune?'

'Well, of course, but it goes on all the time, Mr Brock.' There was desperation now in Simpson's voice. 'It oils the wheels of trade.'

'But it doesn't usually involve a Member of Parliament,' said Dave, fixing the unfortunate Simpson with an unwavering gaze. 'Well, all that remains now is for you to give me the name of the company that secured the contract. And the one that placed the order.'

Simpson had known all along that it would come to this. 'What's likely to happen about all this, Mr Brock?' he asked, switching his gaze to me. 'I mean, will there be a court case?'

'That's a matter for the Crown Prosecution Service,' I said. It was not meant to be helpful, and Simpson was not comforted by it. But then neither was I; I knew that the moment the police began asking questions of an electronics conglomerate, an army of lawyers would appear on the scene intent on frustrating the enquiry at every turn. 'But my main concern is to discover Blakemore's murderer.'

With a gesture of resignation, Simpson drew a pad across the desk and scribbled details of the two companies.

To Dave's amazement, I didn't seem at all surprised at Simpson's revelations.

'It tallies with what we heard from Fat Danny, Dave. What we got from Simpson merely confirms the rumour. Particularly the bit Fat Danny told us about Blakemore being in serious financial trouble.'

'It's a bit more than a rumour, surely, guv?' said Dave.

'Maybe. It's the Aunt Sally syndrome, you see.'

'What in hell's the Aunt Sally syndrome, guv?'

'When people become politicians, they volunteer for it,' I said. 'They put themselves on offer. The moment you become a public figure in this country, particularly a politician, you're asking to be investigated, sniped at, and generally abused. It follows, therefore, that one has to be extremely careful when following up mud-slinging of this sort.'

'Does that mean that we let it rest, then?'

'Not bloody likely, Dave,' I said. 'We'll pursue this bastard to beyond the grave.' I paused to look at my desk calendar. 'Has the coroner released the body yet?'

'Yes, guv.'

'So when's the funeral? Have we heard?'

'Monday, at Brompton Cemetery.'

'Better get your black tie out, Dave, and we'll take a look. Useful things, funerals. All sorts of interesting people turn up.'

'I've made an appointment for us to see Dorothy Blakemore this afternoon, guv,' said Dave.

'Good,' I said. 'I'll be interested in what she has to say. Where does she live?'

'Maida Vale, guv.'

But our interview with Dorothy Blakemore, or Dorothy Edwards as she was now called, was nowhere near as fruitful as I'd hoped.

Although about the same age as the woman who had supplanted her in Hugh Blakemore's affections, Dorothy Edwards had kept the slender figure that had first attracted her former husband. And she knew how to dress. I wondered what Anne Blakemore had that Dorothy Edwards lacked. But I was fairly sure I knew.

'I really don't see how you think I can help you, Mr Brock,' she said, when I had introduced Dave and me, and explained the reason for our visit. 'I divorced Hugh some eight years ago, and I've been remarried for the past six years.'

'When did you last see him, Mrs Edwards?'

'At the High Court in the Strand, the day of the divorce. I told him then that I never wanted to see him again, and I never have.'

'Are you going to his funeral?' asked Dave. It was an unwise question.

'I most certainly am not,' said Dorothy Edwards firmly. 'Furthermore, it may surprise you to know that I do not regret his passing one iota.' A bitter little smile played around her lips. 'Frankly, I'm sick and tired of all the fuss. Ever since Hugh's death, I've been plagued by reporters, in person and on the telephone, trying to extract some salacious titbit for the benefit of their prurient tabloid readers. Every time I leave the house some obnoxious member of the paparazzi emerges from behind a bush and takes a photograph. I just hope that some crisis arises so that they will focus their unwelcome attentions elsewhere.'

I decided to take a chance. 'Were you aware of the rumours that Mr Blakemore had taken bribes?' I asked.

Dorothy Edwards gave me a disbelieving look. 'No, I wasn't,' she said. She remained silent for a moment or two, and then added, 'But I have to say that it wouldn't surprise me in the least.'

We stood up. 'Thank you for your assistance, Mrs Edwards,' I said. 'I doubt that we'll need to bother you again.'

Dorothy Edwards nodded curtly and conducted us to the front door, slamming it before we had even reached the bottom step.

'I don't think she liked him much, guv,' said Dave.

'Don't know what gives you that idea, Dave,' I said. 'Incidentally, I've heard that the Prime Minister and most of the Cabinet are attending Hugh Blakemore's funeral tomorrow. I think we'll have all our team out, just to see if there are any interesting faces that it might be useful to have followed.'

It was clearly time for me to mend fences with my girlfriend. I rang her from the office that evening, and suggested dinner.

'Why don't you come round to my place, and I'll cook,' said Gail.

That was an offer I couldn't refuse. To say that Gail is a superb cook is to underestimate her skill; cordon bleu chef would be a better description. I'd often told her that if she opened a restaurant, she would undoubtedly attract a Michelin star in a very short space of time. But with her typical dry humour, she pointed out that that would mean working every evening. And that from an actress!

Not that Gail was working at all at the moment. Fortunately

for her, she had a rich property developer father called George Sutton who paid her a handsome allowance. He was a pleasant enough fellow, but had a passion for Formula One motor racing, and the land speed record, both of which he talked about incessantly. His wife Sally, a real charmer, with whom he lived in Nottingham, was a former dancer.

Considering that I'd given Gail such short notice, and that she'd had no time to shop, the meal was terrific. She produced a walnut, pear and Parmesan salad, followed by garlic prawns with a mixed salad, and finished off with fresh fruit skewers with fruit sauce and ice cream. And if that wasn't enough, she'd produced a bottle of Malbec to go with it.

NINE

Blakemore's funeral service had been held at Brompton Oratory, and the hearse, followed by the mourners' motorcade, now wound its way from there to the cemetery. Because the Prime Minister and most of the Cabinet were attending the interment at Old Brompton Road cemetery, the Kensington police had stationed themselves in that masterpiece of traffic engineering called Cromwell Place and waved their arms about. The resulting snarl-up, which was to have repercussions lasting well beyond the evening rush hour, succeeded in shortening tempers and, in one case at least, had an adverse effect on the government's chances of re-election.

'What's this cock-up in aid of then, guv?' one disgruntled cab driver asked Dave as we walked towards the cemetery gates.

'It's the Prime Minister and the Cabinet,' said Dave, 'going to a funeral.'

'Is it their funeral?' asked the cab driver hopefully.

I'd seen no point in going to the church and Dave and I had positioned ourselves close to the entrance to the cemetery. A number of Diplomatic Protection Group officers loitered within, backed up by the Firearms Branch that was positioned at various vantage points around the burial ground and on adjacent rooftops, its officers striking threatening poses.

The hearse drew into the cemetery, followed by a long line of limousines, the first of which carried Anne Blakemore and Caroline Simpson. But seated beside Blakemore's widow was a man whom I'd not seen before. It was not Geoffrey Strang.

'I wonder if that could possibly be the Paul Tyler who Fat Danny told us about, Dave.' I beckoned to Kate Ebdon. 'You see the bloke in the car with Mrs Blakemore, Kate? It's the one immediately behind the hearse.'

'Yes, guv.'

'Get someone to stick with him and find out where he goes after this is all over.'

'Good as done,' said Kate, and crossing to where John Appleby was standing, whispered instructions in his ear.

'That's interesting, guv,' said Dave, pointing across the road. 'Blakemore's mother is in a separate car.'

'Hardly surprising though, is it?' I said. 'We know what she thought of Anne.'

Once the tail of the cortège had entered the cemetery, Dave and I brought up the rear. But there was nothing to see that might help us solve the murder of the man now being buried.

A sudden light breeze rippled across the gravestones, sufficient for women briefly to hold on to their hats. In particular, Caroline Simpson appeared to be having trouble with her fascinator.

The clergyman spoke the few words necessary to ensure that Hugh Blakemore was granted a Christian burial, and the obligatory handful of earth was thrown on to the ornate coffin.

And then the crowd began to disperse.

We were back at Curtis Green by two thirty, having lunched in a pub in Old Brompton Road. Young Appleby, who had been deputed by Kate to follow the stranger in Anne Blakemore's car, was waiting for us in the incident room.

'After the burial, sir, Mrs Blakemore and the man who was with her returned to her house in Chelsea in the same car, but before going indoors, he took a grip out of the boot of a car that was parked nearby.'

'I hope you ran a check on it, John,' I said.

'Yes, sir,' said Appleby, frowning slightly. 'It's registered in the name of Paul Tyler. Address in Chichester.' He handed me a sheet of paper. 'Details are all there, sir, together with a description. The man's still there and, judging by the grip, he looks intent on staying for a while.'

I stared thoughtfully at the piece of paper for a moment or two. 'I think we'll pay Mrs Blakemore a visit, Dave,' I said, 'just to keep her informed of the latest developments in our enquiry.'

'Are there any, guv?' asked Dave, looking suitably mystified.

'No, Dave,' I said, 'but that has nothing to do with it.'

It was close to five o'clock the same afternoon when Dave and I called at the Blakemore house in Chelsea, but there was some delay before the door was eventually opened.

A barefooted Anne Blakemore was wearing a thigh-length, white towelling robe and her hair was disarranged. She looked embarrassed to see us on her doorstep. 'Oh! It's you,' she said, but made no move to admit us.

'May we come in, Mrs Blakemore?' I asked.

Still the woman did not move. 'It's not really convenient at the moment,' she said. 'You should have telephoned.'

'I'm afraid it's rather important that we speak to you, Mrs Blakemore,' I said, determined to get a closer look at Tyler.

'Is there something wrong?' Anne's voice quavered slightly. She paused and then said, 'I suppose you'd better come in.' Reluctantly she admitted us.

'There's nothing wrong, Mrs Blakemore, at least nothing that affects you directly.' We followed her into the sitting room. 'But I'm afraid that we have heard some rather disturbing rumours about your late husband,' I began.

'What sort of disturbing rumours?' Anne Blakemore's hands went to the collar of her robe and closed it tightly. 'I suppose you're talking about Gina Watson.'

'Gina Watson? Who is she?' I had intended to discuss the allegations that Blakemore had taken bribes, and gave no indication that I'd already heard the name of the actress that Fat Danny had given us.

'You mean you don't know?'

'The name doesn't mean anything to me. Do you want to tell me about her?' I asked, taking advantage of Anne Blakemore's mention of the woman.

Blakemore's widow gave a frustrated sigh. It seemed like a criticism of my detective ability. 'I knew that woman would be trouble,' she said, sinking down on to a settee. 'She's an actress, you know.'

'Really?' I said, trying not to give the impression that I was fairly conversant with Blakemore's affair with the actress. 'Where does she fit in?'

'She was having an affair with Hugh.' Anne's shoulders slumped. 'And now, I suppose, she's going to sell her story to the newspapers.' The anguish was clear on her face. 'That would be typical of the woman.' She stared at me. 'I hope you'll stop her if she tries to.'

'I'm afraid we have no power to censor the press, Mrs Blakemore,' said Dave.

'Well, someone ought to. The Press Complaints Commission perhaps.'

'Had their affair been going on for very long, Mrs Blakemore?'
I asked.

'Long enough for her to blackmail him.'

'Really?' The conversation was taking an interesting turn,
but one, if anything, that was more likely to complicate things
than simplify them. 'That's a very serious allegation.'

'Blackmail's very serious,' said Anne tersely.

'How did they meet? Your late husband and this actress.'

'Ironically, it was when Hugh tried to help Caroline to get
started in the acting business. God knows how it came about,
but he met this Watson woman and one thing led to another.'
Anne contrived to look sad. 'I suppose I should have known
that would happen. After all, he was married when we met,
so it's hardly surprising that he should have got embroiled
with this woman. If you marry a womanizer, you can hardly
be surprised if he carries on being one, can you?' she added,
in a rare flash of candour.

'Has she contacted you since Mr Blakemore's death?' asked
Dave.

'She wouldn't dare,' said Anne with some force. 'She's
nothing but a common tart.'

'How old is this Gina Watson?' Dave asked.

Anne Blakemore inclined her head to one side and gave a
wan smile that I imagined was intended to provoke sympathy.
'I wouldn't have minded so much if she'd been some empty-
headed bimbo, but she must be at least forty, and that's being
charitable. I call that downright insulting. I mean to say, what
could she possibly have given Hugh that I couldn't?'

'You've met her, then?' I queried, without answering what
I thought was fairly obvious.

'Only the once, and that was at some God-awful reception.
The burden of being a politician's wife,' she added. 'But I
didn't know at the time that Hugh was bedding her, or I'd
have had something to say to the brazen hussy.'

'What was she blackmailing your husband about, Mrs
Blakemore?' I asked.

Anne Blakemore was about to answer when the door to the
sitting room opened and a man appeared.

'Darling, I . . .' The man, dressed in cords and a white, open-
necked shirt, paused on the threshold. 'Oh, I'm sorry,' he said,
'I didn't realize you had company.'

Anne was clearly disconcerted by the man's arrival in the sitting room. 'Er, this is Paul Tyler,' she said, glancing at me. 'He's an old friend of mine.' She returned her gaze to Tyler. 'These gentlemen are from the police,' she explained.

Tyler's sudden appearance came as no surprise to me. That Anne Blakemore had answered the door wearing a towelling robe had indicated to my cynical mind that Paul Tyler was still in the house. And that he and Anne had probably been in bed together. 'How d'you do.' I smiled but made no attempt to stand up.

Anne fiddled with the silver figaro neck chain she was wearing. 'This is Detective Chief Inspector Brock, Paul. He's investigating poor Hugh's murder.' She waved a limp hand towards us as she addressed Tyler.

'A terrible thing, Detective.' Tyler spoke with an American accent, and looked as though he wished he were somewhere else. 'Are you anywhere near finding his murderer?'

'We're closing in,' I said, and promptly changed the subject. 'Have you known Mrs Blakemore long, Mr Tyler?' I asked, attempting to give the impression that I was merely making casual conversation. Frankly, I didn't care how long Tyler had known her, but Hugh Blakemore's death had to have had a motive, and I was duty bound to discover that motive if I could. Tyler might just be it.

The American hesitated long enough for me to deduce that whatever he said was going to be untrue. 'We've been friends for some time,' he said eventually. 'Just friends,' he added lamely. He glanced at Anne. 'Well, if you'll excuse me, honey, I must be going.' He turned to me. 'Business, you know, Detective.' He leaned down, and kissed Anne lightly on the cheek.

'What business is that, Mr Tyler?' asked Dave, his tone of voice implying that he was not really interested.

'Import and export,' said Tyler promptly.

'I see.' Dave nodded. Import and export could cover a great deal of business, including that which was illegal.

'So you've been friends with Mr Tyler for some time, Mrs Blakemore,' I said offhandedly, once Tyler had left the room.

Anne gazed at me thoughtfully. 'Several years, as a matter of fact,' she said. 'He was a friend of my husband's originally.'

'Originally?' I immediately picked on the word, and smiled.

Anne realized that she had given herself away. 'My husband was away a lot,' she said defensively. 'Late-night sittings in the House, and that sort of thing. Paul was always very kind. He would take me to the theatre, and to concerts. Often his daughter Liz would come too. It was all perfectly innocent.' She seemed desperate to convince me that there had been no impropriety between her and Tyler, nor was there now. Unfortunately, her present mode of dress made that more diffi-cult to believe.

'I'm sure it was, Mrs Blakemore. As a matter of interest, how did your husband meet Mr Tyler?'

'Is that relevant?' Anne sounded suddenly hostile. 'I mean, does it have anything to do with Hugh's death?' She paused. 'I see. It's just curiosity, is it?' she continued, in the absence of a response from me. 'Well, I can see what you're driving at, Mr Brock.' She recrossed her legs and tugged at the skirt of her robe. 'If you must know, Paul and I are having an affair. And it started some time before my husband's death.' She sounded almost triumphant, and raised her chin slightly, as if to imply that I'd heard what I'd hoped to hear. She glanced at her wristwatch. 'Well, I'm going to have a drink,' she said. 'Can I get you something?'

'No, thanks,' I said, and watched as the woman walked across to a table and poured herself a gin and tonic. There was already ice in the ice bucket, so I guessed that it wasn't her first.

'Was there anything else you wished to discuss with me?' Composed once more, after her angry outburst, Anne sat down again on the settee opposite Dave and me. 'Apart from Gina Watson, that is.'

'You were about to tell me why she was blackmailing Mr Blakemore,' I said.

'Was I?' Anne looked vaguely at me. 'I think the poor woman's demented.' It was clear that since Tyler's interrup-tion, she had thought carefully about what she had said earlier. 'It was a perfectly innocent contact in the first place. As I said, Hugh was trying to help Caroline, but this woman seemed to think he was keen on her. She threatened that if he didn't leave me and marry her, she'd tell all.'

'Did your husband tell you this?' asked Dave.

Anne frowned. 'I don't know why you're so interested in this woman,' she said.

'I thought you said they were having an affair,' I said, trying to look as though I was confused by the whole business. 'And anything that may help me to find your husband's killer needs to be investigated.'

'Did I say they were having an affair?' Anne shook her head as if trying to recall what she had said. She fussed at her hair, attempting to tidy it. 'Frankly, I've no idea what I am saying. It was the funeral today, and it was a bit of a strain.'

'I do apologize, Mrs Blakemore. If I'd realized, I wouldn't have bothered you. In that case, I won't take up any more of your time.'

Once we were in the street, Dave spoke. 'It didn't take long for Tyler to surface again, guv,' he said.

'And I reckon he was in bed with Anne the moment they got back from the funeral,' I said. 'But I wonder what he really does for a living. Import and export can mean any damn thing.' I opened the door of the car and paused. 'I think I'll get Miss Ebdon on to it, Dave. See if she can find out more about him. And see if she can find out more about Strang's trip to New York.'

'Do you think there's a connection, guv?'

'Maybe. Maybe not. It might just be a coincidence that Tyler's an American, and Strang went to America. I don't like coincidences.'

'What about Gina Watson, the actress, guv?' asked Dave.

'I think we'll have a chat with her,' I said.

'What's happening about Geoffrey Strang?' I asked. My renewed interest in the film-maker threw Tom Challis off balance.

'Well, nothing, sir.' Challis looked puzzled. 'You told me to pull off the obo. Once I told you that Caroline Simpson had moved in with him, you said he was of no further interest.'

'So I did. However, we're still supposed to be finding out who murdered Hugh Blakemore.'

'Are you suggesting that Strang might have had something to do with it, guv?' Challis asked.

'I'm not sure, Tom, but make a few more enquiries about this trip to the States he was supposed to have made at the

end of last year. He said that he was there making a film about
a harbour master or some damned thing. America's a very
good place to find hit men.'

'That's all in hand, sir,' said Challis. 'Joe Daly rang to say
that he'd got a result.'

I glanced at my watch. 'He's probably gone home by now.
I'll see him in the morning.'

As Tom Challis had said, Joe Daly, the FBI agent at the
American Embassy, had already found the answer to the query
that had been lodged with him some time previously.

'You were lucky that he applied for a work permit, Harry.'
The big American waved a hand towards an armchair, and
poured the coffee that was always served when he entertained
visitors. 'If he'd cheated and gone over on a ninety-day tourist
visit, I doubt if we'd've been able to trace the guy. To tell
you the truth the Immigration and Naturalization Service, and
Homeland Security, are sinking under the data they've
collected since nine eleven.' He reached across to his desk for
a file and flicked through the folios. 'But he didn't go at the
end of last year. He was there in March of this year.'

'Interesting,' I said. 'That puts him much closer to the
Blakemore assassination.'

Daly looked up sharply. 'Well, wait until you hear this,' he
said, turning the pages of the file. Although Daly was ostensibly a diplomat, his detective instincts were never far beneath
the surface; twenty-five years of fighting organized crime were
not easily put aside. 'Strang met up with a guy in the New
York harbour master's office, but he didn't see the man himself.
Apparently, nothing was said about making any god-damn
movie.' He turned over another page. 'The guy he saw apparently put him in touch with a hood called Nino Petrosino.'

'You've got that look that says the name means something,
Joe,' I said.

'And some,' said Daly, leaning back with a self-satisfied
grin on his face. 'The guy's got connections with the Cosa
Nostra. But he's only gotten a short rap-sheet because the
Bureau hasn't been able to collar him for anything else.' He
sighed at the apparent injustice of the world.

'Oh, beautiful,' I said. This was precisely the sort of
complication that I could well do without. 'Is that it?'

'Not quite,' said Daly. 'From there, Petrosino introduced him to two other guys.' He planted a podgy finger on the page in front of him. 'Francesco Corleo and Pietro Giacono.'

'Don't tell me. They're tied up with the Mafia too.'

'Yep!'

'Any idea why he met up with these characters, Joe?'

'No idea.' Daly shut the folder. 'But sure as hell they weren't planning a charity ball. Not unless it was their own charity.'

TEN

'I've been thinking about Geoffrey Strang for some time, Dave,' I said, 'and what Joe Daly told me about his activities in New York makes me even more curious.'

'Thought it might, guv,' said Dave.

'I think we'll go and have a chat with Mr Strang, and see what he's got to say about it all.'

'The last time I interviewed you,' I began, 'you said that you went to New York at the end of last year to make a film about the harbour master.'

'That's right,' said Strang, looking puzzled, 'but you said that you wanted to talk to me about a robbery in Golden Square. So, why all the interest in my trip to the States?'

'My enquiries indicate that you went to New York later than that,' I said, declining to answer his question. 'In fact, you were there in March of this year.'

Strang shrugged. 'So I got the dates wrong,' he said.

'Furthermore, although you went there on a work permit, you didn't actually work at all. No film was ever made about the New York harbour master.' I paused. 'According to the New York harbour master's office, that is.'

'I told you that the film was never finished.' Strang shot a concerned glance at Dave. 'The producer went bust.'

'It wasn't even started, let alone finished,' I said. 'Incidentally, what was the name of this producer.'

'I can't remember,' said Strang sullenly.

'You can't remember? And yet you told me that he had paid for your return fare.'

'Watch my lips,' said Strang sarcastically. 'I can't remember his name.' He spoke slowly, emphasizing every word.

I ignored his sarcasm. 'My enquiries of the Federal Bureau of Investigation have revealed that while you were in New York, you met several persons who can only be described as of an undesirable character.' I waited to see what reaction that statement would evoke.

'It's not easy being a freelance in the film business, Mr Brock.' Strang seemed tense in the face of my revelations, and I suspected they had shaken him. Mainly because I'd gone off on another tack.

'I don't imagine it is,' I said, and waited.

'Like I said, the producer went bust, but as I was over there I thought I'd try and save something. I went to the harbour master's office, but they didn't want to know. This guy I saw suggested that there was plenty of scope in New York for making a film about the Italian Quarter. He put me in touch with some more people, but then it all fizzled out. That's when I came home.'

'So, the position is this,' I said. 'You went to New York to make a film about the harbour master. That was a non-starter, so you were tempted to make a film about the Italian Quarter. But that didn't come off either. Have I got that right?'

'Absolutely,' said Strang.

'Or was it to be a film about the Mafia, seeing that you met three Mafiosi?'

'I didn't meet anyone in the Mafia,' said Strang, clearly anguished by my statement. 'Not as far as I know,' he added. 'How can you tell who they are?'

'Well, that's all right then,' I said.

But Strang did not seem comforted by my apparent dismissal. 'I still don't understand why you're so interested in my trip to the States,' he said.

'Because you're a friend of Anne Blakemore, and I'm investigating her husband's murder.'

Dave, who had a contact in show business, eventually managed to trace Gina Watson through her agent. The actress mentioned by Fat Danny, and then by Anne Blakemore, apparently lived at Strand on the Green in Chiswick. But the address proved to be in one of the labyrinth of streets further to the east.

Dave had telephoned to make an appointment, and she had invited us to call at once. 'I'm not working at the moment,' she had said. It transpired that we were fortunate to find her there.

The woman who opened the door was an attractive blonde. Tall and slender, she had a good figure and the poise of an actress. Anne Blakemore had suggested that Gina Watson was about forty, but this woman looked younger.

'Mrs Watson?'

The woman appraised us carefully, and then smiled. 'No, I'm just a friend,' she said, and turning her head spoke to someone inside the flat. 'Gina, I think your policemen have arrived.' She faced us again. 'I was just going,' she added, and then called out a goodbye before easing past us and making her way out of the door.

Gina Watson was indeed in her forties, and although she might have been a beauty years ago, her looks were now fading. Fast. Her long, brown hair was swept up on top of her head and held there, untidily, with a profusion of hairpins. She wore blue jeans and a black Angora sweater. Around her neck was a chunky gold-coloured chain, and the toenails of her bare feet were varnished scarlet. 'Hello,' she said, 'you must be Mr Brock.' Without waiting for an answer, she turned and led the way into the sitting room, leaving Dave to shut the front door.

'You're very trusting,' I said. 'I could have been anyone.'

'Well, you're not, are you, darling?' said Gina. 'Although I must say that you're not like any of the television policemen I've ever worked with. Do sit down, both of you. I was just making some tea. You'll have some, won't you?'

'Thank you,' I said.

'Shan't be a tick.' The woman made an elegant exit to the kitchen, and started to sing something from *Cabaret*.

My gaze was riveted on an enormous, meaningless pastiche, a pseudo-Picasso by the look of it, that occupied most of one wall. Opposite it was a tall bookcase containing a collection of publications about the theatre and films, and a large number of popular novels in paperback. The furniture was of a style that had been fashionable in the 1970s.

'Well, now, I suppose you've come to talk to me about poor Hugh,' said Gina Watson as she pushed a tea trolley into the room. 'Such a tragedy.' She sat down and busied herself pouring the tea. 'Sugar and milk?' she asked, glancing briefly at each of us in turn.

'I understand you knew Mr Blakemore quite well, Mrs Watson,' I began.

'Knew him well?' Gina Watson threw back her head and laughed. 'We were lovers, darling. And do call me Gina. Everyone does.'

'And how long had that been going on?'

Gina leaned back and crossed her legs, looking reflectively at the modernist painting. 'About two years, I suppose. Right up until his death.' She sat forward again, an earnest expression on her face. 'Why?' she asked simply.

I took a sip of tea, and put the cup and saucer down on a side table. 'It may have no relevance at all,' I said, 'but anyone who can tell us about his friends, and the sort of lifestyle he pursued, may be in a position to help us.'

'I murdered someone once,' said Gina. It was an impish, throwaway line.

'Oh, really?' said Dave, but he knew what she was going to say.

'In a play, of course.'

'Of course.'

'But you don't want to hear about the theatre, do you, darlings? I suppose you want to know all about Hugh and me.' Gina gave me a mischievous smile. 'Well, why not? We met at a nightclub. It was a first-night party, although I can't for the life of me remember what the show was now, except that it was a musical, but because he was an MP someone thought it was a good idea to have him along. He was a very personable sort of guy. And very interested in the theatre.'

'In the theatre, or in you?' asked Dave, raising an eyebrow.

Gina laughed. 'You know how to get to the point, don't you, darling?' she said. 'Yes, he was, and he made it obvious. We were in bed by midnight.'

'Where? Here?'

'Good Lord, no! He had a flat in Westminster. He said he'd love to talk to me about the show, but not in a crowded nightclub.' Gina laughed again. 'He wasn't very good at sexual gambits, but I knew what was in his mind. Most men are the same when it comes to sex, you know.'

'I believe you,' I said, and smiled.

'He said something about there being too many press people at the party, and how he had to be careful because he was an MP. I don't know why he was so worried. The only journalists there were theatre critics, and they were more interested in sinking as much free champagne as they could, and chatting up the chorus girls. Perhaps it was being seen with a handful of gay luvvies that concerned him.' Gina shot me an arch smile.

'Where was this flat of his?'

'In a block in Victoria. He said that he kept it because it was convenient for the House after a late-night sitting. Personally, I think he used it for entertaining his women. After all, it wouldn't have taken him much longer to get from the Commons to Chelsea by taxi, would it?'

'His women? Plural?'

Gina laughed again; she laughed very easily. 'I was under no illusions about that, darling,' she said. 'I know a womanizer when I see one, but what the hell? He obviously fancied me and I fancied him. Frankly, I thought it would only be a one-night stand, but a few days later he rang me and invited me out to dinner.'

'He obviously wasn't worried about being seen out with you, then,' observed Dave.

'He may have been,' said Gina, 'because he took me to some small restaurant a few miles out of town. He said that there wouldn't be any journalists there. He seemed to be paranoid about the press. Anyway, he made some ridiculous excuse about having a stepdaughter who wanted to become an actress. But it turned out to be true. At least, I imagine that's what he told his wife.'

'Did you ever meet her? Anne Blakemore, I mean.'

'No. Saw photographs of her. He had one in the flat, and there'd be the occasional pictures in society magazines and in the tabloids of the two of them at some function or another.' Gina paused. 'Oh, just a minute though. I did meet her, along with Hugh at some do, but that was before Hugh and I—' She broke off. 'Well, you know what I mean,' she added with a gay little laugh.

'And were you able to help his stepdaughter?' I asked.

'I told him she should look for a proper job. In the acting business you're out of work more often than you're in it. Unless you get very lucky, of course. But most of us aren't. I managed to put him in touch with a few people, and I think she got one or two walk-on parts in television. It's a hard life, though. Nowhere near as glamorous as most people think.'

I knew that from Gail's experience. Only too well. And that reminded me to ask Gail whether she knew Gina Watson. 'But your relationship with Hugh Blakemore continued, I take it?'

'Yes, much to my surprise. And his, I think.'

'Wasn't it a bit risky? You were both likely to be recognized in public.'

'Now you're flattering me, darling.' Gina smiled sweetly. It was almost sarcastic. 'You may think that because you've been on television a few times everyone will know you, but the nearest I got was some woman in a supermarket saying how much like Gina Watson I looked. That's fame for you.' She laughed scornfully. 'You only have to be off the screen for a couple of months and you're forgotten, believe me. And as for the theatre, well, that's dying. Why go out when you can watch something on the telly? And you can never get a taxi when you want one,' she added reflectively.

'Did Hugh ever mention marriage?'

'No.' Gina's theatrical training enabled her to draw out the word, and make it sound undeniably dismissive.

'Not at all?'

'Not at all. More tea?'

'No thanks,' I said. 'Did Hugh Blakemore ever suggest that he wanted to break off your relationship, Mrs Watson?'

'I told you, call me Gina, darling. I was only married to Frank Watson for four years, but regrettably I made my name during that time, and now I'm saddled with being Watson for all time.' Gina leaned forward and took a cigarette from a box on the coffee table. 'D'you smoke?' she asked, pushing the box towards us.

'Thank you,' I said, and Dave quickly offered the woman a light.

'I shouldn't really, but there's always a part that requires one to smoke so it's impossible to give it up. Seems to be a case of don't smoke, don't work. Still, it might be better now that they've put the kibosh on smoking practically everywhere.' Gina inhaled deeply, blew smoke in the air, and leaned back against the cushions of the settee.

'Hugh Blakemore never said anything about breaking it off, then?' I repeated the question, wondering whether Gina Watson had been trying to avoid it. If Anne Blakemore was right in her allegation that this woman had been blackmailing Hugh, there had to be a reason.

'Only once. Quite recently, in fact. It was just after that business at the prison, when a prisoner got killed. Hugh seemed to think that the press were going to hound him. It was unfortunate really, but it was the same week that we got caught.'

'Caught?'

Gina nodded, a mischievous smile on her face. 'Fiona Savage found us in bed. Here.'

'Who is Fiona Savage?'

'She's the girl who let you in. She's a friend of mine. She's in the business too, and we look out for each other, particularly if either of us is touring. She lives just around the corner and we have keys to each other's flats. I don't know what made her think I wasn't here, but one afternoon she just bowled in, obviously to have a look round and make sure everything was OK. Anyway, she came waltzing into the bedroom and there we were.'

'I imagine that Hugh was not too pleased,' said Dave.

'That's putting it mildly, darling,' said Gina, darting an appraising glance at Dave. 'The poor dear almost had a heart attack. I thought it was screamingly funny, and so did Fiona. But then, I don't care who knows I'm getting laid, or by whom. Anyway that's when Hugh said it was getting too risky. It wasn't his wife he was worried about – he told me once that she was getting screwed while he was away – but, as I said just now, he was paranoid about the press. I told him it was a bit bloody late to worry, but he said he'd have to stop seeing me.' She flicked ash into the ashtray, and smiled. 'But he was back within ten days and in my bed within ten minutes.' She laughed, yet again. 'Men!' she added scathingly.

'She was too good to be true, Dave,' I said, when we were driving back to Curtis Green.

'Well, she is an actress, guv,' said Dave.

'Yes, and I'm sure she was playing a part to perfection just now.'

'D'you think there's anything in this story of Anne Blakemore's that Gina was blackmailing Hugh, guv?'

I shrugged. 'Possibly. But what about? *La Belle* Watson tried to give the impression that it was an idyllic relationship. All sex and nothing else. But, you'll have noted, Dave, that she didn't seem too upset by Hugh's death.'

'So what are we going to do about it?'

But it was not until we were passing through Knightsbridge

that I decided what to do next. 'I think a chat with this Fiona Savage wouldn't be a bad idea, Dave,' I said.

'We'll have to box a bit carefully, guv,' said Dave. 'If they're in each other's pockets, she'll likely go running to Gina and tell her the tale.'

'And that may just turn out to our advantage, Dave,' I said. 'In the meantime, I think we'll have Mickey Lever in, and ask him about how he lost his wallet. And then forgot all about it.'

'What the bloody hell's this all about?' demanded an irate Lever when Dave and I walked into the interview room at Charing Cross police station. 'I ain't done nothing wrong, but just because I've done a bit of bird, you think you can nick me any time you like. And for sod all.'

'It's a hard world, Mickey,' said Dave. 'Is that it for now? You finished bellyaching for the time being?'

'I've a good mind to make a complaint,' said Lever angrily.

'I shouldn't do that, Mickey,' said Dave. 'You're already facing one count of wasting police time. I shouldn't add another to it, if I were you.'

'What's that supposed to mean?'

'I'm talking about you going into Catford nick and telling the station officer that you'd lost your wallet, when you hadn't,' I said. 'And making a song and dance into the bargain. You want to think yourself lucky. In the old days you'd've been nicked for disorderly conduct in a police station. Some of the sergeants I knew would have had you on the sheet quicker than that.'

'So, I made a mistake,' said Lever churlishly.

'I get the impression that you're in the habit of making mistakes, Mickey,' I said, 'if your form's anything to go by, that is.'

'I did think I'd lost it.'

'The plot . . . or your wallet?' enquired Dave.

'Nah, my wallet,' said Lever, clearly not understanding Dave's sarcasm.

'And when did you find it?' I asked.

Lever scratched thoughtfully at the stubble on his chin, attempting to create the impression that he was giving my question deep and careful consideration. 'Must have been a couple of days later,' he said.

'And it didn't occur to you to ring the police station and

tell them you'd found it? For all you know, hordes of policemen may have been out searching for it.'

Even Lever knew that was most unlikely. 'What's this all about?' he asked. 'A big cheese from the CID like you don't go about worrying about geezers what've lost their wallets.'

'No, that's true,' I said. 'But what interests me is that you should have reported this imaginary loss at precisely the time Hugh Blakemore was being murdered in Fulham Road. It's almost as if you were desperate to establish an alibi. To convey to the police that you had absolutely nothing to do with Blakemore's murder.'

'Well I never.' Lever was looking particularly anguished now.

'All right,' I said, and stood up. 'Off you go.'

'Is that it, then?' Lever could not believe that we were just going to let him go. It unnerved him more than if he had been charged with something.

'If I were you, Mickey, I'd keep my hand firmly on my wallet in future,' said Dave.

I'd been working long hours dealing with the Blakemore murder, and when I got home, I felt like a stranger in my own flat.

There was a note on the kitchen table from Mrs Gurney, my cleaning lady. She's an absolute treasure, and I don't really know why she puts up with me. It's probably out of respect for Gail, who stays the night occasionally, and just as occasionally manages to leave some item of underwear in the bedroom that Mrs Gurney washes for her.

> Dear Mr Brock,
> I noticed one or two of your shirts is getting a bit frayed round the cuffs. If you'd like me to have a go at mending them, leave me a note. Otherwise, you might like to buy some new ones.
> Yours faithfully,
> Gladys Gurney (Mrs)

I decided that this was no time to worry about shopping for new shirts.

ELEVEN

When it happened, Caroline Simpson had been enjoying her live-in loving relationship with Geoffrey Strang for just two weeks.

Colin Wilberforce appeared in the doorway of my office. 'Excuse me, sir, but the commander wants to see you.'

I stood up and sighed. If only I'd stayed out of the office until after six o'clock, I'd have been safe. The commander is a strict ten-to-six man. I think Mrs Commander nags him. But if the photograph on his desk were of *my* wife, I'd stay out all night.

'You wanted to see me, sir?'

'Ah, Mr Brock.' The commander always called me 'Mr Brock', unlike all my other guv'nors who used my first name. Never mind, perhaps he thinks I'll respond by using *his* first name; I'm not sure he'd know how to cope with that. He swept off his half-moon spectacles – I'm convinced he wears them in a vain attempt to add *gravitas* to his appearance – and pulled a flimsy sheet of paper across his desk.

'There was a murder this afternoon in Golden Square, and I'm directing you to take over the investigation.'

I was about to protest that I'd already got two murders to deal with – Blakemore and Solly Goldman – but I didn't get the chance.

'The victim was a Geoffrey Strang. I think it makes sense for you to investigate it as I understand Strang had some connection with the Blakemore family.'

Oh, hell! The commander's been reading the paperwork in the incident room again. I should have known; he loves paper.

'What do we know about it, sir?' I asked.

'Only what I've told you, Mr Brock. The CID at West End Central police station are dealing with it at the moment.'

And that was another thing: he never called police stations 'nicks', like the rest of us did.

'Very good, sir,' I said. 'I'll get across there immediately.'

'Keep me informed, Mr Brock.'

The West End Central DCI was called Bernie, and was an old mate of mine.

'I hear you've copped this one, then, Harry,' he said, sounding much too cheerful for my liking.

'What's the SP?' I asked wearily, as we stood surveying the tent surrounding the car containing the dead body of Geoffrey Strang.

'According to a reliable witness, Strang came out of those premises at just before half past three,' Bernie began, waving at the studio where Strang worked, 'and got into his car. He was about to start the engine when a motor cyclist pulled up on the offside of the car and spoke to him. The witness assumed that the motor cyclist was seeking directions. The motorcycle left the scene and Strang remained sitting in his car. After about five minutes, a traffic warden turned up. She started screaming blue murder and called police on her personal radio. The first car on the scene found that Strang had been shot.'

'Did this reliable witness get the number of this motor-cycle? A description of the rider?' I asked

'He was too far away to get the number, Harry, and the description, well, I'm afraid it would fit any motor cyclist. Black leathers and a crash helmet.'

'Lucky the traffic warden didn't arrange to have Strang's car clamped, I suppose,' said Dave.

'It might be worth trying a television appeal,' suggested Bernie.

'I'm always doubtful about television appeals, Bernie,' I said. 'It usually means the incident room staff being tied up with taking calls from people who, when it comes down to it, saw nothing. But I suppose that's all we can do. Anyway, what do we know about the actual killing?'

'A single bullet wound to the temple, Harry. Death was instantaneous, according to Henry Mortlock, the pathologist.'

If Henry Mortlock had said it, it was bound to be correct. 'It's got to be connected to Blakemore's death in some way, Bernie,' I said. 'It's too much of a coincidence not to be.'

'Yes, well, that's your problem, Harry,' said Bernie.

'Have his nearest and dearest been informed of his death?' I asked.

'We don't know who they are,' said Bernie.

'I do,' I said. 'I'll get on to it. Meanwhile, perhaps you'd oversee the removal.'

'Take it as done, Harry.'

Dave and I pulled up outside the Fulham flat that Strang had shared with Caroline Simpson, and it was she who answered the door. She was wearing a man's white shirt – one of Strang's, I suppose – and nothing else.

'Yes?' She looked enquiringly at us, and was, I suspected, somewhat disturbed by Dave. Being six foot tall, well built and black, he tended to have that effect on people.

'Miss Simpson?'

'Yes.'

'We're police officers, Miss Simpson.' I introduced Dave and me, and explained that we were investigating the murder of her stepfather. She did not appear too surprised by this revelation.

'What d'you want with me, then?' Caroline asked. 'You'd better come in,' she added, as an apparent afterthought.

'I understand that you share this accommodation with Mr Geoffrey Strang.' I couched my words carefully. In these days of political correctness it is easy to cause offence; people are very touchy about status and relationship.

'We live together, if that's what you mean,' said Caroline, unimpressed by my stilted phraseology.

'In that case, I'm afraid I have some bad news for you.' I spoke gently, but I knew there was no easy way to do this. In my view telling people that someone close to them has just been murdered is probably the worst part of a policeman's job. Although telling parents that their missing child is dead at the hands of some paedophiliac maniac is even worse.

Caroline sensed what was coming next. 'Is it Geoffrey?' she began, an expression of panic suddenly gripping her.

'I'm afraid he's dead, Miss Simpson.'

'Oh, my God!' Caroline's face drained of colour and she stared unseeing at me. I imagined that she was having trouble trying to take in the sickening news I'd just broken to her. She began to sway and for a moment it looked as though she might faint. 'I don't believe it,' she whispered, and began to shake violently.

Dave took her elbow and steered her towards an armchair. 'You'd better sit down,' he said, and disappeared to the kitchen to get a glass of water.

'What was it?' asked Caroline. 'A car accident?'

'No, Miss Simpson, I'm afraid he was shot,' I said. 'His body was found in his car. In Golden Square, near where he works, I understand.'

Caroline stared blankly at me. 'D'you mean he committed suicide?'

'It doesn't appear so.' I was loath to reveal any of the circumstances of Strang's death. At least, not yet.

Suddenly the appalling truth struck Caroline. 'D'you mean he was murdered?' Automatically she took the glass of water from Dave, and drank it down in one go.

'It's difficult to say at this stage, Miss Simpson,' I said cautiously, although there was no doubt in my mind.

'But who would do such a thing?'

'I'm afraid we know very little at the moment, Miss Simpson, but if you feel up to it, there are one or two questions I'd like to ask you. To start with, are you aware of anyone who might have wanted Mr Strang dead?'

'No, of course not.' Caroline shook her head vigorously. 'He was mature, kind and amusing. I don't think he had a care in the world.'

'I understand that he was a friend of your mother, Miss Simpson.' I posed my tentative question to see what reaction it would produce.

Caroline looked up, her eyes blazing through her tears. 'Until he met me,' she said vehemently. 'He was sleeping with my mother, but I took him off her.' There was a look of triumph on her face at having stolen Strang from Anne. But then Caroline was half her mother's age, so I imagined it was an unfair contest.

'I think that'll be all for the time being, Miss Simpson,' I said, as Dave and I stood up. 'But we might have to see you again at some future date.'

Despite the apparent lack of love between her and her mother, I subsequently learned that later that evening Caroline had thrown a few things into a bag and taken a taxi to her mother's home in Chelsea. Presumably so that they could console each other at the loss of a mutual lover.

*   *   *

Strang's car had been taken to the Metropolitan Laboratory at Lambeth and, when Dave and I arrived, it was in the process of being thoroughly searched by a team of forensic scientists who specialized in the examination of motor vehicles. The senior forensic practitioner overseeing the operation was Linda Mitchell, attired as usual in her white coveralls, and overshoes.

'What have you got, Linda?' I asked.

'No more than you'd expect, Mr Brock,' said Linda. 'So far, that is.'

'And what would I expect, Linda?'

'Nothing, Mr Brock. And that's exactly what you've got.' Linda permitted herself a rare smile, and then relented. 'But we haven't finished yet. There's always the possibility of something turning up.'

And with that, I had to be satisfied, for the present. I knew that if there was anything of evidential value, Linda Mitchell and her team would find it. 'Keep up the good work, Linda,' I said. 'By the way, is there any word on the mud found in the getaway Mondeo that was used after the Blakemore shooting? The one that belonged to Miss Atkinson – that was found in Richmond Park?'

Linda shook her head. 'We've nothing to compare it with,' she said. 'Nothing significant. We tried the soil immediately around where the vehicle was found, but the lab people said it didn't match. If you can find some mud that you think might tie the vehicle to a particular place then I'll get them to give it another run.'

'Thanks, Linda,' I said, 'but I doubt it will tell us anything even if you do find a match.'

'We can't have motor cyclists marauding around London shooting people,' said the commander, when he sent for me the following morning. He had a way of simplifying outrageous crimes as if it were beyond his comprehension that they had not been solved.

'I'm doing my best to put a stop to it, sir,' I said, risking a reproof for sarcasm. The last thing I needed right now was a lecture on the theory of criminal investigation from someone who knew little about it. There was, however, an old copy of Hans Gross's *Criminal Investigation* on his bookshelf.

'The Commissioner's not at all pleased.' The commander ran a hand across the polished, bare surface of his desk. It was one of his less appealing characteristics that he invariably invoked the imagined opinion of someone more senior than he. I'd have preferred it if he'd said *he* wasn't pleased.

'Neither am I, sir,' I said.

The commander ignored my sardonic comment. 'Apparently the Justice Secretary's been asking some quite pointed questions about the progress of the Blakemore enquiry,' he continued. 'That an MP can be shot down in a London street is quite unacceptable.'

'That anyone can be shot down in a London street is unacceptable,' I said, 'no matter whose life it was.'

The commander slowly realized that I was agreeing with everything he said. But that was not quite why he'd sent for me.

'Well, what's happening, Mr Brock?' There was a note of exasperation in his voice.

'Enquiries are continuing, sir. With vigour.'

'Yes, well, I hope we're going to see some arrests soon,' said the commander. 'Do you need any more assistance? Any more men?'

'No, sir, nor women,' I added mischievously.

'Yes, women, of course.' The commander hated being caught out on matters of what the Bramshill Police College whiz-kids incorrectly called gender diversity.

'I've got a damned good team working on it.' Sensing that the interview was over, I stood up. 'But I'd be obliged if you didn't mention it to them. I don't want them getting ideas above their nick.'

I stirred absent-mindedly at the cup of coffee that Joe Daly's secretary had placed in front of me. 'I more or less put it to Strang that I thought his story of visiting New York to make a film about the harbour master was untenable,' I said.

The American Embassy's legal attaché laughed. 'And some,' he said. 'What did he say about the three guys he met over there?'

'I didn't put the names to him, but he denied meeting anyone connected with the Mafia,' I said. 'Not that I think he would recognize a Mafioso if he met one, he was far too naive.

But it's interesting that only two days after my interview with him he was murdered.'

'So, what can I do to help, Harry?' The big FBI man drew a pad of paper across his desk.

'I'd be interested to know if any one of the three hoods you mentioned has been missing from his usual haunt during the last three days.'

'Holy cow!' said Daly, and shook his head. 'D'you think that one of them might have come over for the express purpose of taking out this guy Strang?'

'Or even Blakemore,' I said, hoping I was wrong. This enquiry was getting much too complicated. 'But funnier things have happened, Joe.'

'I'll have to look up their names again.' Daly cast about on his cluttered desk looking for a file.

'Nino Petrosino, Francesco Corleo and Pietro Giacono,' I said.

Daly looked up in surprise. 'How in hell's name d'you remember names like that, Harry?' he asked.

'I'm a Scotland Yard detective,' I said. 'Thanks for the coffee.'

'Get outta here, you Limey bum,' said Daly with a laugh.

I decided it was time to pay a visit to the electronics company named by Charles Simpson as one of his clients. And I also decided not to make an appointment. I prefer not to give notice of my intentions, if I can avoid doing so. And in this particular case, I thought there might be some advantage in arriving unannounced.

The receptionist was distinctly aloof. 'The managing director does not usually see anyone without an appointment,' she said, and continued to fiddle with some paperwork. But she was not as confident as she tried to appear, and probably thought that these two well-dressed men might just be interested in placing a lucrative order, and that by stopping them from seeing the boss, that order might be lost.

'I'm Detective Chief Inspector Brock of Scotland Yard,' I said, putting her out of her misery, 'and this is Detective Sergeant Poole.'

The receptionist glanced casually at my warrant card and stood up. 'If you care to wait a moment, I'll see what I can do.

But he is very busy,' she said as she disappeared through a door at the rear of the foyer.

Dave glanced at me, eyebrows raised. 'Protective, ain't she, guv?' he said.

'Aren't they all?' I rejoined. 'Makes me wish I'd got a secretary.'

The receptionist returned seconds later. 'Come this way, please,' she said, clearly irritated that the managing director had overruled her attempt at access control.

'We meet again, Mr Brock.' The man who rose from behind the large desk was none other than Paul Tyler whom I'd last seen at Anne Blakemore's house in Chelsea. Tyler walked round his desk and shook hands. He glanced at Dave. 'We've met before too, haven't we?' he asked.

'Yes,' said Dave, as we accepted Tyler's invitation to sit down.

'Well, Mr Brock, and what can I do for you? More questions about poor Hugh's death?'

'In a way,' I said. Rather than surprising Tyler, it was me who had been caught wrong-footed. Although I had told Kate Ebdon to do a background enquiry on Tyler, she had yet to report her findings, and I was annoyed at being unprepared. But I wasn't annoyed with Kate; I doubt that she'd have expected to find Tyler at the company, and I now wished that I had asked Simpson for the name of his contact here. And, sure as hell, this wasn't what I'd expected when Tyler had described his commercial activities as 'import and export'. Nevertheless, I outlined what Simpson had told me about the contract Tyler's company had secured. With the aid of Hugh Blakemore.

Although I'd not named his informant, Tyler identified him immediately. His eyes narrowed. 'That bastard Simpson put you up to this, didn't he?' he said.

'We never reveal the names of people who give us information,' said Dave.

'You don't have to,' said Tyler, now clearly a little worried that the police had arrived unheralded, to ask what could well be embarrassing questions. 'There's only one guy who could have told you about that.'

I decided to abandon any further pretence at shielding my informant. 'Mr Simpson has suggested that you paid

Hugh Blakemore a substantial bribe,' I began, 'to influence certain persons to put this contract the way of your company.' Simpson hadn't quite put it like that, but I hoped it would rattle Tyler's cage a little.

'I don't know what the hell he's talking about,' said Tyler angrily. 'There were a lot of expenses involved in this thing. Simpson's public relations outfit specializes in political lobbying. The people who work for clients like us have to travel all over the world, and you can't put them up in two-bit hotels. It costs money, one hell of a lot of money. Believe me, Mr Brock, none of this comes cheap, but in the end it's worth it.'

'So the name of Hugh Blakemore was never mentioned?' I queried. It appeared that Tyler was putting the onus back on Simpson, as far as any question of bribery was concerned.

'Not in that context,' said Tyler, but immediately looked as though he wished he'd kept quiet.

'In what context then?'

'It was Blakemore who put me in touch with Simpson. I'm an American, you see—'

'Yes, so I gather,' I said. Tyler's nationality had been quite apparent from our last meeting. Anyway, it would have been difficult for him to deny his origins, given the strong Bronx accent with which he spoke.

'And I'm not too familiar with the way these things work. Not on this side of the pond anyway. Hugh suggested Simpson and said that he was good at what I wanted, and was the guy to see. He said that we could put our trust in him, and that he'd do a good job for us.'

'And did he?'

'Yeah, sure. Well, we got the contract, didn't we?'

'And there was no suggestion of bribes.'

Tyler gave a sardonic smile. 'Nope,' he said, 'but I didn't arrive here on a banana boat, Mr Brock. Every company has a slush fund, despite all the bullshit you read about moral rectitude. And when you get a whacking great bill from a public relations company, you don't ask too many questions. As far as I was concerned, the account from Simpson was for services rendered in pushing our product. And, like I said, he did a good job.' He paused. 'What's this got to do with Hugh's murder, anyway?'

'I don't know that it has anything to do with it,' I said. 'But it may have.'

Tyler leaned back in his high office chair, perfectly relaxed. 'You know, I suppose, that Simpson's still shafting Anne.'

'Really?' I'd long since ceased to be surprised at anything, but I found this latest snippet of information hard to believe. I thought, in fact, that Tyler was trying to sully Simpson's reputation because of the tales he'd been telling us. 'But they were divorced eight years ago.'

'So what? It happens.' Tyler leaned forward again, an earnest expression on his face, and lowered his voice. 'Between you and me, Mr Brock, Anne's a nympho. And a lush. Her whole idle life is one round of sex, booze and drugs. Blakemore was having it off with some actress, so Anne reckoned, and she was doing ditto with Simpson.'

'And you?' I queried.

Tyler smiled. 'Yeah, and me. And that guy Strang before Caroline snatched him from on top of her mother.'

'What d'you know about Strang's murder? Anything?'

Tyler shrugged. 'Only what I read in the papers, but why should you think I know anything?'

'You'd met him presumably.'

'Yeah, sure I met him.'

I took a calculated gamble. 'He went to the States in March, apparently to make a film about the New York harbour master.'

'Yeah, I know.'

'Did you have any hand in that?'

'Only that I put him in touch with Simpson. Anne asked me if I could help. As Simpson had been useful over our contract, I thought he might be able to give the youngster a hand. Not that I thought he stood much chance.'

'Oh? Why was that?'

'Because America is stiff with people who want to get into the movies. Whether it's acting, or camera work, or directing, or even running coffee for the stars. There's no room for a Limey with hardly any experience. Every waitress and every busboy in LA is a wannabe actor.'

'I see. As a matter of interest, Mr Tyler, how did you meet the Blakemores?'

'At the American Embassy. It was some junket for expatriate businessmen. Hugh and Anne were there. We got chatting and when Hugh wandered off to talk to someone, Anne put it to me straight.'

'Put what to you straight?' asked Dave, an amused expression on his face.

Tyler switched his gaze to Dave. 'She propositioned me. Said she'd like to see me again. Said she'd always loved Americans and wanted to discuss our great country.' He spoke sarcastically. 'Well, Detective, a nod's as good as a wink.'

'She said that you took her to the theatre, along with your daughter,' I said. 'Liz, I believe?'

Tyler laughed outright. 'Liz isn't my daughter. She lives with me. Started out as my secretary, but . . .' He held his hands out, palms upwards. 'I guess you know how it is.' Suddenly he tired of the interview. 'Was there anything you really wanted to see me about, Mr Brock, or was this just a little enquiry into my sexual habits?'

'Not specifically, Mr Tyler. As you know, I'm investigating the murders of Hugh Blakemore and Geoffrey Strang. Anyone who knew them, or Anne Blakemore, may have some information that could be useful to me. Even if they're unaware of it.' I stood up. 'However, I'll not detain you any longer. Your young lady in reception told me that you're a very busy man. Thank you for your valuable time.'

TWELVE

As Dave and I were driving back to Curtis Green, I rang Kate Ebdon on my mobile.

'Kate,' I said, 'find out what you can about Charles Simpson and his business. I think there's more to that smooth bastard than immediately meets the eye. But be discreet. I don't want Simpson to know that we're taking an interest in him. Not until I'm ready to have another go at him. But then I want to be armed with as much ammunition as we can muster.'

'Are you going to shoot him, then, guv?'

'Chance would be a fine thing,' I said.

Kate assembled a small team of officers. It took about three days, but at the end of that time, she was in possession of as much information as she was likely to get without alerting Charles Simpson to police interest.

'I've had a full report prepared, guv,' said Kate, sitting down opposite my desk. She held up a five-page document.

'I'll read it later, Kate,' I said. 'Just give me the basic facts.'

'Lives in Chorleywood, just outside the M25,' Kate began, resting the report on her knee. She had no need to refer to it; she had familiarized herself with its contents before coming to see me. 'A house that's reckoned to be worth about a million and a half. The whole works: swimming pool, tennis courts, six bedrooms, each with an en-suite bathroom—'

'I think I've got the picture, Kate. And all this from public relations?'

'It's difficult to say, guv,' said Kate.

'Meaning?'

'The public relations company that he heads is owned by another company. That in turn belongs to yet another company. In other words, he's managed to build a corporate maze. I think the Fraud Squad and Revenue and Customs would spend days, if not weeks, trying to unravel it. But the interesting thing about his public relations company is that it appears to have been running at a loss.'

'It might just be the way big business works these days, Kate,' I said, but something about the Simpson set-up worried me. 'I think we'll leave that for the moment. Simpson's business practices might be dubious, but somehow I don't think that they have any bearing on Hugh Blakemore's murder.'

'One of the lads had a word with the local copper,' continued Kate. 'They're lucky enough still to have a beat duty constable assigned to the area. This PC said that Simpson's got a Rolls Royce and a Mercedes, plays golf a lot, and has frequent parties. Apparently there are always lots of attractive young women about the place. And not always the same young women, either. But apart from appearing to possess a personal harem, there's nothing adverse.'

'How disappointing,' I said. 'Nevertheless, I think I'll see him again.'

But two days later, and before I was able to interview Charles Simpson again – the public relations man was out of the country on business – I received a call from Anne Blakemore. Although obviously anguished, she declined to discuss on the telephone what was concerning her.

Dave and I arrived at the Chelsea house a little before noon. Hugh Blakemore's widow appeared to have dressed especially for our visit. She was attired in an emerald green dress, black tights and high-heeled shoes. 'Do come in, Mr Brock,' she said, and ushered us into the sitting room. She stood at the drinks table as we sat down. 'Would you care for a drink?' she asked.

'No, thank you,' I said, answering for both of us.

'Well, I'm going to have one,' said Anne, and prepared herself a gin and tonic. I noticed that the ice bucket was already full. It seemed to bear out what Tyler had said about the woman being an alcoholic.

'You seemed very concerned about something when you telephoned, Mrs Blakemore,' I began.

'It's Paul,' Anne blurted out. 'He's gone, disappeared.'

I suppressed the spark of interest that this statement had aroused, and responded blandly. 'And what makes you think that he's disappeared?' I asked.

Anne sat down on a sofa facing us, and took a sip of her drink. 'I tried telephoning him all day yesterday, but I only got his answering machine.'

'Was this his home number you tried?'

'Yes, it was.'

'He could just have been out somewhere, and it's hardly grounds for thinking that he's disappeared,' I said. 'Did you try his office?'

Anne looked sharply at me. 'His office?'

'Yes. The electronics firm of which he's managing director.' I was not prepared to believe that Anne was unaware of Tyler's business enterprises.

'Oh, that. Yes, but they merely said that he'd taken a few days off.'

'Well, there you are then,' I said. I was mildly irritated at having my time wasted by a hysterical woman.

'But he was supposed to come and see me yesterday afternoon and—' Anne stopped abruptly.

I was tempted to add, 'And stay the night,' but thought better of it. 'Perhaps some urgent business has cropped up. Abroad maybe.'

Anne shook her head. 'That sort of thing's happened before,' she said, 'but he's always let me know if he was going to break an appointment. Even so, his daughter Liz is always at home. But she doesn't seem to be there either.'

I contained a smile at that. Either Anne Blakemore did not know of the relationship between Tyler and his former secretary, or she chose not to reveal it to us. But the fact that Liz had gone as well interested me, and I began to wonder whether Tyler was more involved with the deaths of Blakemore and Strang than had, at first, been apparent. And it could have been my questioning that had caused the American to vanish.

'Where does Mr Tyler live?' I asked, although I'd already been told that the American lived in Chichester.

Anne confirmed the address that I'd been given by Kate Ebdon. She stood up and, crossing to the drinks table, refilled her glass. 'Are you sure?' she asked, holding the gin bottle in the air.

'Quite sure, thank you,' I said, and noted that there was no trace of a slur in the woman's speech, and that she walked back to the sofa without the least sign of a stagger. She obviously had a high level of tolerance for alcohol.

'I really am very worried, Mr Brock.'

'Where did you meet Mr Tyler, Mrs Blakemore?' I asked.

Tyler had given us one version of their meeting, but I never missed an opportunity to cross-check any information that came my way. And Anne had avoided the question when I'd put it to her on the day that her late husband was buried.

'At the American Embassy, years ago. We'd been invited because Hugh was an MP. We had to go to simply hundreds of these things, and a frightful bore they were too.'

To my surprise her account of the meeting bore out what Tyler had told me. I was surprised because almost everyone we'd come across so far seemed to be devious when it came to answering even the most straightforward of questions.

'How many years ago was that, Mrs Blakemore?' asked Dave.

Giving the question some thought, Anne Blakemore leaned her head back so that her gold medallion necklace slipped inside the top of her dress and nestled between her breasts. With a nonchalant gesture, she flicked it out and leaned forward again. 'I suppose it must have been about two years ago,' she said. 'But then he was away for a few months. I don't know where he went, and I didn't think I'd see him again. But then he dropped in, out of the blue, a day or two after Hugh died.'

'So, in fact, he's disappeared before.'

'Yes, but this is different. He was supposed to come up to London and—' Once again Anne stopped suddenly when about to disclose the reason for Tyler's proposed visit, but then she abandoned her caution. 'He was coming to spend the night with me,' she said, careless of what I may think about it. She seemed to have forgotten that she'd previously told me that she and Tyler had been conducting a long affair. What was more, she'd obviously forgotten how she was dressed when we called on her immediately after her husband's funeral. Or perhaps she thought I hadn't noticed. Fat chance!

I stood up. 'I'll get the Sussex Police to look into it, Mrs Blakemore,' I said.

Anne Blakemore stood up too, and laid a hand on my arm. 'That's terribly good of you, Mr Brock,' she said. 'I'm most awfully worried.'

'Think nothing of it,' I said. But I wasn't doing Mrs Blakemore a favour; I was very interested in discovering why Tyler had disappeared so soon after he had been interviewed.

And I had no intention of allowing the Sussex Police to look into the matter: I was going to have one of my own officers deal with it. Or even deal with it myself.

After Dave and I had lunched at my favourite Italian restaurant, I found Kate Ebdon waiting to see me. 'I don't know whether it's of any interest, guv,' she said, 'but I've heard a whisper from a snout that Mickey Lever's disappeared from his usual haunts. He's the villain who was banged up with Kenneth Johnson when he got topped by Hugh Blakemore.' She gave me a mischievous grin.

'Yes, I know who Mickey Lever is,' I said, 'and I'm beginning to wonder why it is that everyone I speak to either gets murdered or runs away.'

I'd decided to take a personal interest in the possible disappearance of Paul Tyler. If, in fact, he had disappeared, I was anxious to know why. I had also taken the precaution of obtaining a warrant to search his home from the City of Westminster district judge on the grounds that evidence of Blakemore's murder might be found.

It was an elegant, detached house a few miles to the north of Chichester. Set back from the road and shielded by conifers, it boasted a double garage and was surrounded by well-tended lawns and flower beds. I suspected that Tyler employed a full-time gardener.

Dave rang the doorbell and we heard it ringing somewhere in the depths of the house. But there was no answer. We walked right around the property, and peered through the windows, but there was no sign of life in any of the ground-floor rooms.

'Well, there doesn't seem to be anyone here, Dave,' I said, after we'd looked through the window of the back door to the garage and found no cars inside.

'Better break in, then, guv,' said Dave. 'I mean, he might be lying dead upstairs,' he added with a grin.

There seemed no alternative to that, and we had a perfectly valid warrant.

I telephoned Sussex Police headquarters and asked for the services of an officer with a battering ram.

Minutes later a local area car arrived complete with the equipment for which I'd asked.

'What's the score, then, sir?' asked the PC wielding the ramming device.

I explained briefly what we were about, and showed the officer the warrant.

'Let's do it, then,' said the PC, happily wielding his rammer. With one deft swing, he bludgeoned open the front door. 'There you are, sir,' he said, standing back. He turned to his colleague. 'Jim, radio headquarters to let them know that the burglar alarm has probably been activated, and to pay no attention. Tell them we're on scene and dealing.'

Dave and I walked from room to room. There were no signs of a hurried departure: no dirty dishes in the kitchen sink, no unmade beds, no dirty linen in the large basket in the dressing room and, significantly, no towels, clean or dirty, in the bathroom, which was *en suite* to the master bedroom. The entire house was clean and tidy and it looked as though Tyler and Liz had prepared carefully for their departure.

We returned to the large sitting room that ran along the rear of the house, and had windows on three sides. Dave stooped to inspect the DVD recorder. It had not been set. He turned his attention to the answering machine and played back the four messages that had been recorded. Moments later the increasingly anguished voice of Anne Blakemore filled the room, imploring 'Paul darling' to get in touch with her.

Dave pressed the redial button on the telephone; he knows about these things. 'Sorry to disappoint you, guv,' he said, 'but the last number called was for the speaking clock.'

Finally, Dave dialled 1471, but a recorded voice announced that the last caller's number had been withheld. 'Reckon they've done a runner, guv,' he said.

I turned to the Sussex PC. 'D'you know much about the guy who lives here?' I asked. 'Name of Paul Tyler.'

'Not a lot, sir. We've had calls from time to time from neighbours complaining about noisy parties that have gone on well into the night. Once, there was a shindig going on round the swimming pool. Loud music and lots of birds in bikinis drinking champagne. And that was at two o'clock in the morning.' The PC sighed. 'How the other half live, eh, sir?'

However, I declined to leave the matter there, and determined to make a few local enquiries. But it was to no avail.

The few near neighbours, and they were not very near at that, either pretended to know nothing of Tyler, or had not seen him for days. The only local resident who added to that sparse information was a middle-aged woman with straight grey hair who gave the impression that she enjoyed minding everyone else's business. But even she was unable to volunteer any more than that Mr Tyler and his 'daughter' always kept themselves very much to themselves. And, no, she added in response to Dave's question, they did not seem to entertain.

But I suppose she didn't want to upset Tyler, and made no mention of the parties. Knowing human nature as I do, I decided she was probably the one who'd complained to the police. And when I asked the local PC, he confirmed it.

Back at Tyler's house, I surveyed the property yet again. 'I think we'll get a fingerprint team down here, Dave,' I said.

Without further ado, Dave dialled the number on his mobile and relayed my request. 'Be here within the hour, guv, probably sooner,' he said.

Exactly one hour later, Linda Mitchell's fingerprint expert was lifting prints from those places in the house likely to have been used by Tyler and Liz, rather than by a visitor.

Back at Curtis Green, I decided that I would pay another visit to Gina Watson, the late Hugh Blakemore's former paramour. I sent for Kate Ebdon. 'Give Gina Watson a ring and tell her we're coming to see her, Kate,' I said, pointing to my telephone.

'*We*, sir?' queried Kate.

'Of course,' I said. I intended to talk to the actress again about her relationship with Hugh Blakemore, and attempt to discover whether she'd been blackmailing him. And I decided that, on this occasion, I'd take Kate Ebdon with me; her forthright attitude might just get beneath the surface of Gina Watson's theatrics. 'I reckon you'll think of all the questions I don't think of.'

'I'll give it my best shot, guv,' said Kate, and tapped out Gina Watson's number. When the call was answered, she asked for the actress. She listened for a short while, scribbled down some details, and replaced the receiver. 'Fiona Savage answered the phone, guv. She said that Gina Watson doesn't live there. But she gave me Gina's number. It's in Brighton. I'll do a subscriber check.'

'How very interesting, Kate,' I said. 'In that case we'll pay Ms Savage a visit and see what's going on. Leave the subscriber check for the moment; Fiona Savage will give us Gina's address.'

Fiona Savage answered the door, paused for a moment, and then said, 'Oh, it's you,' as she recognized me. 'I'm afraid Gina isn't here.'

'I know,' I said. 'She doesn't live here, does she, Miss Savage?'

'What makes you think—?'

'You told my officer when she rang, about an hour ago.'

'Oh! Was that you?' The woman gave Kate an embarrassed glance.

'May we come in?' I asked.

'Of course.' With a resigned shrug, Fiona Savage opened the door wide, and stood back to allow us to enter.

'Why d'you imagine that Mrs Watson should lead me to believe that she lived here, Miss Savage?' I asked. 'It is *Miss* Savage, is it?'

'Yes.' The woman nodded. 'Actually we share. She stays here if she's in a show in London, and this is the address her agent has for her. She owns the flat, and has her own bedroom, although she spends most of her time in Brighton.' She glanced at Kate. 'Gina rang me the other day and said that she would be using the flat to talk to you. She said that you wanted to talk to her about a burglary. She said it would be more convenient for you to come to Chiswick.'

'I see. And where was this burglary supposed to have taken place?'

'Well, in Brighton, she said.' Fiona Savage looked distinctly uncomfortable.

'Interesting,' I said, 'particularly as burglaries in Brighton are dealt with by the Sussex Police, not the Metropolitan.'

Fiona Savage was sitting tightly bunched in an armchair opposite Kate and me. 'I really don't know then.' She appeared to be as mystified as I was by her friend's subterfuge.

'I am investigating the murders of Hugh Blakemore and Geoffrey Strang,' I announced. 'That's why I wanted to see her.'

'Good heavens! I had no idea.' Fiona's hand went to her mouth, and she paled visibly. 'But does that mean that you think she had something to do with them?' She had clearly been shocked by my statement.

'I'm not thinking anything at the moment,' I said, 'except to wonder why Mrs Watson should have pretended to live here. I don't see the point of it. You say she lives in Brighton.'

'Yes, on the outskirts really. She's got quite a big house in Preston. But she wasn't pretending she lived here. As I said just now, she owns the flat, and sometimes uses it.'

'Is she appearing in anything at the moment?'

'No,' said Fiona immediately. 'She doesn't do very much these days. Between you and me, I think the acting business has become a bit *passé* as far as she's concerned. She doesn't have to work, you know. She's a very wealthy woman.'

'Really? The proceeds of acting?' I knew that was unlikely. From what my girlfriend Gail had said, if you'd acquired wealth from treading the boards, everyone would have heard of you. And Gina Watson's name hadn't meant anything to me until I'd starting enquiring into Blakemore's murder.

Fiona laughed. 'No chance,' she said. 'Not from the sort of things she's done lately. She did one or two London productions in the past, but these days she's mostly in rep if she does anything at all. She only has very occasional parts on television, but usually she does voice-overs. As a matter of fact, I think her last visual television appearance was about seven years ago. And that was only an advert,' she added cruelly, and cast a quick glance at Kate Ebdon who had spent the whole time coolly appraising her.

'When I was here last, Miss Savage, Mrs Watson was telling me about her relationship with Hugh Blakemore.'

'What relationship?' Fiona contrived a look of surprise, but the look carried little conviction. I would have thought that an actress could have done better.

'Mrs Watson claimed that you once discovered her in bed with Mr Blakemore. Here.'

Fiona's mouth opened. 'What on earth could she have been talking about?' she asked. 'Gina's never slept here with a man.'

'Miss Savage.' Kate Ebdon spoke for the first time since arriving at the flat. She had been fully briefed by me on the way to Chiswick, and now decided that she would intervene. 'We're investigating two murders, not judging people's morals.'

Fiona switched her gaze to the woman detective. 'I realize that,' she said quietly.

'And we don't like people obstructing us in those enquiries,' Kate continued. 'Frankly, I don't give a damn if Gina Watson slept with a dozen men.' By now, Kate had deliberately emphasized her Australian accent so that it sounded vaguely threatening.

'She swore me to secrecy,' said Fiona lamely.

'Why should she have done that?'

Fiona shrugged. 'She said he was an important man, an MP, and that he was married, and if it got out that he and Gina were lovers, it could damage his career. That's why she would use the flat. That and the fact that Hugh wouldn't go all the way to Brighton.'

'So you did find them in bed here.'

'Yes.' Fiona looked down at the carpet and kept her eyes lowered.

Kate made an inspired guess. 'Did you arrive by accident? Or did Gina Watson suggest that you return at a specific time, the time, in fact, that you found them?'

Fiona Savage's head jerked up. 'How did you know that?' she asked.

'I didn't. You just told me,' observed Kate drily.

'Yes, she did, now you come to mention it. I was rehearsing that morning, and Gina said she would be out of here by three. She asked me to return at that time because she wanted to get away, and I did.'

'But presumably Mrs Watson has a key to her own flat. Why should she have wanted you to return before she left?'

'Thinking about it, it was a rather silly request. She comes and goes as she pleases. She wouldn't normally wait for me to come home.'

'So, the real reason was that Mrs Watson wanted you to find her and Hugh Blakemore in bed together.'

'I suppose so.'

'Did she introduce you?'

Fiona laughed nervously. 'It was hardly a propitious moment for introductions,' she said. 'Neither of them had any clothes on.'

'How did you know who he was then?'

'Gina told me afterwards. That's when she pleaded with me not to tell anyone.'

If that was the case, why on earth should Gina Watson have told her friend who he was? But it was obvious that she had planned the whole thing. Perhaps it was to give her a hold over Blakemore.

'When did this incident occur?' I asked, taking the questioning back again.

Fiona glanced at the large painting before looking back at me. 'About a year ago, I suppose. Perhaps a little longer.'

'Do you know of any other men that Mrs Watson entertained here?' I asked, even though Fiona had previously denied it. But that was when she was still lying. It was obviously worrying her that she was being asked to reveal her friend's intimate secrets, but the fact that we might have thought that Gina was involved in a double murder had clearly alarmed her. The thought had probably crossed her mind that we might think, that in sharing Gina's flat, she too was involved. 'There was another man that I knew she was seeing. A younger man – younger than Gina, that is – who she raved about once or twice.'

'Do you know his name?'

'No, I don't think she ever mentioned it. But she did say he was something to do with making films.'

I gave no indication that she might have been referring to Geoffrey Strang, although as an actress Gina must have known a lot of people in the film business. 'Perhaps you'd let me have Mrs Watson's address in Brighton,' I said, as we stood up. 'And I'd be grateful if you didn't mention this conversation to her.' But that was a vain hope. I had no doubt that Fiona Savage would be on the phone to Gina Watson the moment we left.

THIRTEEN

'Nice legs that girl had got, hadn't she, guv?' said Kate impishly, as she shot me a sideways glance.

'Probably,' I said, without turning in my seat. In fact, I'd found Fiona Savage extremely attractive.

'What happens next, guv? A visit to Brighton?'

'Yes, Kate,' I said, 'and I want you to come with me. I reckon having a woman in on the conversation might just produce the sort of information that Gina Watson wouldn't share with a man.'

'From what Fiona Savage was saying, that's about the only thing she wouldn't share with a man,' said Kate drily. Pulling into a lay-by, she took out her mobile, and tapped out the telephone number of Gina Watson's Brighton house. But when the phone was answered, she made the excuse of having got a wrong number, and apologized. 'She's there, guv,' she said.

After a hair-raising hour of what Kate called positive driving, we drew up outside Gina Watson's house in Preston.

When Gina opened the front door she gazed impassively at the two of us. 'Hello again, darling,' she said after a pause, and glanced apprehensively at Kate. 'For a moment I thought you were those awful people who try to convert you to some obscure religion.' She spoke breathlessly and made little theatrical gestures with her hands. 'You'll have to excuse how I look, but I was just dashing around with the Hoover.' She was wearing a white T-shirt, a denim skirt and mule sandals. 'The demands of Thespis don't leave one a great deal of time for spring-cleaning, you know.' She paused. 'In fact, darlings, you may be able to help me. I'm being considered for a part as a woman detective in some forthcoming TV thing. It's terribly exciting. I've not done anything like that before.'

But Gina's comment was interesting in view of what Fiona Savage had told us about her, that she wasn't doing much in the way of acting these days.

'Oh, right,' said Kate, unimpressed by the woman's performance so far. I hoped that she wouldn't make one of her cutting remarks about how female police officers were portrayed on television. I knew from her previous comments on the subject that she could be very critical. 'What's it called, this TV play?'

Gina appeared slightly flustered. 'I can't remember,' she said. 'Fancy that. Me an actress, and I can't even remember the title, let alone my lines. I've got the script knocking about somewhere.' She glanced around as if hoping it would suddenly materialize.

The room into which Gina had showed us was sumptuously furnished. In the centre of a large Axminster carpet that almost completely covered the wood-block flooring, stood a mahogany occasional table with cabriole legs. Against one wall there was an Edwardian cabinet bookcase, also in mahogany. Two hide settees jutted out from an open fireplace, and several other pieces of good-quality furniture, strategically placed around the room, bore a profusion of small ornaments. The overall impression was that Gina Watson was not short of money.

'Nice place you've got here,' said Kate.

'Thank you, darling,' said Gina, waving a hand towards the settees. 'Do sit down and tell me what you want to talk about.' But as I was about to start, Gina fluttered her hands again. 'Oh, what must you think of me? You must have some coffee first.' And she disappeared through an archway on the far side of the room. 'I shan't be long,' she called out. 'It's already made.' There was a clattering of crockery, and minutes later the actress reappeared with a tray on which were a cafetière, three cups and saucers, cream and sugar. 'Now,' she continued, as she busied herself pouring coffee, 'how can I help you? But if you've come to talk about poor Hugh, I've told you all I know.'

'Have you? Everything?' I looked searchingly at the actress.

'Everything I could remember, yes. Why? Is there something else that you think I might be able to assist you with?'

'You didn't say that Mr Blakemore helped you buy this house, and furnish it,' said Kate, taking a wild guess, even though the only indication that that might have been the case was Fiona Savage's suggestion that the Watson woman's money had not come from her acting career.

Gina Watson looked around. 'Oh, now where have I put my cigarettes?' she said. 'Ah, there they are.' She stood up and took a packet from the mantelshelf, and offered it to each of us, but we both declined. 'Yes, he did help out. Such a nice man.

I shall miss him terribly. I didn't think it was important to mention it, really.' She was clearly flustered by the question, and it was apparent that her mind was racing feverishly.

'Why should he have done that, Mrs Watson?' Kate persisted.

'Do call me Gina, darling. Everyone does.'

'OK, Gina, but why should he have done that?'

The actress drew deeply on her cigarette and expelled smoke towards the ceiling. 'We had a very special thing going,' she said. 'I think he was on the point of leaving his wife and suggesting that we got married.'

'Did he ever talk about that possibility?' Kate crossed her legs, and I noted the feline look of envy Gina Watson gave them. Instead of her usual jeans and shirt, Kate was, for once, wearing a dark suit, and a white blouse with a jabot. Recently, she had been dressing that way when interviewing those she described as well-heeled witnesses.

'He hinted at it, yes.'

'But you told me that he'd never mentioned it,' I said.

'Well, he didn't, not in as many words,' said Gina. 'But a woman can always tell. Don't you agree?' She shot a glance in Kate's direction.

'Not in my experience,' said Kate brutally.

'You also told me that Mr Blakemore was very concerned the day that Fiona Savage found you and him in bed in Chiswick,' I said.

'Well, of course he was, darling. He was a married MP, and absolutely terrified that someone would find out, and that it would be all over the newspapers. You know what those people are like.'

'In that case, why did you arrange for Miss Savage to arrive at the very moment when you knew that she would find you both at it?'

'Why on earth should you think that?'

'It's true, isn't it?' Kate was determined to get at the truth of the actress's relationship with Blakemore.

Gina Watson suddenly looked immeasurably sad, almost as if she had just read stage directions telling her to adopt a sympathy-invoking pose. 'I was afraid of losing him,' she whispered.

'How would being found in bed by a third party stop him from running away?' asked Kate pointedly. 'More likely to have scared the pants off him, I should've thought.' She paused. 'But I suppose they were off already,' she added.

'Ah, but you didn't know him, my dear.' Gina cast her eyes down and clasped her hands gently together in an attitude of supplication, but it was fairly evident that Kate's hammed-up Aussie twang was disturbing her. 'I shouldn't say this really, but I'm sure that an attractive young woman like you will understand.' She looked up hopefully. 'I was trying to force him into making a commitment.'

'And did he?'

Gina shook her head. 'Quite the reverse. It panicked him into leaving. He couldn't get out of my flat fast enough.'

'And I suppose that's the last you saw of him?' asked Kate innocently.

'I'm afraid so.'

Kate reached down for her handbag, took out her pocket-book and made a pretence of thumbing through its pages. It was a device; she had made herself thoroughly familiar with Dave's notes of our interview with Gina Watson. 'When you were telling Mr Brock about this, Gina, you said, "But he was back within ten days and in my bed within ten minutes".' She closed her pocketbook and gazed unwaveringly at the actress.

'Did I really? Oh dear! I must have been confusing that occasion with another.'

'So there was another similar occasion, was there? When you and he were discovered in bed, I mean.' Kate was not going to let this woman off the hook easily.

'Well, I—' Gina Watson broke off and glared angrily at her interrogator.

'Or was the other occasion when you and a younger man, a man in the film business, were found together? What was his name?'

'It's none of your business who he was. Anyway, it's over.'

'Suit yourself.' Kate shrugged, and taking a guess that it had been Geoffrey Strang, added, 'But it would be over anyway, considering he's dead.'

'Look, what is all this about?' asked Gina, looking to me for sympathy. 'I didn't have anything to do with Hugh's death, if that's what you're getting at. So why all the questions about my love life?'

'It's a bit like a jigsaw,' said Kate. 'Until we've got all the pieces, we shan't have the full picture. We don't really care what the two of you did, but if Mr Blakemore was being blackmailed, it could be relevant.'

'Blackmailed? My God, what a suggestion.' Gina Watson raised her eyes to where the gallery would have been had she been on stage.

'I understand from Fiona Savage that you share the flat with her, Gina,' Kate said.

'That's true, but I'm not often there. But why have you been bothering Fiona?'

'As I said just now, we need to acquire as much information about Mr Blakemore as possible. If we're to discover who murdered him.'

'Oh, I see.' Gina seemed about to give in. 'It's the tax, you see.'

'The tax?' Kate raised her eyes in disbelief.

'As an actress, I pay tax under Schedule D, and I was afraid that you might have wondered about my money if I'd invited you down here. After all, you're all in it together, aren't you? Tax inspectors, policemen, customs officers.'

'So this story about you and Fiona living round the corner from each other, and having keys and looking out for each other was all a load of old moody, was it?' demanded Kate, intent on proving that Gina Watson was a liar.

'You're all against people like me,' said Gina, and began to cry, softly. 'Oh, I do miss him,' she mumbled.

'When you've finished the histrionics, Gina, mate,' said Kate, 'I've a serious suggestion to put to you.'

Gina composed herself again, very quickly, and shot a bitter glance at the Australian DI. 'Well?'

'*You* were blackmailing Hugh Blakemore, weren't you? Was it just the money, or was there some other motive?'

Even I was taken aback by Kate's forthright question, but I stayed silent.

Cue indignant outrage.

'How dare you make such an accusation. Hugh and I were lovers. And because he respected me so much, he made me gifts. Very generous gifts.' Gina waved a hand around the room. 'Much of what is here came from him.'

'As a price for your silence, Gina? As a price for your not going to the newspapers with a kiss-and-tell story?'

'That's preposterous.'

'He told you that he'd had enough, and that he wanted to break it off, didn't he? So you arranged one last meeting at Chiswick, and set up Fiona Savage to find the pair of you in bed, because the only way you could hold on to a good thing was to put the black on him.'

Gina Watson leaped from her settee, and pointed melodramatically towards the door. 'Get out, both of you. I refuse to sit here in my own home and listen to these wild accusations any longer.'

As the front door slammed behind us, and we walked down Gina Watson's drive, Kate turned to me. 'Guilty as hell, guv,' she said, 'and she's a piss-poor actress.'

'Yes,' I said thoughtfully, 'but I think we'll have a word with the local Inspector of Taxes, just the same.'

We stopped off for a meal on the way back to London, and then drove around the M25 until we reached the junction nearest to Forest Hill.

Although Mickey Lever was said by Kate Ebdon's informant to have disappeared, we still had hopes that his girlfriend had remained at the terraced house that the two of them had occupied. And so it proved to be.

'Hello, Melanie,' said Kate, when the stripper came to the door.

'Oh, it's you again. What d'you want now?'

'We want to ask you some questions,' said Kate.

Melanie, accustomed to frequent visits from the police, turned and walked indoors, leaving us to follow her. 'What is it this time?' she asked listlessly. 'If it's Mickey you want, the bastard's buggered off and left me with a load of bills. Despite having five grand in the bank.'

'Where's he gone?' asked Kate.

'Search me. I haven't a clue. He just took off about ten days ago, but I don't know where he's gone.' Melanie sat down on a worn armchair. She was wearing a miniskirt that was, at most, fourteen inches from waistband to hem. Her scarlet blouse was knotted under her breasts leaving a bare artificially tanned midriff, and she wore sheer black tights and white, stiletto-heeled shoes. She crossed her legs and tried to yank her inadequate skirt down an inch or two, something she would not have bothered to do had I brought a male detective with me.

'I think you do know where he is, Melanie,' said Kate.

'Well, I don't.' Melanie Gabb was apprehensive in the presence of this Australian woman detective. She had had dealings with policewomen before – particularly this one – and hadn't enjoyed the experience. 'If I did, I'd tell you. Mickey ain't done me no favours, believe me.'

'You said he went about ten days ago,' said Kate. 'When, exactly?'

Melanie frowned. 'It was a Wednesday.'

Ten days ago on a Wednesday was the date of Strang's murder. And at the very time Strang was shot, Lever was at Charing Cross police station being interviewed by Dave and me. *What an alibi!*

'Are you sure it was a Wednesday?' I asked. That Lever should have gone missing on that day interested me enormously. It must have had something to do with the grilling we gave him.

'Of course I'm sure. I was in late the night before. About one in the morning, I s'pose.' Melanie's voice adopted a whining tone.

'What's that got to do with it?' asked Kate.

'I was working, up West. Doing a striptease cabaret at a retirement party for a load of bloody coppers, if you must know. And when I got back, Mickey was in bed, pissed, if his snoring was anything to go by.' Melanie lapsed into silence, apparently convinced that she had told us all we wanted to know.

'Just get on with this fairy tale, will you,' said Kate.

'Well, when I woke up in the morning, Mickey'd gone, and I ain't seen hair nor hide of him since.'

'Did he leave a note, or has he rung you since?' asked Kate.

'No, not a bleedin' word. Good riddance, I say.' Melanie scratched irritably at the arm of her chair. 'Anyway, what you want him for?'

'Did he ever mention a man called Strang, Geoffrey Strang?'

Melanie shook her head. 'No, he never,' she said. She looked up sharply. ''Ere, ain't he the bloke who got murdered the other day? I saw it on the telly.'

'That's right,' said Kate. 'On Wednesday, the thirty-first of July. The day your beloved Mickey did a runner.'

And it seemed that he'd disappeared immediately after leaving the police station.

'Oh, my Gawd!' said Melanie. 'D'you think he done it, then?'

'If he didn't, why has he vanished?' asked Kate. But both Kate and I knew that he couldn't have been directly involved in Strang's murder.

'I thought he was doing a job some place.'

'So did we,' said Kate drily.

'Poor little cow,' said Kate, as we arrived back at Curtis Green. 'I don't think she knows a damned thing, guv.'

All in all, it had not been the most satisfactory of days. Although we had come near to getting an admission from Gina Watson that she had been blackmailing Hugh Blakemore, we had not quite got what we wanted. But even if we had, it would have been no indication that she'd had any part in his murder. If anything, quite the reverse. Blackmailers don't generally kill the goose that lays the golden egg.

And as for Mickey Lever, even though he was in custody at the time, he might have had some hand in the killing of Geoffrey Strang; perhaps he had commissioned someone else to do the job. But there was no apparent motive. And, frankly, Kate Ebdon, who knew him better than I did, didn't think he had the mental ability to set up a job like that.

But his disappearance annoyed me nevertheless. 'I want Lever found, Kate,' I said, 'and I don't care what it takes to find him.' And then I added, 'And Paul Tyler as well, while we're about it.'

Kate took a photograph from her pocket and laid it on my desk. 'Mickey Lever, guv,' she said.

'I do know what he looks like, Kate.'

Kate chuckled. 'Yes, guv, but the clerk at the Jobcentre, whom Lever allegedly saw at the time of the Dartford Post Office van robbery, doesn't know what he looks like.'

'Get to the point, Kate.'

'I played a hunch, guv. I showed him Lever's criminal record photograph. And that's not the guy who went into the Jobcentre, even though he gave Lever's name and address.'

'That's very dishonest.'

'Shall we nick him when we find him, guv?'

'No, Kate,' I said. 'It may be more useful to us to let him roam free for a while.'

FOURTEEN

'Fingerprint Branch haven't got any trace of Paul Tyler, guv,' said Dave, as he entered my office and sprawled in my armchair. 'Either in its main index or in scenes-of-crime. Assuming, of course, that the fingerprints lifted from his drum in Chichester are his.'

'Which was to be expected,' I said glumly. 'That being the case, I wonder why he disappeared. Of course, he could be innocent, I suppose,' I added.

'Yes, sir,' said Dave.

'Anything else?'

'British Telecom's records of Strang's phone bill show that he made an interesting call during the evening following your interview with him, guv.' Dave waved a sheaf of paper.

'Who did he call, Dave?'

Dave handed me the printout of Strang's record of telephone calls. Alongside the number that had attracted his attention, he'd pencilled in the name of the subscriber. 'Mind you, guv,' he said, 'it's only an indication that the number was called, not that Strang actually spoke to the person he was calling.'

'I wonder what it was about.'

'We could ask,' said Dave.

'Yes, we could, Dave,' I said, 'but at this stage we need more than that. For the time being, I think we'll just tuck it away and remember it. For future reference.'

Next, I sent for Kate Ebdon. 'Kate, I want you to use as many resources as you can spare to hunt down Paul Tyler and Mickey Lever. I want to know why those two have gone missing. But be discreet about Tyler; he is, to all intents and purposes, a respectable businessman, and he may have a very good reason for going away somewhere, like he's fed up to the back teeth with darling Anne. But as far as Lever's concerned, I don't care how much noise you make. In fact, the more you let it be known that I want to talk to him, the more likely it is to panic him into doing something stupid. Not that he'd have much difficulty in doing that.'

Those matters put in hand, I decided that Dave and I would see the grieving widow Blakemore once more.

'Have you found him, Mr Brock?' asked Anne Blakemore, the moment she had the front door open.

'No, we haven't, Mrs Blakemore,' I said, as Dave and I followed the woman into the house.

'What on earth can have happened to him?' Anne sounded genuinely distressed.

'We searched his house at Chichester,' I said, as Dave and I sat down on one of the sofas, 'and he appears to have made an orderly departure.'

'What does that mean?' Anne raised an eyebrow.

'It means that he doesn't seem to have gone in a hurry. The house was clean and tidy, as though he had been preparing to go on holiday.' I recalled a previous conversation that I'd had with Blakemore's widow. 'Last time I was here, you said that, on one occasion, Paul Tyler went away for a few months, but returned just after your husband's death.'

Anne looked vacantly at me. 'Yes, that's right.'

'Have you any idea where he went then?'

'No, no idea. Why?'

'It's just that he might have gone there again,' I said.

'Oh, I see,' said Anne. 'Do you know if his daughter has gone too? Liz.'

I decided that it was time Anne Blakemore knew the truth about Paul Tyler's relationship with Liz. 'Liz is not his daughter, Mrs Blakemore,' I said.

'Not his—?' Anne broke off, staring at me. 'Well, who is she?'

'She's the woman he lives with.'

'But that's ridiculous. She's only about twenty-seven at the most. Who on earth told you that?'

'Paul Tyler did,' I said, 'when I interviewed him last. At his office.'

'Well, the cheating, two-timing little bastard,' exclaimed Anne furiously and, rising majestically from her chair, made her way to the drinks table. She turned. 'I suppose I can't interest you in a drink, can I?' she asked.

'No, thanks.' I was amused at Anne's earthy outburst, but recalled that she was, after all, the daughter of a Dagenham cinema usherette. Essex girl had surfaced.

Anne sat down again, took a deep draught of her gin and tonic, and stared into the glass for a moment or two. Then it all came out. 'The reason that Paul went last time was because of a row between him and Hugh.'

'What was the row about?'

'Me,' said Anne, glancing up to meet my eyes.

'Would you like to elaborate on that?'

'My ex-husband and I were . . .' Anne let the sentence tail off, unwilling to reveal any more evidence of her promiscuity.

'You and Charles Simpson were occasionally sleeping together,' said Dave in matter-of-fact tones.

'How did you know that?' demanded Anne, staring malevolently at Dave.

'We were told.'

'By whom?' Anne snapped out her demand.

'It doesn't matter who told us,' I said. 'Is it true?'

Anne took another sip of her gin and tonic before looking up. 'Yes,' she said quietly. 'We were very discreet, but somehow or another Hugh found out, or at least suspected it. Apparently he confronted Charles about it, and Charles, who was convinced that Hugh couldn't possibly know, told him that it was Paul Tyler that I was having an affair with. That's what the row was about.'

'I'm sorry,' I said. 'You've lost me.'

'Charles told Hugh that Paul and I were lovers. I told you that Paul was very good to me, taking me to the theatre and that sort of thing. Anyway, Hugh confronted him here one afternoon, and there was an almighty row. Hugh said that, as a Member of Parliament, he had considerable influence, and told Paul that if he didn't stop seeing me, he'd have him deported back to America.' Anne drained her glass and stood up to refill it. 'I don't think he could have done, and anyway, I thought that was pretty rich, considering that Hugh was screwing that Watson woman.' All of that was said with her back towards me as she poured herself another drink. She turned and made her way back to her seat. 'That's the actress I told you about.'

'So Paul Tyler disappeared, did he?' I asked.

'Yes.'

'And you've no idea where he went?' I repeated my previous question.

'No, none at all.'

'One last question, Mrs Blakemore. Was your husband in debt?'

'In debt?' Anne Blakemore scoffed. 'My dear Mr Brock, we were practically bankrupt.'

One of the useful snippets of information that Kate Ebdon and I had discovered when we interviewed Melanie Gabb was where Mickey Lever had his English bank account. But in order to obtain further particulars of the account, given that Lever was not wanted for a specific offence, was difficult. At least, through proper channels. I spoke to Alan Cleaver, my detective chief superintendent.

Cleaver, using his influence with the chief security officer at the bank – a retired CID commander – arranged to be notified of any drawings that Lever made using his cash card. Normally such transactions are cloaked in secrecy, but as Cleaver had convinced the former policeman that I needed to question Lever about his possible involvement in two murders, the bank was more willing to assist than it would have been normally. It's called 'the old boy net'.

I'd pondered the problem of Paul Tyler's sudden departure from Chichester. I'd had enquiries made of the electronics company of which he was managing director, but the company secretary was able only to suggest that Mr Tyler had taken a short holiday. The MD, he had said, had taken a week or two off and, no, he had no idea where he'd gone. But it was not unusual for him to take a short break from time to time. I did, however, wonder what he was up to.

'Dave, you said that there was no trace of Tyler's fingerprints in SO4.'

'Neither was there, guv.'

'But we don't know for certain that the prints that were obtained were those of Tyler and his lady friend, do we?'

'I said that, sir,' said Dave, 'but knowing Linda Mitchell, she'd have taken them from places unlikely to have been touched by visitors to the house.'

'But they could have belonged to the previous occupants, couldn't they?'

'It's possible, I suppose, but according to records at the local authority, Tyler has been paying council tax from that address for over five years. So, even with the worst cleaning woman in the world, I can't imagine that any of the previous occupants' dabs would still be there.'

'Still possible, though,' I said, 'particularly if Liz is not very good at housework either.' I paused. 'Incidentally, have you got a surname for her?'

'Middleton, guv. Elizabeth Middleton. There's no trace of her in any of our records.'

'Nationality?'

'British, born twenty-eight years ago in Hertfordshire. I got young Appleby to do a birth search at the General Register Office in Southport. Liz was Tyler's secretary at one time, but she's been living with him for about three or four years now.'

'I don't know, Dave,' I said, 'but this case seems to be abounding with people blessed with the most extraordinary sexual appetites.'

'You can say that again, guv.'

'Have a word with Joe Daly at the American Embassy, and ask him if he'd be so good as to send those prints across to the FBI. I know they're only partials, but you never know what might turn up.'

I next turned my attention to Mickey Lever. It was natural enough that we should have gone after him following Blakemore's murder, particularly once we'd discovered that he, Kenneth Johnson and Peter Crowley had been mates when they had been banged up in Melbury prison at the time of Johnson's death.

However, confirming that he wasn't terribly bright, he'd gone into Catford police station at the very time Blakemore was being killed, and made a fuss about a supposedly lost wallet. But he'd not visualized that his little ploy would back-fire on him so badly that I would give him a going over at Charing Cross police station.

Furthermore, the crude alibi Lever had faked at the Jobcentre, and the resultant failure of the Kent police to pin the Dartford Post Office van robbery on him, had probably made him too cocky, and he doubtless thought he was in the clear.

And so he'd decided that it was time to vanish.

But, as with most of Lever's ventures, his departure had not been planned. Apart from enjoying the irony of doing a

runner while Melanie Gabb was shedding her clothes for a
load of legless coppers at some retirement party, he'd given
no thought whatever to where he was going to go.

One thing was certain though: by dint of an All Ports
Warning, we'd made sure that he could not leave the country.
At least, that was it in theory. On those rare occasions when
he'd passed through an airport in the past – usually on a
package flight to the 'Costa del Crime' in Spain – he'd always
been stopped and questioned. Given his limited intelligence,
he probably hadn't worked out why this should have happened.
Even if he'd realized that his natural furtiveness, his mode of
dress, and the fact that he had 'villain' written all over him
were the reasons, there was nothing much he could have done
about it.

Given all that, there was no doubt in my mind that Mickey
Lever was, in a manner of speaking, marooned in the United
Kingdom. Maybe. One of the problems of All Ports Warnings
is that an officer might be heavily engaged in dealing with
one suspect on the list, thus allowing others to escape the net.

However, I knew nothing of Lever's thought processes, such
as they were, although with my long experience in the CID,
I might have taken a fairly accurate guess.

The first report to reach me, via DCS Cleaver, showed that
Lever had drawn a hundred pounds from an ATM in Catford.
The second, of a similar drawing in the Waterloo area, came
the day after. Two days later, another hundred pounds was
drawn from the same Waterloo cash machine.

'It looks very much as though Lever is holed up in the
Waterloo area, guv,' said Dave. 'But what are we going to do
about it?'

'It'll be a hellish waste of manpower if it doesn't come off,
Dave, but I think the only answer is to get as many of our
people out in that area for a couple of days. Particularly in
the region of the ATM he's used twice.

It was then that I got a telephone call from Joe Daly at the
American Embassy.

'Harry, I think you ought to hightail it up here. I've got
some interesting news for you.'

'The prints your guy handed me, Harry, the ones you think
belong to Paul Tyler . . .'

'We're not sure they are his, Joe,' I said.

'I sure hope to hell they are,' said Daly, 'because the guy whose dabs you gave us is one Tony Palladio and he's wanted by the New York Police Department.' He opened a file. 'They kindly sent a photograph of him.' He passed the print across his desk.

I examined the photograph, and handed it to Dave. We both agreed it was Paul Tyler.

'What do the NYPD want him for, Joe?'

'How long you got, Harry?' Daly chuckled, and went on to list Palladio's 'alleged' involvement in drugs, prostitution, protection rackets, the numbers game and tax evasion. He ended by saying, 'Oh, and just to round it off, the NYPD want him for murder.'

'Sounds like a nice all-American guy,' I said.

'Yeah, thanks, Harry.' Daly made a sour face.

'When did Tyler start this wicked career of his, Joe?'

'He's been at it for years, Harry,' said Daly, 'but the Bureau never got enough to nail him until the murder – and that's what caused him to take off – about five years back. Took out some rival in a blaze of machine-gun fire. Just like Chicago,' he added and sounded almost wistful.

'Well,' I said with mock severity, 'I take a poor view of you allowing him to escape and foul up our green and pleasant land.'

'Yeah, sure,' said Daly. 'Er, how soon can we have him back?'

'We've got to find him first, Joe. Start the extradition proceedings if you like, but in view of his form, he must be a front runner for involvement in the murders of Hugh Blakemore and Geoffrey Strang.'

'Oh, Jesus!' said an exasperated Daly. 'You really think so?'

'Anne Blakemore said that Tyler had a run-in with Hugh,' I said, 'and that Hugh threatened Tyler with deportation. In view of what you've just told me, that seems to give him a bloody good motive for murder.'

Daly drained his coffee cup. 'You remember the three Mafiosi whose names came up in connection with Strang?'

'Nino Petrosino, Francesco Corleo and Pietro Giacono,' I said.

Daly laughed. 'I don't know how you do it, Harry. Yeah, those three guys. D'you want that I should make enquiries to see if Tyler – alias Palladio – had any connections with them?'

'Joe, how can I ever thank you?'

'I drink bourbon,' said Daly. 'If Tyler is convicted, how long's he likely to go down for over here?' He sounded gloomy at not being able to lay hands on his wanted man for some time.

'Life,' I said, 'if we can prove that he conspired to have Blakemore killed. And if we can tie him into the Strang murder, life again.'

'Big deal,' said Daly.

FIFTEEN

The information that Joe Daly had received from Washington, and had passed on to me, that Paul Tyler, alias Tony Palladio, was a racketeer wanted for murder, did not necessarily mean he had had anything to do with Hugh Blakemore's death or, for that matter, the murder of Geoffrey Strang.

If I were to suggest to Tyler, when eventually he was arrested, that he might have had a hand in either of those killings, all Tyler had to do was deny it. There was no proof, and it now appeared that Tyler was a sufficiently experienced criminal not to make admissions.

I knew that I would have to get further evidence. I glanced at my watch and rang for Kate Ebdon. 'We're going to see Mrs Blakemore,' I said, 'to tell her the sad news about Paul Tyler.'

Anne Blakemore did not seem at all pleased to see me again, but reluctantly admitted Kate and me. Once again, Kate had dressed up. With the practised eye of 'a lady who lunches', Anne evaluated the cost of the woman detective's clothes and, if her expression was anything to go by, seemed surprised that they were of such good quality.

'Well, Mr Brock, and what is it this time?' she asked. Oddly, she seemed disconcerted by the presence of the woman officer.

'I want to talk to you about Paul Tyler, Mrs Blakemore,' I began.

'You've found him, then.' Anne Blakemore sounded weary, but tried to give the impression of hope. She waved a hand towards the armchairs. 'You'd better sit down,' she said, and seated herself opposite us, in the centre of the large sofa where she usually sat.

'No, we haven't found him,' I said and, as briefly as possible, outlined a little of what the police knew of Paul Tyler's background. I decided, at this stage anyway, not to mention that he was wanted by the United States authorities, or that they would be seeking his extradition. If Anne Blakemore was in touch with the fugitive American, I didn't want her warning him. Neither did I yet suggest to her that Tyler's record made him a suspect in the murder of her husband.

'What on earth are you talking about?' demanded Anne imperiously, when I'd finished. 'I've never heard such rubbish.'

'I'm afraid there's no doubt, Mrs Blakemore,' I said. 'I've received full details, and a photograph, from the FBI.' I paused. 'The Federal Bureau of Investigation,' I explained.

'I do know what the FBI is, Mr Brock,' said Anne softly. In contrast to her earlier haughtiness, she now appeared completely drained by what I'd just told her.

'Has he been in touch with you in the last few days, by any chance?' I posed the question quietly.

'No, he hasn't.' There was not a moment's hesitation in Anne Blakemore's reply. I imagined that, although disinclined to admit it to the police, she was now seeing Tyler in an entirely new light. She probably realized that Tyler's disappearance when Hugh had threatened him with deportation – and his return immediately after Hugh's murder – had some sinister basis. And it must have hurt, more than my revelations about his criminal past, that Tyler had happily bedded her while all the time he was living with Liz who he'd told her was his daughter. 'But if he does—'

'You'll let me know,' I said, by no means certain that she would. I'd already made arrangements for Anne Blakemore's house to be under constant surveillance until Tyler was arrested.

'Of course.' Anne stood up. 'Well, I'm going to have a drink. Will you join me, Mr Brock?'

'No, thanks,' I said.

'How about you, my dear?' said Anne to Kate. Her patronizing attitude, and her confidence, returned as quickly as it had evaporated.

'No, thank you,' said Kate.

'On second thoughts, neither will I.' Anne glanced at her watch and sat down again. 'What's going to happen about poor Paul, then?' she asked.

'That rather depends on what he says when we find him,' I said.

Anne shook her head. 'I just don't believe any of this, you know. I don't believe it,' she said, her jaw muscles tightening quite noticeably.

'I understand that you told Mr Brock the other day that you'd known Paul Tyler for some years,' said Kate. Apart from refusing a drink, it was the first time that she'd spoken at any length.

Anne looked mildly offended that Kate had posed a question. Nevertheless, she replied. 'Yes, I did, but does that have anything to do with this ludicrous nonsense about his being a gangster, or whatever it is you're suggesting?' Anne looked at Kate, once more openly inspecting her dress and her shoes, and studying the gold earrings she was wearing.

'Would I be right in thinking that you first met him about four or five years ago?' Kate's query sounded innocent enough. 'Rather than the two years you previously told Mr Brock.'

Anne Blakemore's eyes narrowed. 'Yes, it was about four years ago.' She decided not to argue any more. Having lost her husband and a former lover, Geoffrey Strang, within weeks, and learning that another lover was now supposed to be a criminal, she suddenly appeared deflated by the whole business.

'Not long after he came to this country from America, I presume.' Kate continued her questioning quietly and persistently.

'Yes.'

'Did he tell you anything about what he had been doing over there?'

'Nothing.'

'He told you nothing, or he said he'd been doing nothing?'

'He told me nothing,' snapped Anne, seemingly irritated by Kate's necessary pedantry.

I was sitting back in my chair, studying Anne Blakemore. Now, more than ever, I was convinced that she was better informed about Tyler's background than she was prepared to admit. And I wondered if she was not being open about him because she was, in some way, involved with Tyler in the death of her husband. But there was plenty of time to attempt to establish that.

'He just turned up, did he?' asked Kate. 'Just like that.'

'No, he didn't just turn up.' Anne began to sound annoyed, and spoke her reply tersely. 'I told you, Mr Brock,' she said, glancing at me with a frosty smile, 'that he was a friend of my late husband. And I told you that we met at the American Embassy.'

'That was a bit chancy, in the circumstances. His going to
the American Embassy,' said Kate. She sensed that Anne was
trying to steer the conversation back to me, mistakenly
believing that, as a man, I would be more sympathetic towards
her. Unfortunately for her, Anne did not realize how futile
such a ploy was.

'I still don't see that how we met has anything to do with
you,' said Anne. 'He was a perfect gentleman and, as far as
I knew, a respectable businessman. Frankly, I don't believe
all this about him being a criminal. I think you people must
have got him mixed up with someone else.'

'We're trying to discover who was responsible for the
murder of your late husband,' said Kate. She, like me, knew
that the fingerprints lifted from the Chichester house left no
doubt in our minds about Tyler's identity. If he had had nothing
to do with Blakemore's murder, unlikely though that was, then
it would be an incredible, and cruel, coincidence. But the fact
that Tyler had disappeared so very soon after I'd interviewed
him, tended to lend weight to my suspicions.

'Oh, my God!' Anne gave an exasperated sigh, as if she
were dealing with two complete fools. 'You're not for one
moment suggesting that Paul might have had a hand in that,
surely. It was two men on a motorcycle. It was in all the newspapers. And on television,' she added, as if to emphasize the
veracity of the reports of her husband's murder.

'Yes,' I said. 'That's correct. One of the two men on the
motorcycle actually shot your husband, but I'm convinced that
he was a professional killer who didn't know Mr Blakemore
personally. And I want to know who paid him. As far as I can
see, the actual killer would have had no reason to commit the
murder other than for financial gain.'

Anne Blakemore tossed her head. 'You're surely not
suggesting that Paul had anything to do with that, are you?'
she repeated. 'That's quite preposterous.' She stared at me in
amazement, more than ever convinced that we were blunder-
ing idiots. I didn't mind her thinking that. Sometimes, playing
the stupid cop paid dividends.

'We'd just like to talk to him about it,' I said.

'Well, if you think Paul had anything to do with the murder
of my husband, you'll just have to do that, won't you?'

I stood up, indicating that the interview was at an end.

'I didn't say that Mr Tyler had anything to do with the murder of your husband, Mrs Blakemore. I merely suggested that he may be able to assist us in our enquiries.'

I subsequently discovered that immediately after we'd left, Anne Blakemore telephoned Charles Simpson, her ex-husband.

I decided that it was now time to obtain warrants from a crown court judge to inspect the bank accounts of the late Hugh Blakemore, Anne Blakemore, Paul Tyler, Charles Simpson and, for good measure, Gina Watson the actress. I was by no means certain that I'd learn anything from them, but I had a distinct feeling that they could reveal a motive for Blakemore's murder and in turn the death of Geoffrey Strang. I was sure in my own mind that the allegation of accepting bribes that Simpson had levelled against Hugh Blakemore, backed up by Fat Danny the journalist, and to a certain extent by Tyler, was at the root of the murders. I was interested too to know if there was any validity in Anne Blakemore's claim that her husband had been blackmailed by Gina Watson and, if so, whether that had any bearing on the killings.

Finally, I directed Kate Ebdon to prepare an application to the Home Secretary to have an intercept placed on Anne Blakemore's telephone. But I was not confident of it being granted. Anne was, after all, the widow of an MP, and I was cynical enough to think that that might just sway the Home Secretary's decision – against the application.

But, in that, I was wrong. The Home Secretary sent for me.

'Mr Brock, do take a seat.' The Home Secretary indicated an armchair with an urbane flourish and then sat down opposite me. 'This application for a telephone intercept warrant . . .' He had the document on his knee. 'Do you think there's anything in this suspicion of yours about the man Tyler?'

'I shan't know until I talk to him, sir,' I said, 'and as he's disappeared that won't be possible until he's apprehended. However, that aside, he is wanted on an extradition warrant to answer a charge of murder in the United States.'

'And you have reason to think that he may attempt to contact Mrs Blakemore?'

'I do, sir,' I said. 'They were lovers before Mr Blakemore's death, and continued their affair afterwards. At the same time as Mr Blakemore was conducting a liaison with an actress.'

That information had not, of course, been included in the application.

'Were they really?' The Home Secretary's face broke into a broad grin. It always amused him to hear of the sexual peccadilloes of his colleagues. Or their wives. 'And you think that Mrs Blakemore may still be seeing this Tyler fellow?'

'I would say it's a strong possibility, sir.'

'Very well, Mr Brock.' The Home Secretary crossed to his desk, took out his pen and scrawled his signature on the bottom of an official document. 'There's your warrant,' he said, handing it to me.

I next made a point of seeing Charles Simpson again.

'Did you enjoy your trip?' I asked.

'Not really,' said Charles Simpson. 'New York at this time of year is to be avoided, I can assure you. Too hot and sticky.'

'It was business then?'

Simpson laughed. 'I wouldn't go to New York for a holiday in midsummer,' he said. 'Come to think of it, I wouldn't go at any time if I didn't have to.' He toyed briefly with a sheaf of computer printouts and tossed them into a tray. 'I hope you won't think me rude, Mr Brock,' he continued, 'but I do have rather a lot of catching up to do.'

'I shan't keep you long,' I said. 'But I was wondering why you didn't tell me that Paul Tyler was your contact at this electronics firm you were acting for.'

'Didn't I?' Simpson raised his eyebrows in surprise. 'There was no ulterior motive,' he said. 'It must just have slipped my mind. Did it matter?'

'Not really,' I said. At the time, I'd been furious to be confronted by Tyler without being prepared for it. 'Has he been in touch with you recently?'

'No.' Simpson did not hesitate. 'Our business is over and done with. There's no reason for us to contact each other.'

'Oh!' I said. 'That's interesting.'

'Why's that?' asked Simpson.

'He didn't seem very happy with you when I spoke to him.'

'Really? I can't think why.'

'He particularly didn't like your suggestion that he'd paid Blakemore a substantial bribe.'

'Oh, I didn't say that, surely?'

'When I put it to you that Blakemore took bribes, you said that that was one way of putting it. That seems pretty plain to me, Mr Simpson.'

'Ah!' said Simpson, his fingers playing a brief tattoo on the desktop. 'That was perhaps a little indiscreet of me. But I did say that it was only something I'd heard.' He sounded nervous.

'So you did,' I said, 'but when I spoke to the people at the company that had put the contract out for tender, they denied categorically that their meeting with Blakemore had been on an improper footing.'

'Well, I suppose I should have expected that,' said Simpson half-heartedly. 'I didn't know for a fact that money had changed hands.'

'That's probably as well,' I said. 'From what I hear it is a company of great integrity. In fact, if they even suspected you were making such allegations, I'm sure they would embark on some sort of legal process. For slander probably.'

'Oh!' Simpson did not seem too worried at the prospect. But although he was more familiar with modern business practice than me, I suspected that such an action wouldn't get off the ground. Mainly because the company wouldn't want the publicity that would attend such an action.

'You know, of course, that Tyler has vanished,' I said.

'Vanished? Really?'

'You mean that Mrs Blakemore hasn't told you?'

'I haven't spoken to Anne for ages,' Simpson lied.

'In that case, I can tell you that there's a warrant out for Paul Tyler's arrest,' I said.

'Good God!' It was obvious that Simpson was shaken by that piece of news. 'Not in connection with this bribery business, is it?'

'What bribery business?' I asked, smiling. 'No,' I continued, 'for the murder of a business associate.'

'Christ!' Simpson appeared shocked. 'What's that all about?'

'I don't know,' I said, pleased that, as I'd not told Anne Blakemore that the Americans wanted Tyler, she'd been unable to pass it on. 'I dare say that someone made some unfounded allegation against him.'

In the annals of crime, it is frequently members of the uniform branch who arrest dangerous and much-wanted criminals. In the past, great armies of detectives have carried out searching enquiries, talked to countless informants, maintained observations for days on end, and spent fortunes gleaning information in public houses only to find that a young patrolling constable arrests the man they have all been seeking. And that turned out to be the case with Mickey Lever too.

Lever was running short of money: the balance of his current account was now dangerously low. Another fifty pounds and it would be exhausted. That, of course, was provided that Melanie Gabb had not somehow got her hands on it. He had unwisely left a chequebook behind at Forest Hill, and although the account was in his own name, he did not think that Melanie was above a bit of forgery. As for his Swiss bank account, the police were still holding all the documents.

Thoughts of Melanie Gabb reminded him of the other shortage that was becoming a nagging problem to him: the lack of female companionship. Now that he was on the run, he knew that he could not return to Melanie. The police were bound to be watching the house.

Now though, Lever was living in a crummy bedsit next door to a prostitute, but he had no intention of paying her even if he could have afforded to. He had caught sight of the girl once or twice and although she was not a beauty, she had a certain coarse sexual allure that seemed to improve each time he saw her.

Accustomed all his life to taking what he wanted, that afternoon Lever walked straight into her room without knocking.

'Come in, why don't you,' said the girl sarcastically, as she looked over her shoulder and recognized the man who had lived next door for the past two or three days. Wearing a pair of faded blue jeans and naked from the waist upwards, she was washing out her underclothes in the inadequate washbasin.

Lever walked across to her. 'Sharon, ain't it?' he asked and, putting his arms around her waist, moved his hands up to cup her breasts. 'How about being neighbourly?'

But Sharon was a street-fighter: in her game she had to be. She immediately began to scream at the top of her voice and, with a quick downward thrust of her forearms, she knocked Lever's hands away. In one swift, flowing movement, she turned and brought her knee up between his legs; it was a very accurate, very powerful and very painful blow.

With a cry of agony, Lever fell to the floor clutching his genitals. 'Christ!' he moaned, 'Oh, Christ!'

Sharon stood over him, hands on hips. 'You have to pay to touch, duckie,' she said and kicked him in the ribs. 'Now, piss off out of it or I'll call the law.'

But the noise of the disturbance, and Sharon's screams, had already attracted the attention of the owner of the shop beneath her room. He promptly telephoned the police and told them that the girl in the room above was being murdered.

The first officers on the scene – a man and a woman – burst into Sharon's room to find that, far from leaving, Lever had only managed to crawl across the floor and was now sitting with his back to the wall, moaning and clutching himself between the legs. Sharon, still bare-breasted, was standing over him wielding the old Metropolitan Police truncheon that she always kept handy for situations such as this one.

'You all right, love?' the woman officer asked Sharon. In the circumstances it seemed an unnecessary question.

'Yeah,' said Sharon, 'but I'm not too sure about this guy.'

'What happened?' The male PC joined in.

'Bastard tried to rape me,' said Sharon, never one to understate her case.

The policeman took the truncheon from her. 'Where did you get this from?' he asked, examining the crown and the letters 'MP' that were stamped into the wood.

Sharon laughed at him. 'If I told you, he'd never forgive me,' she said.

The woman officer, who had been busy on her personal radio, walked across to where Lever was sitting. 'Ambulance is on its way,' she said.

Lever looked up. 'I don't want no ambulance,' he groaned, aware of the danger that going to hospital would put him in. 'I'll be all right.'

'Suit yourself.' The woman officer shrugged and took out an incident report book. 'Now, what happened?' she asked.

Sharon began an account of Lever's arrival in her room and went on to embellish what had actually occurred.

'I didn't try to take her jeans off,' protested Lever. 'Anyway, she's only a tom,' he added, which endeared him neither to the woman PC nor to Sharon.

'Prostitutes have their rights, too, you know. So just be quiet,'

said the woman PC and continued to extract details of the
assault from Sharon. 'You willing to come to court and give
evidence?' she asked, tapping her book with her pen.

Sharon scoffed. 'You kidding? No, just get the creep out
of here.' She glared down at Lever. 'Next time, I'll cut 'em off,'
she promised.

The PC helped Lever to his feet. 'Where d'you live?' he
asked.

'Next door,' said Lever, leaning heavily against the wall.

'Next door?'

'Yes. The room next to this one.' Although relieved that
Sharon intended to take the matter no further, Lever, nonethe-
less, was not thinking clearly. If he had been, he would have
given a false address.

'You ever done anything like this before?' asked the PC.

'No, never.'

'What's your name?'

'Er, Peterson.' It was the first name that came into Lever's
head, but he had hesitated just long enough for the policeman
to be suspicious.

'You got any proof of that?' The PC was wondering whether
he had caught a rapist. There had been at least two rapes in
the last fortnight that were still on the books at Kennington
Road police station as unsolved.

'Why d'you want proof?' Lever was beginning to get edgy
in the face of the constable's persistence.

'Right, let's go next door.'

'Look here—' began Lever.

The policeman took an aggressive step closer. 'If you want
to be nicked, right now, for indecent assault, I shan't hesitate,'
he said.

'But Sharon said—'

The policeman pulled Lever towards the door. 'She's a prostitute, mate,' he said, 'and if we say she'll come to court,
she'll come to court. We can always get a witness summons,
and she can't afford to upset the police, you know. Now, we'll
go and have a look in your room.'

And that was it. Lever's bank card was on the chest of drawers.

Colin Wilberforce entered my office. 'A bit of good news, sir.
Lever's been arrested on Kennington Road's ground.'

'Who nicked him?'

'A couple of PCs who were called to a disturbance, sir. Apparently he indecently assaulted a tom living in the next room.'

I laughed. 'He was never much good at being a villain,' I said. 'Where is he?'

'Kennington Road nick, sir.'

'What's the SP?' I asked.

Colin gave me a quick résumé of the incident, and finished up by saying, 'They did a check on the PNC and found he was wanted.'

'It's all coming together,' I said, although I was by no means certain that we were anywhere near solving the murders of Blakemore, Geoffrey Strang, or, for that matter, Solly Goldman. 'Colin, perhaps you'd arrange for the Kennington Road police to transfer Lever to Charing Cross nick. In the meantime, Dave and I will have another word with Lever's live-in stripper.'

SIXTEEN

'What the bleedin' hell d'you want this time?' demanded Melanie Gabb aggressively.

'Your Mickey's been nicked,' said Dave.

'What for?' asked Melanie, who had been kept in total ignorance of Lever's activities over the past week or so. Not that there was anything new in that.

'He tried to rape a prostitute at Waterloo,' said Dave. He thought that was a better explanation than telling her the real reason for his arrest. 'And she kicked him in the balls. You might say he met his Waterloo.'

But that *bon mot* went over Melanie's head. 'Serve the bastard right,' she said, and laughed outright. 'I'm surprised he could get it up,' she added dismissively. 'Have you found out where he got all that cash from?'

'No,' said Dave, 'but I've a feeling he'll tell us before the day's out.'

'Well, you can tell him that if he comes home, I'll kick him in the balls as well,' said Melanie. 'How long are you going to keep him?'

'About twenty years, I should think,' said Dave. 'But while we're here, we'll have another look round.'

'Ain't you s'posed to have a warrant for that?'

'Not if we have your permission,' said Dave.

'Well, I ain't giving it.'

'Thanks very much.' Dave took out his pocketbook and spoke aloud as he made a note. 'Occupant gave her permission for a search to be conducted.' He closed his book and put it away. 'We'll try not to untidy the place too much,' he said. It was a sarcastic comment; the house was a tip.

'You're wasting your time. He ain't been here.'

'So you say,' said Dave.

But Mickey Lever's stripper was right when she said we were wasting our time. We found nothing of interest.

* * *

Dave and I seated ourselves at the table in the interview room at Charing Cross police station and awaited the arrival of Lever. Moments later, his bowed figure shuffled slowly into the room.

'What's wrong with you, Mickey?' asked Dave. 'Had an accident?'

'Some tart kicked me in the balls,' said Lever, 'as if you didn't know.'

Dave laughed. 'Well, I've got news for you, Mickey, old son. If Melanie ever sets eyes on you again, the same thing's likely to happen.'

'What's she been saying?' asked Lever as he lowered himself painfully into the chair opposite us.

'She's still very unhappy about your sudden wealth, Mickey.'

'What are you on about?'

'I'm talking about the five grand you've got in a Swiss bank account.' I produced the documents we'd seized when we first searched Lever's house.

'I've got nothing to say,' said Lever. 'And I want a brief.'

'You can have a solicitor, Mickey,' I said. 'In fact, in your position I strongly recommend it. But let me explain one or two things first. I am minded to charge you with conspiracy to murder Hugh Blakemore and Geoffrey Strang—'

''Ere, leave off,' said the anguished Lever. 'I never had nothing to do with that. You know that. I was in Catford nick reporting the loss of me wallet when that happened.'

'So you were,' I said. 'An extraordinary coincidence. Particularly as you didn't lose your wallet in the first place.'

'You ain't got nothing on me,' said Lever desperately. 'I couldn't have had nothing to do with Blakemore's topping, and I've never heard of—' He broke off. 'What d'you say his name was?'

'Geoffrey Strang. He was murdered in Golden Square. Shot to death while sitting in his car.'

'Oh, yeah, I remember seeing about that. That was when I was in the nick talking to you.' Lever could not disguise the look of triumph at having got one over on the Old Bill.

'Right, let's start again,' I said. 'Where did the money come from?'

'I ain't saying.'

'In that case, I'll tell you, Mickey,' I said, taking a calculated guess. 'You were paid a substantial sum of money, £25,000 to be exact, to set up the murder of Hugh Blakemore. I suspect that you hadn't the bottle to do it yourself, but you'll still go down for life. You accepted a contract to top Blakemore and paid two hoods to ride their motor bike down to Fulham and shoot him. That was the twenty grand that went out of this account.' I tapped the documents that still lay on the table. 'Ten grand just before the murder, I should think, and the other half when the job was done.'

Lever scoffed. 'What a load of bleedin' toffee,' he said.

'So, the situation is this,' I continued. 'Either you tell me the name of the man who put out the contract, or you'll go down for it yourself. On the other hand, if you care to do a bit of explaining, it might just be possible, and I put it no higher than that, to persuade the judge to give you a lesser sentence. But one way or another, Mickey, you're looking at a fairly lengthy stretch on the other side of the wall.'

'Are you threatening me?' asked Lever truculently.

'On the contrary, Mickey, I'm trying to help you. So let's have the name of the individual who put out the contract and we'll see what can be done.'

Lever looked up, an expression of despair on his face. 'I can't do that, Mr Brock,' he said. 'If I grassed, I'd get topped meself.'

'Well, it's your funeral, Mickey,' said Dave, deploying an apt metaphor which did little to comfort Lever.

'What d'you think, guv?' asked Dave, when Lever had been returned to his cell.

'He's well involved, Dave. And he's put himself in the frame by refusing to name the bloke who put out the contract. If he hadn't had anything to do with it, he'd have said so. But he admitted his part by saying that he'd be topped if he grassed.'

'So how are we going to identify the paymaster, guv?'

'Or pay*mistress*, Dave,' I said.

'D'you think she's involved in all this? I can't really see Anne Blakemore commissioning a hood like Lever to kill her husband. He's a pretty weak link.'

'Funnier things have happened,' I said. 'And if an amateur set it up, they might have thought that Lever was a shrewd operator.'

'You must be joking, guv,' said Dave. 'Well, at least we'll be able to look at her bank account shortly.'

'Amateur or not, Dave, d'you honestly think that any one of the accounts we're going to examine will show a payment to M. Lever, Esquire, for twenty-five grand? There's not a cat in hell's chance.'

'What's next then, guv?'

'Find Paul Tyler and talk to him, Dave. And we'd better be quick about it because we've either got to charge Lever or let him go. I'm happy to put him on the sheet for conspiracy to murder, but once we've done that, we can't ask him any more embarrassing questions. And I rather think he's got a lot more to tell us. We'll have another go at him later this evening.'

Now that Lever had been arrested, the officers who had been searching for him were deployed in the hunt for Paul Tyler.

But he was a different quarry entirely from Lever. There was no chance that a sophisticated criminal of Tyler's calibre would be found in a sleazy rooming house in a place like the Waterloo area of London. A much more likely place would be a West End hotel, but I suspected that he might already have left the country. Despite putting out an All Ports Warning, I knew that it was still possible for a suspect to slip through the net.

One thing was sure though: he would not have gone to America. But we realized the futility of trying to check airline manifests. We'd tried that before and knew it to be a hopeless task. Apart from the speed at which such records were destroyed, there was nothing whatever to prevent a passenger who was determined to escape from booking in under a false name. Or having his secretary do it for him.

Nevertheless, officers of my team pursued their enquiries with vigour. We hoped that Tyler, having been unnerved by his interview with me, would have hesitated to present himself at an airport. Even if he possessed a false passport, there was always the chance that he may be recognized, particularly as his photograph had been obtained from the FBI and circulated to police officers at ports.

We put Paul Tyler's name on the Police National Computer, and in the *Police Gazette*, the daily publication that listed those wanted by, or of interest to, the police. Then we sat

back and played a waiting game. There was little else we
could do.

Mickey Lever was slouched despondently in his chair when
Dave and I entered the interview room again. Having given
the small-time crook an hour in which to think about his
predicament, I was intent on talking to him once more.

'Well, Mickey?' I sat down and offered Lever a cigarette.

'I've got nothing to say.' Lever exhaled smoke and waited.

'When I spoke to you earlier, Mickey, you admitted that
you had undertaken a contract to have Hugh Blakemore
murdered—'

'I never.'

'And further admitted,' I went on, as though Lever had not
interrupted, 'that if you named him, you would likely get topped
yourself.' I paused. 'Or would it be a case of naming *them*?'

'Look . . .' Lever sat up and pinched out the end of his cigarette before putting it in his pocket. 'I might have said that,
but I ain't saying no more. It's more than me life's worth,
God's honest truth.'

'D'you really think that you can be got at in here?' I asked.

'It's not here I'm worried about,' said the distressed Lever,
'it's what'll happen to me if I get banged up on remand.'

'Ask for Rule 43,' I said. Lever was an ex-prisoner and
knew that Rule 43 was the regulation under which vulnerable
informants, along with other inmates who needed protection,
were segregated from the main prison population.

'Pah!' Lever snorted. 'If you believe that'll make any differ-
ence, you'll believe anything.'

'Let's try it from the other end, then,' I said. 'You arranged
for two men – I'm presuming they were men – to murder
Blakemore. Now, who were they?'

'You must be joking,' said Lever. 'The same thing could
happen. In fact, it'd probably be more likely if I told you who
they were.'

'So, you're prepared to have this lot on your own, are you,
Mickey?'

'Don't see as how I've got much option,' said Lever
miserably.

'You could save yourself a lot of grief if you turned Queen's
Evidence.'

'How would that help?' There was a flicker of interest in Lever's eyes as he posed the question.

'You would have to admit your part in this business, Mickey,' I said, 'and name your co-conspirators. That would enable me to obtain corroborative evidence to put before the court following the arrest of your accomplices. If you gave evidence for the Crown it might result in your being given a considerably lesser sentence than you would otherwise have been given. Of course,' I went on, and I always hated having to advise suspects of the dangers of this course of action, 'if the court declines to believe you, you could still go down for the full whack. However, if you agree to cooperate, I dare say that we could arrange a new identity for you so that you could disappear.'

'What about the five grand I've got stashed away? Would I be able to keep that?'

I shook my head. 'I doubt it,' I said. 'If it's shown to be the proceeds of crime, it may well be seized.' But I knew that there was no machinery whereby the court would be able to lay hands on money lodged in a foreign country, particularly Switzerland.

'Well, that's bloody rich, that is,' said Lever. 'And s'posing I don't say nothing? What am I likely to cop for this little lot?'

'The same as if you'd topped Blakemore yourself, Mickey. Cruel old world, isn't it?'

For some moments, Lever stared down at the table. 'I think I'd better talk to a brief,' he said finally, as he looked up to stare at me.

'Very wise of you, Mickey,' I said. 'Very wise.'

'Bank statements, sir,' said Kate. 'One account in the name of Hugh Blakemore, and the other in Anne's name.'

'Anything surprising, Kate?' I asked.

'Not really, guv. As Mrs Blakemore told you, Hugh Blakemore was practically on his uppers. Even his parliamentary salary each month wasn't enough to pay off his overdraft. Not by a long chalk. And up until about three months ago there were substantial, regular payments to Gina Watson.'

'What d'you call substantial, Kate?'

'About two grand a month.' Kate plucked a couple of pages

of Blakemore's statement of account out of the pile resting on her knee, and handed them to me. 'Then they stopped. Of course, if anyone had asked, he'd probably have told them that she was employed as a researcher or something. Apparently all MPs do that.' She glanced at another statement. 'But Mrs B seems to have had quite a lot in her own account.'

'None of which comes as any surprise,' I said. 'What about the Watson woman?'

'Loaded, guv.' Kate picked out Gina Watson's statement from the pile. 'Looks as though Blakemore was keeping her.'

'Keeping her quiet, more likely,' I suggested. 'And Tyler?'

'Not very much in his, surprisingly, but I'm by no means sure that we've found all his accounts. His sort of villain usually spreads his money about. Something to do with tax, I expect.'

'Yes,' I said. 'Most American hoods know that Al Capone eventually went down for tax evasion.'

'And then we come to Simpson, guv. Prosperous businessman, but all apparently kosher from what we found. But we know he's got several companies.'

'And that's it, is it?' I asked.

'Not quite.' Kate picked up another piece of paper. 'I thought I'd keep the best bit for last. Tyler telephoned Anne Blakemore early this morning.'

'And?'

'She asked him where he was. He said that he was out of town on business, but avoided telling her exactly where. She then told him about your visit and that you'd told her about his criminal past in the States. He said that you'd got the wrong guy.' Kate glanced up. 'Surprise, surprise,' she said with a grin. 'Anne then accused him of two-timing her by pretending that Liz was his daughter. Tyler put on a wonderful performance of being outraged by the allegation, and said that Liz was definitely his daughter, and that the police were trying to make trouble for him, and that he'd sue you for slander.' I laughed at that. 'Finally,' Kate concluded, 'Anne said that the police kept pestering her, and asked when she would see him again. Tyler said soon, and that he wanted to sort out this case of mistaken identity.'

'He'll have a job,' I said.

Kate laid the transcript of the telephone conversation on

my desk. 'There are a few more bits and pieces, sir,' she said, 'but nothing of any consequence.'

'Just one thing,' I said. 'Where was he telephoning from?'

'I knew you'd spoil it, guv'nor,' said Kate. 'He was talking from an unregistered mobile phone.'

'That reckons,' I said. 'So the intercept we had put on Anne's phone didn't help.'

'No, guv,' said Kate, as she gathered up her papers.

Mickey Lever had thought long and hard about the situation in which he now found himself, and after a brief conversation with a solicitor – one he had picked at random from the list of duty solicitors willing to counsel persons detained at police stations – he asked if he could talk to me again.

'Been thinking about your future, then, Mickey?' I asked.

'That's not funny,' said Lever.

'What have you got to tell me?'

There was a long pause. It appeared that Lever was still uncertain whether to tell me anything more about his involvement in the death of Hugh Blakemore. But then he decided. 'The geezer what approached me was Geoffrey Strang,' he said at last.

'Well, that's bloody convenient, I must say,' I said. 'He's dead. Did you have him topped as well, by any chance?'

'No, I never,' said Lever angrily. 'D'you want to hear this or not?'

'Don't get your knickers in a twist, Mickey,' I said. 'Get on with it.'

'He come and saw me just after I got out of Melbury. I dunno how he found me, but he did. He said as how he knew all about what had happened in the nick, what with Blakemore knocking poor old Kenny down the stairs, and him doing his head, like. And he said that certain persons wanted him took out because of it. Well, I said as how I didn't want nothing to do with it. I mean, topping's heavy, ain't it?'

'Final, really,' murmured Dave.

'He said that twenty grand was available for anyone what was willing to do the job, and that there was five grand in it for me. Or more if I could get the job done cheaper.'

'So you put an ad in the newspapers asking for the services of a couple of assassins, did you?' suggested Dave.

I was beginning to disbelieve the whole of Lever's story, and determined to find out which solicitor had advised him, confident that his advice had been to tell the police a pack of lies.

'Look, this is straight up, Mr Brock,' said Lever. 'Nah! I put the word out, discreet like, that there was some good gelt about for anyone what was willing to do the job. Well, eventually a couple of geezers what I knew said as how they'd be willing to take it on. So I give 'em half on account—'

'Half what?' I asked.

'It was like you said. Half the twenty grand. And the other half when the job was done,' said Lever, confirming my original guess. 'Well, them's the usual terms, ain't they?'

'Very businesslike,' said Dave drily.

'And I said I never wanted to know nothing more about it except when the job was coming down, so's I could row meself out, see?'

'By going into Catford nick and making a fuss?'

'Yeah!' Lever sighed. 'That weren't too clever though, was it?'

'No,' I said. 'All you succeeded in doing was to bring yourself to notice. Which was a shame, because I'd had you down as not being bright enough to set up a job like that. I'd rowed you out already. But you going to the nick to make a report about a missing wallet suddenly made me think that you were implicated in the shooting. Blokes like you always steer clear of police stations.'

'I never had nothing to do with the topping, Mr Brock, honest,' said Lever imploringly, probably realizing that he had made far too many mistakes and, not for the first time, wishing that he had not got involved. He must have known that he'd be a suspect and had taken what he thought were clever steps to create an alibi.

'All that remains now, Mickey,' I continued, 'is for you to give me the names of the two hoods who did the job.'

'No way,' said Lever hurriedly. 'That's all I've got to say. Like I said yesterday, there ain't no chance of me grassing on them. They'd have me, sure as God made little apples. I only told you about Strang because he got his comeuppance, and he can't do me no harm.'

'Talking of which,' I said, 'what d'you know about Strang's death?'

'Nothing, guv'nor. Stand on me,' said Lever. 'I've never topped no one in me life, and I never knew Strang was going to get his. That weren't nothing to do with me. Anyway, I was in here, talking to you, when that job went down.'

And, for once, I believed him, although I was still doubtful about Strang's involvement. That he was dead made him much too easy a patsy for my liking.

Sam Marland, one of the Yard's most senior fingerprint officers, arrived in the incident room just as I was having a look at the latest, mostly useless, information from members of the public. 'Harry,' he said, 'I am the bearer of good tidings.'

'Come in,' I said, and led the way to my office. 'It's about time I had good news. What've you got, Sam?'

'D'you remember the BMW motorcycle that was used in the Blakemore shooting?'

'Not likely to forget it,' I said. 'What about it?'

'And the Ford Mondeo that was found abandoned in Richmond Park?'

'Get to the point, Sam.'

'It had two sets of leathers and two crash helmets in the boot.'

'Yes, I remember, Sam.'

'There was a patch of blood on the leather strap of one of the helmets, about a centimetre in diameter. The thief must've cut himself at some time during the job. We didn't pay too much attention to it at first, but one of the lads decided to have a go at developing it and, bingo, we got a partial off it. And the bonus is that the lab reckon they might have enough for DNA comparison from the blood.' Marland laid a small piece of film on my desk. 'The microfiche of one Kevin Fagan,' he said. 'Who has several convictions for crimes of violence.'

'And about to get one more,' I said. 'What a very suitable name.'

Immediately following Sam Marland's visit, I ordered the preparation of a list of Kevin Fagan's associates whose names appeared on his criminal record. The records of those associates were then examined and the names of more associates collated. The Serious and Organized Crime Agency was alerted and three more names added; and CID officers throughout the Metropolitan Police District were contacted urgently and asked to supply any further information about the man I now wanted to interview.

Within twenty-four hours, we'd amassed no fewer than fifteen names, each of whom had a criminal record of his own.

Finally, I sought the assistance of the Flying Squad, and all their available members were mobilized. From their bases at Barnes, Lea Bridge Road, Finchley and Tower Bridge, eighty of the Squad's one hundred and seventy officers, supported by armed officers from the Yard's Firearms Branch, sallied forth into the great Metropolis to make the arrests.

Within three hours of the start of the operation, thirteen of the fifteen suspects were in custody at various police stations around the Metropolitan Police District. The other two, who were not at the addresses shown on their files, would come later, of that I was sure.

And there was a dividend: a substantial amount of stolen property, drugs and firearms had been recovered. Even if the prisoners were exonerated from any involvement in the deaths of Hugh Blakemore and Geoffrey Strang, they would still have a lot of explaining to do. Not that that was my concern.

At five in the morning, the principal suspect, Kevin Fagan, had been dragged, at gunpoint, from his bed in Purley and taken, on my instructions, direct to Belgravia police station where I intended to interview him personally.

But before leaving Curtis Green, I ordered the removal of Mickey Lever to Belgravia police station. Putting all our eggs in one basket, so to speak, would save a lot of time.

SEVENTEEN

Over the years, it has frequently happened that police involvement in events of grave importance – events that should be treated with great seriousness, if not reverence – have developed into high farce. In short, a monumental cock-up. And so it was with the arrest of Paul Tyler.

I was on the point of leaving for, I hoped, a late supper with Gail, when the telephone rang.

'It's Inspector Matt Ferguson of the Diplomatic Protection Group, sir.'

'And what can I do for you, Mr Ferguson?'

'I'm on duty at one of the Middle Eastern embassies, sir, at a cocktail party,' said Ferguson, and named the particular embassy.

'Really?' I was beginning to think that I'd gone wrong somewhere in my career.

'I think your man Paul Tyler is here, sir. I saw his photograph in the *Police Gazette*.'

'What in hell's name is he doing at an embassy?'

'I've had a look at the guest list, but his name doesn't appear,' said Ferguson. 'Embassies get a lot of gatecrashers at these functions. They've usually been associated with the diplomatic world at some time or another, albeit tenuously, and just stroll in, bold as brass. Seem to have a nose for these junkets. I reckon they never buy a meal or a drink during the season. You can always spot them. Grab a glass the moment they get through the door, and make straight for the eats. I've mentioned it to various embassy staff two or three times, but they don't seem to be bothered. Incidentally, this man Tyler is here with a young lady.'

'What does she look like, Mr Ferguson?'

The DPG inspector described a woman who could easily have been Liz Middleton, the woman Tyler had passed off as his daughter – to Anne Blakemore, at least. But then again, she could as easily be one of a hundred other young women.

'If I bring a couple of my officers up to the embassy,

Mr Ferguson, perhaps we can work something out.' But God alone knew what that something might be; diplomatic privilege and diplomatic premises are tricky subjects.

'No problem, guv'nor. I'll have a word with Sid Jenkins, the chief security officer. He's ex-DPG. He might be able to come up with an idea.'

Fortunately, Kate Ebdon, Charlie Flynn and Tom Challis were still in the incident room. I rounded them up and, not without some misgivings, told Charlie to get us to the embassy as quickly as possible.

'Matt Ferguson, sir,' said the immaculately suited man standing at the entrance. He indicated a man next to him. 'And this is Sid Jenkins. As I told you on the phone, he used to be with the Group.'

'What's the form, Matt?' I asked.

'It's a bit tricky, guv, being diplomatic premises. I'm not sure whether this guy can be arrested in here. It's possible it'd affect the validity of such an arrest. But I've had a word with the ambassador, and he's quite happy for us to escort Tyler out of the building – on the grounds that he wasn't invited – and he can then be arrested in the street.'

'Sounds good to me.'

We followed Ferguson into the building where the ambassador and his wife were still greeting late arriving guests.

'Ambassador, this is Detective Chief Inspector Brock of Scotland Yard. He's here to deal with the problem I mentioned earlier.'

The bearded ambassador, attired in an ornate *galabieh* and *kaffiyeh*, shook hands. Standing beside him was an attractive Arabian woman, quite a bit younger than the ambassador, whose kaftan was of a magnificent embroidered silk. 'I cannot begin to express my gratitude for the way in which Scotland Yard looks after us, Chief Inspector. Mr Ferguson tells me that you have come to remove an uninvited ruffian.'

'Indeed, sir,' I said. 'The man, if it is him, is wanted for murder in the United States.'

'As I have diplomatic privilege, I could just have him shot, Chief Inspector.' The ambassador gazed at me with a twinkle in his eye. 'It would save you a lot of trouble, would it not?' He threw back his head and laughed.

'That would be very helpful, sir,' I said, going along with the ambassador's little joke, 'but I rather want to talk to him about a couple of murders that occurred in London.'

'Oh, I see. However, Chief Inspector, that won't stop me from having a bit of fun at the American ambassador's expense next time I see him.'

'With your permission, sir, my officers and I will escort this man from the embassy so that we can arrest him outside.'

'I'm most grateful,' said the ambassador. 'Please feel free to have a drink while you're here. We don't drink alcohol ourselves, of course, but we always like to cater for our Western friends.'

Declining the diplomat's offer of drinks, we moved away from the ambassador and his wife, and Ferguson discreetly pointed out the man he believed to be Paul Tyler. '*Is* that him, guv?' he asked.

'Yes, you were quite right, Matt,' I said, 'and that's probably Liz Middleton he's talking to, not that I've seen her. But who's the man they're chatting to?'

'That's James Parfitt. He's with the Conference and Protocol Department of the Foreign and Commonwealth Office. He's always on duty at these parties.'

'Nice job he's got,' said Kate Ebdon.

'I'll have a quick word with him,' said Ferguson. 'Just to let him know what's going on.'

But before the DPG inspector could make a move, Parfitt spotted him and walked across. Glancing at me and my officers, he asked, 'What's going on, Matt?'

'You were talking to an American just now, James. Fellow of about forty-five to fifty. Had an attractive girl with him.'

'Yes,' said Parfitt. 'He's not an American though. He's a Canadian, name of Sheridan. I've often seen him at embassy functions. He's something to do with electronics. Does a lot of international trade.'

'I'm sorry to disappoint you, James,' said Ferguson, 'but he's not Canadian. He's an American Mafioso called Paul Tyler and he's wanted for murder in New York. There's an extradition warrant in existence for him.' Indicating me, he added, 'This is Detective Chief Inspector Brock, and he's about to arrest him.'

'Oh, Christ!' muttered Parfitt, 'you can't arrest him in here. These are diplomatic premises, and there'll be the most awful row about it. Diplomatic notes to the Foreign Secretary and all that sort of thing.'

Ferguson sighed. 'Give me credit for knowing something about diplomatic law, James,' he said.

'Yes, of course. Sorry,' said Parfitt. 'So, what are you going to do?'

'I've arranged for the ambassador to chuck him out. Metaphorically, of course. One thing the Arabs take a dim view of is harbouring murderers.'

Parfitt still did not seem too happy. 'Well, I hope you know what you're doing, Matt,' he said, and walked away, obviously wishing to have nothing to do with such an unsavoury incident.

I turned to Kate. 'When I give the signal, Kate, you, Tom and Charlie close in on Tyler and escort him from the embassy.'

Kate approached Tyler and told him she was a police officer. But the American was not in the least perturbed. 'Well, well,' he said, oozing urbane charm. 'I sure meet the police in some strange places, but,' he went on, pre-empting Kate's next statement, 'if you've any thoughts about arresting me in here, let me tell you that these are diplomatic premises.'

'I know that,' said Kate. 'And so does the ambassador. So we're going to eject you, at His Excellency's request, and then I'm going to arrest you outside.'

For a brief second, Tyler studied Kate. 'I don't think so, Inspector,' he said. Suddenly, and with surprising agility, he lunged to his immediate left and started running.

Tyler's manic trail was marked by shouts and screams as he manhandled guests out of his way. Firstly, he collided with a portly German who promptly lurched backwards and hit a long table laden with food. Despite its pure white tablecloth and ornate display of international food, it was only a trestle table. It collapsed under the German's assault, and he promptly fell backwards into a large pyramid of profiteroles, squashing them and squeezing the cream out of them, to the detriment of his expensive Savile Row suit.

A passing waiter, slipping on the spilled cream, was the next victim. His tray of champagne flew up in the air and overturned to drench the wife of a Japanese second secretary, and ruin her dress in the process. She screamed, and then protested loudly that she did not expect to find 'Ingrish rarger routs' in an embassy.

An Arab, his *kaffiyeh* displaced so that it covered his eyes, clutched blindly at a Turkish woman envoy. In a vain attempt to keep his balance, his hands clawed at her ample bosom. With total disregard for endangered species – crocodiles or Arabs – the Turkish diplomat hit the unfortunate Arab on the side of the head with her heavy crocodile leather handbag, causing him to cannon into a bishop. A member of Mossad, the Israeli secret service, who was masquerading as a first secretary, discreetly photographed the incident on his mobile phone, regretting that he could not record the resultant threats of diplomatic sanctions.

But Tyler had no real chance of escaping. As he reached the swing door to the kitchens, a burly waiter, blissfully unaware of all that was happening beyond, flung it open. As usual, given that such doors are very heavy, he pushed it violently, striking Tyler full in the face. The American staggered backwards, his nose immediately starting to bleed profusely.

Flynn and Challis seized Tyler by the elbows and, lifting him bodily, carried him to the door.

Kate returned to the ambassador. 'I'm most awfully sorry about the disturbance, sir,' she said. 'But these things sometimes don't go according to plan.'

The ambassador shook Kate's hand vigorously. 'My dear Inspector,' he said, 'please don't apologize. This is the first really enjoyable evening I've had since being accredited to the Court of St James. Such wonderful entertainment.'

Outside in the street, the handcuffed figure of Paul Tyler was leaning against a car. His white shirt was bloodstained, and a large bruise was developing on the side of his face.

DS Flynn looked at Kate. 'They'll never believe he walked into a door, guv,' he said.

'Paul Tyler,' I said, 'I'm arresting you on a warrant for a murder committed in New York on . . .' When I'd finished, I glanced at DS Challis. 'Run him across to the nearest hospital and get him patched up, Tom, and then take him to Belgravia nick. I'll talk to him in the morning.'

'Mr Brock.' The figure of James Parfitt came running out of the embassy.

'Yes?'

'I think you ought to know,' said Parfitt breathlessly, 'that there'll be a terrible to-do about that rumpus in there. Very likely a note from their government.' He paused. 'Well, *governments*, I should say, considering how many diplomats were assaulted, albeit inadvertently.'

'My dear Mr Parfitt,' I said, secure in the knowledge that the ambassador had expressed his delight at the 'entertainment', 'I'm sure you'll be able to smooth things over. Have a word with His Excellency, when he's stopped laughing. That's what you Foreign Office chaps are for, isn't it? Smoothing things over.'

A very brief message was awaiting me when eventually I returned to the Yard after the arrest of Paul Tyler. Joe Daly at the American Embassy had telephoned to say that further enquiries of the FBI office in New York had revealed that Paul Tyler, alias Tony Palladio, was a known associate of Nino Petrosino, Francesco Corleo and Pietro Giacono, the three Mafiosi whom Geoffrey Strang had contacted when he was in America.

'I think we're starting to get somewhere, Dave,' I said.

Kevin Fagan, and the other twelve suspects arrested by the Flying Squad in their dawn swoops, had been lodged at Belgravia police station. The prisoner shown on Fagan's record as his principal associate, a man named Barry Todd, was also among those arrested. But Fagan's partial fingerprint on the strap of the abandoned crash helmet was the only evidence to link any one of them to the death of Hugh Blakemore. So far.

Immediately following those arrests, a team of my own officers began searching the premises where the prisoners lived. Detective Sergeant Challis was in charge of the search of Fagan's abode in Purley, and Detective Sergeant Flynn led the team ransacking Barry Todd's terraced house in that densely populated area between Melfort Road and London Road in Thornton Heath.

Alerted by Colin Wilberforce that some money-grubbing bystander had telephoned the press, and a television camera crew had arrived on the scene, I turned on the television in my office. The interviews with people living nearby were hilarious: most of them expressed the view that Todd was a quiet sort of fellow and kept himself very much to himself. Little knots of interested neighbours loitered nearby, exchanging rumours, the strongest of which, a hungry TV reporter discovered, suggested that Todd was a mass-murderer and that the police were about to bring out bodies. An opposing camp sought to convince their listeners that he was a Middle-Eastern terrorist of some description.

Charlie Flynn returned triumphant from searching Todd's house at Thornton Heath. 'We found this, guv,' he said, displaying a pistol wrapped in oilskin.

'Where did you find it, Charlie?' I asked.

'In an outside lavatory along with a disused lawn mower, an old motor tyre, two or three half-empty cans of paint, and a sack, guv. The pistol was discovered in the overhead cistern.'

'They never learn,' I said, shaking my head.

'There's a woman called Donna Gibson who lives with Todd, guv. We interviewed her briefly at the local police station, but I'm convinced that she knew nothing whatever of Todd's activities. She was released on police bail.'

A traffic division – sorry, traffic OCU – motor cyclist was sent for and within forty minutes the weapon, still wrapped in its oilskin, was on the bench of Hugh Donovan, the senior ballistics officer at the Metropolitan Laboratory. But he did not touch it, not until Sam Marland, the fingerprint expert, had done his work.

The two men worked assiduously, bearing in mind that they were constrained by a time limit. It was now nine o'clock at night; Fagan and Todd had been arrested at six thirty that morning, and the clock was running. Unless they were charged by six thirty the following morning, we'd be obliged to release them, or come up with a damned good reason for seeking to extend their detention.

But when I heard that the firearm found at Todd's house had not only fired the rounds taken from the three murder victims, Blakemore, Strang and Goldman, but also bore the fingerprints of Fagan and Todd, I knew that there wouldn't be too many problems about holding my two star prisoners.

Both Fagan and Todd took advantage of the system that provided them with free and prompt legal advice, and the following morning found them seated in separate interview rooms. Each was in consultation with a solicitor who was confidently waiting to do battle with the wicked police.

It came as something of a surprise, therefore, when I took each prisoner, in turn, to the custody sergeant.

Todd's solicitor addressed me. 'My client is totally bemused
by this outrageous arrest, Chief Inspector,' he said, 'and I
demand that he either be charged or released immediately.'

'Certainly,' I said, and nodded to the custody sergeant.

'Barry Todd,' said the sergeant, 'you are charged in that on
divers dates you did murder Hugh Blakemore, MP, Geoffrey
Strang and Solly Goldman. Against the Queen's Peace.' He
fixed his gaze on Todd and cautioned him. Looking back at
the solicitor, he added, 'Does your client wish to say anything
in answer to the charge?'

The dumbfounded solicitor, who had assured Todd that he
would mount a vigorous defence on his behalf, shook his
head. 'No,' he said.

But Todd decided to say something. 'Did that bastard Lever
grass on us?' he asked.

The custody sergeant wrote down the prisoner's answer.

Kevin Fagan appeared next, and he too was charged with
the same three murders.

Fagan also wanted to know if Lever had informed on him,
and got the same response as Todd.

'And on what evidence do you base these ludicrous charges,
Chief Inspector?' demanded Fagan's lawyer.

'The evidence will be made available to defence counsel
as and when the Crown Prosecution Service decides to release
it,' I said.

And with that I left the custody sergeant to complete the
unnecessarily vast amount of documentation that is involved
in the charging of prisoners.

Fagan turned on his solicitor. 'What a useless prick you
turned out to be,' he said. 'Get lost.'

I was quite satisfied that Fagan and Todd had no defence
to the killing of Blakemore, Strang and Goldman, but I was
still a long way from discovering who had commissioned them
to undertake those murders.

'Where's Tyler, Dave?' I asked as we walked down the
corridor of the high-security section of the police station.

'Cell number four, guv,' said Dave.

EIGHTEEN

Tyler was incredibly cheerful considering that he was facing extradition on a murder charge, a cheerfulness probably engendered by the belief that his money could buy him out of his present troubles.

'Well, fancy seeing you again, Mr Brock,' said Tyler sarcastically, as he stood up and shook hands. He had been allowed to send for a change of clothing to replace the bloodstained suit and shirt in which he had been arrested, and was attired in a plum-coloured sweatshirt and a pair of chinos. There was a purple bruise on one side of his face, and his nose was swollen.

'Mr Tyler,' I began. I saw no point in being other than polite to the prisoner. 'I want to talk to you about the murders of Hugh Blakemore and Geoffrey Strang, and possibly Solly Goldman.'

'You gotta be joking,' said Tyler, contriving a masterful expression of surprise. 'I had nothing to do with that. And I never heard of Goldman.'

'No?' I queried. 'Strang went to the United States in March of this year, supposedly to make a film about the New York harbour master.'

Tyler laughed. 'Yeah, I know. It was a bum steer.'

'Did you assist him in any way?'

'Not really. He was dead set on doing this thing, and I told him he was wasting his time, but he never listened. I gave him a couple of grand and a few names of contacts who might've been able to help him. It's always useful to know someone when you go to a strange place and, believe me, Mr Brock, they don't come much stranger than New York.'

'I take it you're not from New York.'

'No, sir. I was originally, but now I've a place in Chicago. The east coast holds no attractions for me any more.'

In view of what I'd learned from Joe Daly, that came as no surprise. Nor, for that matter, that he was now domiciled in Chicago, once the stamping ground of Al Capone. Although,

in view of the amount of time he spent in England, I doubted
that he saw very much of the Windy City.

'Who were these people you put Strang in touch with,
Mr Tyler?'

'Oh, hell, I don't remember now. Just a few guys who're
friends of mine. Guys who know the scene, who know their
way round the Big Apple. Some of them have got interests
in the film business. I thought they might have given him a
push-start. You know how it is.'

'I think I've got the general idea.' I sensed that Tyler was
unwilling to admit anything to me. But, given his background,
that was hardly surprising.

'Yeah, well, I'll tell you what I know. Anne and I were
having a bit of a fling.' Tyler made a gesture of surrender with
his hands. 'But I guess you knew that already,' he said. He
had obviously forgotten having admitted his liaison with Anne
when last I spoke to him. 'And she asked me if I could help
this Strang guy on account of he was a friend of her daughter's.
You met Caroline?'

'Yes,' I said. 'I have made her acquaintance.'

'Yeah? Well, I did what I could, as a favour to Anne, but
I reckon the biggest favour I did to Strang was to tell him he
was wasting his time. The film business in America is buttoned
up tight, believe me. I knew he'd get no place.' Tyler shrugged.
'Anyways, like I said, I gave him a couple of grand to finance
his trip, and wished him *bon voyage*.' There was an eloquent
pause. 'He was back within days. Can't say I was surprised.'

'The last time I saw you, you said that you'd referred Strang
to Simpson.'

'I did? Yeah, well, that's right.'

'But you can't remember the names of any of the people
you put him in touch with.'

Tyler screwed up his face, giving the impression that he
was thinking hard. Eventually he offered a couple of names
together with the addresses of nightclubs in the Italian Quarter
that they were supposed to frequent.

But I knew that the names would be false, and so it proved
to be; when Joe Daly attempted to have them traced, the New
York FBI agents were unable to find anyone who had heard
of them, let alone who knew them.

I decided to give Tyler a helping hand. 'How about Nino

Petrosino, Francesco Corleo and Pietro Giacono for a start?'
I asked. 'I would suggest, Mr Tyler, that those were the names
you gave Strang.'

'What in hell are you asking me for if you already know?'
snapped Tyler, disturbed that I'd obviously been talking to the
'Feds', as he always called the FBI.

'Just refreshing your memory, Mr Tyler.'

Tyler calmed down again, and decided to change the
subject in an attempt, I imagined, to avoid further questions,
the answers to which might possibly be incriminating – or
the absence of answers would be. 'What about this business
I've been arrested for, Mr Brock?' he asked. 'You don't think
they're really going to extradite me for that, do you? It's a
load of baloney.'

'I'm afraid I can't discuss that matter, Mr Tyler,' I said.
Convinced that I'd obtained from the American all that I was
going to get, I added, 'But I can tell you that the extradition
warrant is based on a charge of murder allegedly committed
by you in New York in 1995.' I paused. 'That was when you
were calling yourself Tony Palladio, of course.'

Tyler laughed, long and loud. 'They're not still trying to
pin that rap on me, are they?' he asked. But this time, the
bravado was manifestly false.

'However,' I continued, 'to get back to what I was talking
about just now, I'm not altogether satisfied that you had nothing
to do with the murder of Hugh Blakemore.'

'Hey! Now hold it right there—'

'Just let me finish, Mr Tyler,' I said. 'On your own admission, you were having an affair with Anne Blakemore. She's
told me that it started some time before her husband's death.'

'So what?' asked Tyler churlishly. 'Happens all the time.
There's nothing new in that sort of thing.'

'It seems that your activities in the States have attracted
quite a lot of attention, mainly from the diverse law enforcement agencies that seem to abound in that part of the world.
According to the FBI, you have the sort of associates – some
of whom I have just mentioned – who might have been interested in a contract to murder Blakemore. However, it would
seem that they wisely decided to decline the offer.'

'That's slander,' said Tyler angrily.

'So, sue me,' I said. 'However, I shall continue to make

enquiries into any possible connection you might have had
with Hugh Blakemore's death – and Strang's for that matter.
I now know that one of our native villains, Mickey Lever, at
the instigation of Geoffrey Strang, procured the services of
two others, namely Kevin Fagan and Barry Todd, to carry out
those murders.'

'Never heard of them,' said Tyler. Certainly, from his
demeanour, the names appeared to mean nothing to him, but
not only had Tyler been interrogated by the police on many
occasions, Joe Daly had told me that he had a reputation for
being a pretty cool poker player.

'I understand from Anne Blakemore that her late husband
threatened to have you deported, Mr Tyler,' I said. 'Now that
sounds like a pretty good reason for wanting him out of the
way, particularly when one looks at why the New York police
are so desperate to get you back.'

'He was bluffing. There was no chance of him pulling that
off. Hugh sometimes thought he was more important than he
truly was.'

'You don't think that, as a Member of Parliament, he might
have found out about your record, and the warrant which the
NYPD held for you?'

Tyler shrugged. 'Maybe,' he admitted, 'but if he did, why
didn't he shop me to the authorities? I can tell you this,
Detective Brock, with hand on heart, I didn't have him killed.
I just disappeared for a while. And that was for Anne's sake.
I didn't want her getting in bother with her old man.'

'Curious coincidence that you came back immediately after
Blakemore's death, isn't it?'

Tyler laughed. 'Well, sure as hell, I wasn't going to come
back before. Look, I'll level with you. Sure, I knew about the
NYPD warrant, and the last thing I wanted was to get sent
back to the States. So I decided to lie low for a bit. Get out
of the way. Liz and me took a cottage in Cornwall for a few
months and after that—'

'That would be Liz Middleton, would it?'

'Yeah, sure.'

'How did you run your business during that time, Mr Tyler?'

'Wonderful things, laptop computers, BlackBerrys, and the
Internet,' said the American. 'Anyway, the firm knew where
I was.' He paused, and laughed. 'But I'd sworn them to

secrecy. Anne knew where I was, though. I called her from time to time.'

I found that interesting, given that Anne Blakemore had denied knowing where Tyler was, or that she'd heard from him. 'How much money did you give to Anne, Mr Tyler?' I asked.

'What makes you think I did?' Tyler's answer was level, controlled, and gave no hint of surprise at my sudden change of tack.

'Her bank statement shows that she received several substantial payments from you.'

'How the hell did you get to see her bank statements? That's a violation of her civil rights.'

'Then I suggest you take it up with the Crown Court judge who issued the warrant,' I said.

'They were loans. She was short of money, and Hugh Blakemore was being bled dry by some actress he was screwing.'

'D'you know that for a fact?'

'I guess so. It was Anne who told me.'

'It would seem, therefore, that Anne Blakemore's only interest in you was money,' I suggested. 'It's the only thing that really counts in her life, isn't it?'

Tyler shrugged. 'You may be right about that, Detective,' he said, 'but so what? She was a damned good lay, drunk or sober.'

'Be that as it may,' I said, 'I shall be further interviewing Anne Blakemore about this matter. I'm far from convinced that she is an innocent party to her husband's death.'

'She'd never be able to set up something like that,' Tyler scoffed. 'Like I said, she's a lush and a nympho. The only thing she can plan is where the next shot of gin's coming from.'

'I have a feeling that when all the evidence is laid before her, she'll abandon you, Mr Tyler. I think she'll throw you to the wolves in order to save her own neck. In fact, I'm absolutely certain that she'll leave you to face charges on your own.'

It was that comment that prompted Tyler's outburst, and he wasted no time in denigrating his erstwhile lover.

'Now listen up,' Tyler began. 'First of all, I had nothing to do with any of the murders you're talking about. And as for

Anne, well, like I said, she's a lush and a nympho. More often than not, she was smashed out of her mind when I got there. And it was obvious that she wanted me for one thing, and one thing alone.'

'I'd never have guessed,' put in Dave.

'Difficult to miss,' said Tyler. 'Usually when I visited her, she'd obviously been drinking and she insisted that we took a bottle of champagne up to the bedroom with us. She was a passionate and animated lover, but even so she never seemed to be satisfied. I knew that she was entertaining Simpson as well as me, which was probably as well. I always rated myself in bed, but I just couldn't keep up with her. She wasn't only a lush, she was a nymphomaniac. Most times when I arrived all she had on was a robe, and she'd lead the way straight upstairs. On one occasion, she answered the door nude. Would you believe that?'

'Yes, I would,' I said. Tyler was merely confirming the view I'd formed of Anne Blakemore at our first meeting.

'And, like I said, there'd always be a bottle of champagne in an ice bucket.' Tyler smiled at the recollection. 'Right by the bed.'

'Did she ever talk of marriage?'

'Too right she wanted marriage, and she'd talked of "getting rid" of Hugh, but I thought she meant to divorce him, citing that slut of an actress Hugh was screwing. But what she really wanted was money.' Tyler shrugged. 'OK, so I was prepared to finance her – paying for my pleasure, if you like – but there was no way I'd have married her. She was a greedy broad, but I was having fun. However,' he finished by saying, 'I was on the point of leaving her anyway and, incidentally, Liz too. As a matter of fact, I'd got tired of the pair of them, and I've begun to romance a young New Zealand girl who's just started to work for me as a secretary. I'm thinking of making her a sleeping partner.' Tyler afforded himself a sly grin at his little joke.

'That's all very interesting, Mr Tyler,' I said, 'but I intend to continue my investigation and if I find evidence, I shall not hesitate to charge you with the murders of Blakemore and Strang. If not Solly Goldman.'

'Now you listen up good, buddy,' said Tyler, all pretence at courtesy and reasoned conversation abandoned. 'I've been investigated by the FBI, the NYPD, the Internal Revenue

Service, the Drug Enforcement Agency, and Alcohol, Tobacco and Firearms.' He paused. 'Even the Sheriff of Lone County – which is some place you've probably never even heard of – tried to pin a rap on me. And none of them managed to screw me down. So a Limey cop like you ain't got a prayer.'

'I take it you don't wish to make a statement then,' I said.

'You're damned right I don't. And the next time you come nosing round this excuse for a god-damn station house, you'd better have some hard evidence because I'll have a mouthpiece sitting right here in the room.'

I nodded. 'I think if I were in your position, Mr Tyler,' I said, 'I would adopt exactly the same attitude.'

NINETEEN

'd been extremely disappointed by my interview with Paul Tyler. I'd not expected a confession from the man, but I'd come away without anything upon which I could even base further investigation. Tyler had admitted giving Geoffrey Strang money for his trip to New York, and had not denied furnishing him with the names of three Mafiosi contacts, even though he hadn't actually acknowledged that they had Mafia connections. But that did not amount to conspiring with Strang, Lever, Fagan and Todd to murder Blakemore. There was certainly no evidence to connect him with the killing of Strang, and even less to implicate him in the death of Solly Goldman.

Back at Curtis Green, I listened once again to the recording of my interview with the man. 'Well, Dave,' I said, 'I think we've reached an impasse. Somehow, we've got to get this thing moving.'

'So, what's next, guv?' asked Dave.

'A small handful of frightening powder, Dave,' I said. I telephoned Kate Ebdon, and outlined exactly what I wanted done. 'And ring me when it's all set up.'

The call came an hour and a half later, and Dave and I left immediately to return to Belgravia police station.

Seated in an interview room, Anne Blakemore was radiating fury, indignation and disdain – all at once. Immaculately dressed in a tangerine linen suit that must have cost a fortune, she looked completely out of place. 'What is the meaning of this outrage?' she demanded imperiously as Dave and I entered the room. 'Sending that wretched woman to arrest me. To arrest *me*.' She was spluttering with rage now, but I wondered whether it was an act to cover the apprehension she felt at the enquiry having been placed on a formal footing in the austere surroundings of a police station.

'I would appreciate an explanation, Chief Inspector,' said the silver-haired man seated beside Anne.

'We've not met,' I said, although I guessed who the man was.

'I'm Mrs Blakemore's solicitor,' he said, and handed me a business card.

'Your client has not been arrested,' I said, 'as I'm sure you're aware. Detective Inspector Ebdon merely asked her to come to the station for an interview. An interview that, for her own protection, will be recorded.'

'Tosh!' snapped Anne. 'It was pretty obvious to me that I had no option. Me, the wife of a Member of Parliament.'

Dave placed tapes in the recorder and announced the date and time, and who was present.

'You are, in fact, the *widow* of an MP, Mrs Blakemore,' I said, as I sat down opposite her. In view of what I'd learned about her sexual exploits, I had no sympathy for the woman. 'I interviewed Paul Tyler this morning, and he made several admissions which cause me to believe that you might have been a party to your husband's death.' That was far from true, but I'd got to the stage where I had to start pushing this woman a little if I was to get anywhere.

Anne's hand went to her neck and she began playing nervously with her gold locket. 'What on earth are you talking about?' There were two high spots of colour on her cheeks now. 'This is preposterous,' she continued. 'I think you should know that I still have a lot of influential friends at Westminster. And in the City.'

'It would be better if you let the officer finish, Anne,' said her solicitor quietly.

'What Paul Tyler had to say, in my view, implicates you, and you are therefore entitled to know of it,' I continued.

'I'm not interested,' said Anne. 'It'll all be lies.'

'Nevertheless, I shall tell you what he said, Mrs Blakemore.' I'd known from the outset that Anne Blakemore was not going to be an easy woman to interview, much less one from whom I would obtain a confession. Not that it mattered. I glanced at the solicitor who was sitting back in his chair, perfectly relaxed, and listening intently.

'As you wish,' said Anne. She was sitting sideways to the table, her legs crossed, staring at the door.

I glanced down at my notes. 'Tyler claims that he first met you some years ago.'

'Of course he does. I told you that. It's no secret,' said Anne cuttingly.

'Anne, *please*,' implored the solicitor, afraid that Anne's display of temper would show her in a bad light. I guessed that he wanted to know what I knew, aware that a chief inspector does not make serious accusations against the widow of an MP without possessing very credible evidence.

'Well, it's true,' said Anne crossly. 'I don't know why I had to be brought here to be told something I already know, and that I've already told you about.'

'Tyler claims that, despite the fact you were already having an affair with your ex-husband, Charles Simpson, you readily embarked upon an affair with him. He describes it as a torrid affair. He spoke of visiting you regularly, usually in the afternoon, and went on to say that you could hardly wait to get him into bed. He says that on many of those occasions you answered the door wearing just a robe and nothing else.'

'It's all lies,' said Anne, despite her solicitor's restraining hand on her arm.

I ignored Anne's constant interruptions. 'But you continued to carry on your affair with Simpson, even though you were having sexual intercourse with Tyler at every available opportunity.' I paused. 'I'll read you what he said.' I turned a page or two of the transcript until I found the place. 'Ah, here we are. Tyler went on to say, "Usually when I visited her, she'd obviously been drinking and she usually insisted that we took a bottle of champagne up to the bedroom with us. She was a passionate and animated lover, but even so she never seemed to be satisfied. I knew that she was entertaining Simpson as well as me, which was probably as well. I always rated myself in bed, but I just couldn't keep up with her. She wasn't only a lush, she was a nymphomaniac."'

Anne turned to her lawyer. 'Do I have to listen to this libellous rubbish, Richard?' she screamed at her solicitor, the fury evident on her face.

'The officer is quite within his rights to tell you what's been said about you, Anne,' said the solicitor calmly, 'and I really think you should listen to the whole thing.' He was a skilled lawyer and had already begun to suspect that I had little or no evidence against his client.

'Whose side are you on?' Anne snapped.

The lawyer ignored Anne's outburst and directed his next

request to me. 'I'd appreciate a copy of that statement, Mr Brock,' he said mildly. 'The statement of one co-conspirator against—'

'Are you suggesting that Mrs Blakemore is a co-conspirator?' I asked.

'Of course not.'

'Then she's not entitled to a copy of what Tyler said, unless she makes an admission. Incidentally, Tyler did not make a written statement. What I have here is a transcript of the recording of the interview.'

The lawyer said nothing. He'd tried it on, but failed.

'According to Tyler, both he and Simpson were lavishing money on you in a way that your husband could not afford,' I continued. 'Tyler claims that you were besotted with him and wanted to marry him because of the lifestyle he could offer you. But there was one impediment: your husband Hugh Blakemore. It was then that you began to evolve the idea of having him killed.' I broke off my narrative. 'I can now tell you that the New York Police Department wishes to extradite Tyler in connection with a murder that took place in New York in 1995.'

That appeared momentarily to stun Anne, but she recovered quickly. 'And I told you that you've got the wrong man. And if the way you've gone about finding my husband's murderer is any indication of your efficiency, that comes as no surprise to me.'

'We learned some interesting facts about Mr Tyler, or Tony Palladio, as he's better known to the FBI,' I continued.

'This is preposterous,' said Anne. 'I don't believe a word of it. I just don't believe it.'

'I think you know a lot more about Paul Tyler than you're prepared to admit,' I said. 'In fact, I've come to the conclusion that you've known who he really is for some considerable time.'

'It sounds as though you've been investigating me,' said Anne, raising her chin.

'We *have* been investigating you, Mrs Blakemore,' I said, determined not to be put off by the woman's lofty attitude. 'In fact, we know quite a lot about you. That you were born and brought up in Dagenham, that your father was a baker and your mother a cinema usherette. And we know that you worked in Covent Garden and then in public relations, where you met your first husband—'

'This is disgraceful,' shouted Anne.

'You were no innocent abroad, Mrs Blakemore. I suggest that you were perfectly aware of Paul Tyler's background, knew that he was a criminal, and knew also that he was wanted for murder in the United States. I imagine that you were not only excited by that, but saw Tyler as a useful tool to further your plan. But there was a danger that the murder could have led to an investigation into your affair with him which, I gather, was pretty much of an open secret around Westminster anyway.'

'Hugh was playing fast and loose, too. He was a woman-izer of the worst possible sort. There were dozens of women—'

'Anne, please don't say anything,' said the solicitor, clearly worried that his client was about to incriminate herself. 'In any event, immorality is not a crime—'

'Oh, shut up, Richard,' replied Anne. 'I'm not going to sit here and take this without defending myself. Which, inci-dentally, is what I'm paying you to do.' She fixed the lawyer with a censorious gaze. 'Not that you've helped much so far. All you've done is to tell me what the police may or may not do. Why don't you start working for me?'

'There'll be ample opportunity for that later, Anne.' The solicitor sounded weary of the whole business, and I almost felt sorry for him. But then I thought about the fat fee that he would undoubtedly be charging for his attendance at the police station, and did not feel quite so sorry.

'And as you could not risk allowing Tyler to go to America, for the reasons I've outlined, you concocted a scheme to send Geoffrey Strang instead. That had the additional advantage of putting a distance between yourself and the murder.' I put down my notes. 'Strang was a weak character, Mrs Blakemore, and was besotted with you. That was before he took up with your daughter, of course. But at the time, he would have done anything for you and, when you asked him to go to New York and set up the murder of your husband, he went, willingly.'

Anne Blakemore suddenly exploded. 'I'm not going to sit here and listen to any more of this nonsense,' she screamed. Her face went red, the flush slowly creeping down to meet the neckline of her jacket.

'Anne, you really must control yourself,' said her lawyer. 'You'll have a chance to say anything you want to in just a moment. Not that you need to say anything at all.'

Anne turned on her solicitor. 'I'm not putting up with it,' she cried, 'and, furthermore, I don't need your unhelpful advice any more. You can go.'

'But Anne—'

'I no longer need your services, Richard. Is that clear? You're dismissed. Now get the hell out of here.' Anne raised her arm and pointed at the door like a wronged woman in a Victorian melodrama. Then she turned her wrath on me. 'And I'm going too,' she announced imperiously.

'I'm afraid you're not, Mrs Blakemore,' I said. 'If you insist, then I shall have no alternative but to arrest you.'

'This is deplorable, deplorable,' yelled Anne. She turned once more to her solicitor. 'I've told you to go,' she said. 'You're useless.'

With a sigh, the solicitor stood up, resting a hand on his briefcase as he did so. 'I hope you know what you're doing, Anne,' he said.

'I certainly don't need your help, Richard. You've done nothing for your £250 an hour, so just fuck off out of it.'

At last the Dagenham woman was showing out.

For the benefit of the tape-recording, I announced that the solicitor had left the interview room and then resumed my accusations. 'You convinced Paul Tyler that if he didn't go along with your scheme, your husband would have him deported. Tyler believed it and gave Strang the names of the right people to contact, and some money—'

'You can hardly blame me for that,' interrupted Anne.

'In addition to the sizeable amount you gave Strang to cover the contract for the assassination.' I went on as though Anne had not spoken, but I'd no proof that Strang had actually received any money from Anne, and passed it on to Lever. 'Tyler told him to get in touch with Nino Petrosino, Francesco Corleo and Pietro Giacono, all of whom are known to the FBI and the New York police as criminals and Mafiosi. The FBI now knows that these people were approached by Strang. They also believe he told them that he was acting on your behalf and that you had put out what they call a contract on your husband's life.' It was pure guesswork.

As far as I knew, the three men I'd mentioned had refused to say anything.

'I had nothing to do with it,' said Anne.

I glanced across at Dave. 'Sergeant.' He knew that I could never remember the words of the caution.

'Yes, sir,' said Dave. 'You do not have to say anything, Mrs Blakemore, but it may harm your defence if you do not mention when questioned something which you later rely on in court. Anything you do say may be given in evidence.'

I decided that the delivery of a formal caution might just concentrate the woman's mind sufficiently to bring forth the truth. Apart from which, this woman was no ordinary criminal and I wasn't prepared to take any chances. Despite her peremptory dismissal of her solicitor, I knew that if she ever came to trial some of the best legal brains at the bar would be marshalled in her defence.

Suddenly all the arrogance left Anne Blakemore and she leaned back in her chair, deflated. 'I didn't have anything to do with it,' she repeated. She had a vacant expression on her face now. 'And I've no intention of going to prison for something I didn't do.' She let out a great sigh, and her shoulders slumped. 'But I'll tell you what I do know. In fact, I'm tired of the whole business. Tired of being harassed by you people, tired of Paul Tyler . . .'

'You did know about his past, didn't you, Mrs Blakemore?'

Anne nodded in a resigned way. 'Yes, but only recently. It was after you'd been to see him that he told me all about it. He thought that you'd heard from the FBI. That's why he disappeared.'

'Why should he have thought I knew?' I was interested to know what exactly had alerted Tyler.

'He told me one evening, when we'd both had a lot to drink. He said that one of those friends in New York that you mentioned had telephoned him and warned him that the FBI were making enquiries about Geoffrey Strang's visit to America. I suppose poor Paul put two and two together and thought that he was about to be arrested.'

'Do you wish to make a written statement about all this, Mrs Blakemore?' I asked.

For a few long moments, Anne Blakemore stared at me. 'If you like,' she said eventually, and began dictating her statement to Dave.

Unfortunately, her testimony proved to be far from the damning indictment that I'd hoped for, and the flow of it was frequently broken by Anne's outbursts. 'He's having an affair with a young New Zealand girl now,' she said, the break in her voice clearly indicating that she had been hurt by it. 'It's pure sex,' she claimed, 'nothing else. The girl's only twenty-two, for God's sake.' From time to time, she stared at me, as though willing me to understand. 'I mean, what can a man in his fifties possibly have in common with a child like that if it's not sex? And she wasn't the first, you know, Mr Brock. There have been others.' She laughed suddenly, almost hyster-ically. 'I should know. After all, he and I . . .' Her face clouded, and she started to ramble. I wondered how much she'd had to drink before being brought to the police station. 'I found out that Geoffrey Strang was sleeping with Caroline, and had cast me off. As if that wasn't hurtful enough, Paul told me that he was pretty sure that Caroline was on drugs. He knows about these things, you know.'

According to the FBI, Tyler certainly did know all about drugs. And I had no doubt that Anne Blakemore was incensed when Strang had spurned her in favour of her own daughter.

'But by then, there was nothing I could do. Everything seemed to go wrong.' Anne suddenly covered her face with her hands and burst into tears. 'First Hugh,' she mumbled between sobs, 'then Geoffrey. And now Paul's been arrested.' She looked up at me, seemingly unconcerned at the image her tear-stained face was presenting. 'I've got no one left,' she moaned miserably.

'Would you like something to drink, Mrs Blakemore?' I asked, unmoved by this display of emotion, and convinced that it was a device to seek sympathy. 'A cup of tea or coffee, perhaps?'

Anne shook her head. 'No,' she said, 'but I could use a gin and tonic.'

'I'm sorry. No alcohol.'

'A cigarette, then.'

I opened my case and placed it on the table. Dave inter-rupted his writing to produce his lighter, held the flame to the woman's cigarette, and waited for her to continue.

'If I'd known what he was planning, perhaps I could have stopped him.' Suddenly Anne Blakemore appeared to accept that Tyler had been involved in the death of her husband. Unused to smoking often, she puffed nervously at her cigarette. 'But I didn't know that's what he was going to do. Why did he do it? Was it to punish him for treating me so badly?' All logic seemed now to have vanished from her narrative that, at best, had been somewhat disjointed. 'I didn't know Geoffrey was going to America to arrange it, and I didn't know that Hugh was going to be killed.' She began to sob hysterically, her clenched fists pummelling the table in front of her. 'If only I'd come to you when it all started,' she mumbled through her tears. 'But I didn't know anything.' She stared imploringly at me. 'Honestly, I didn't know.'

'Well, that was a monumental waste of time, Dave,' I said, when he and I returned to Curtis Green. Finally convinced that the whole interview had been a pointless exercise, I'd told Kate to take Anne Blakemore back to her Chelsea home.

When Kate returned, she appeared in the doorway of my office.

'What is it, Kate?'

'I've just had a phone call, guv.' Kate closed the door and accepted my invitation to sit down. 'As you know, I've been leaning on some of my snouts in the West End over this Goldman shooting.'

I nodded. 'Yes?'

'I've been tipped off about a guy who runs a strip joint in the area. I think he's prepared to give up the name of the hoods who've been putting the arm on him. But he's terrified and, furthermore, he won't accept my assurances that he'll be protected, or that we're not intent on shutting him down. I think if you were to have a word with him, he may just surrender the bloke we want.'

'Lead me to him, Kate,' I said.

TWENTY

'Who's this character we're going to see, Kate?' I asked, as Kate and I strode past the tawdry facades of Soho's vice community; a community that sold sex and sex aids, explicit videos and magazines, and exploited young women who thought that divesting themselves of their clothing before a lascivious audience was the first step on the ladder to stardom.

'Lou Gannon, guv.' Kate had told me previously, but I wanted to be absolutely certain. It's not a good idea to get a valuable informant's name wrong. 'He's been running a fairly legitimate strip club for some years now. I checked with Clubs and Vice, and they've got nothing on him. Doesn't rip off his clients, doesn't sell mock champagne at inflated prices, and won't have the customers propositioning his girls on the premises. Mind you, what they get up to privately is their business.'

Teetering on high stiletto heels in the doorway of Gannon's club was a tall, striking blonde. She wore a top hat, an evening dress tailcoat over a skintight black satin leotard, and the inevitable black fishnet tights. From time to time, she twirled a small cane with a silver knob. 'Lots of lovely naked girls,' she said, as we approached.

'Gets monotonous, doesn't it?' commented Kate.

'We don't normally see ladies in here,' said the blue-chinned bouncer.

'Well, you're going to see one now,' said Kate, wafting her warrant card under the man's nose.

Gannon's office was in an upstairs room from where, through a two-way mirror, he kept a watch on his continuous stage show below. Near his left hand was a bell-push that would immediately summon a couple of 'heavies' to deal promptly with any disorder, including those clients who thought they could climb on to the stage to help his girls to disrobe.

'Mr Gannon, I'm Detective Chief Inspector Brock of Scotland Yard, and I understand you know DI Ebdon.'

'Please sit down,' said Gannon, rising to his feet and peering at us through thick-lensed, heavy horn-rimmed spectacles. He was short, with a completely bald head and podgy, ringed fingers. Without enquiring whether we wanted a drink, he poured three substantial measures of whisky into tumblers. 'Thank you for coming, Mr Brock.'

'I understand that you've been troubled by people trying to sell you insurance, Mr Gannon,' I began as I sampled the club owner's Scotch.

Gannon smiled, but it was not a smile of amusement. 'That's one way of putting it, Mr Brock. But I run a straight club here.' He gave an expressive shrug of his shoulders. 'All right, so the Church of England might not approve, but it supplies a demand, and if I didn't provide a strip show, someone else would. But it's tasteful and there's no prostitution. I don't run a brothel, and the drinks I sell are at reasonable prices, for Soho anyway. And they're legal. No bootlegging from the continent, I assure you.'

'I believe you, Mr Gannon,' I said, forbearing to point out that I wasn't a customs officer. 'So who are these people?'

'Two guys came in here one evening, about a week ago. They told me that Solly Goldman had been topped, and they suggested that it was because there were elements in the village who were causing trouble, and that they could provide me with what they called "cover" so that it wouldn't happen here. At a price, of course. I told them that my staff were more than capable of taking care of any trouble.'

'What did they say to that?'

'They laughed, Mr Brock, and said that my people might be able to deal with the odd drunk or two, but what they were talking about was real trouble.'

'Did they suggest what sort of trouble, Mr Gannon?'

'Oh, yes.' Gannon smiled bleakly. 'They mentioned one or two places in the area that had caught fire, and others that had been vandalized wholesale. They left me in no doubt that if I didn't cooperate, the same thing would happen here.'

'So what did you do?'

'I paid up. What else could I do?'

'You could have come to us,' I said.

Gannon swirled his whisky round in his glass and stared pensively into it for a moment or two. He looked up. 'I don't mean to be rude, Mr Brock,' he said, 'but what can the police do? You can't be here all the time, and even if you were, what would that do for my business? The sort of people who come in here are respectable. Bank managers and accountants, solicitors, businessmen. I even saw an MP in here once.'

'Was that, by any chance, Hugh Blakemore, Mr Gannon?'

'Yes, it was. The MP who was murdered. But people like him, and the others I mentioned, don't want to get into trouble, and with the police here they'd probably think it was about to be raided. Names in the papers, Mr Brock, names in the papers. You know what I'm saying?'

I waited until Gannon had poured more whisky. 'It wouldn't have come to that, Mr Gannon,' I said. 'I'm afraid we don't have enough policemen to guard places like this, but we can do something about stopping these people. We need cooperation, though. And that means names.'

'That's the bottom line, isn't it?' Gannon knew that it would come to this, and his puffy face took on a pallid hue.

'Well?'

Gannon spread his hands. 'People like me who run places like this,' he said, waving a hand around his office, 'don't generally talk to the police, but they do talk to each other. We might cut each other's throats when it comes to business, metaphorically speaking.' He laughed nervously. 'But when it comes to watching each other's backs, we usually work together.'

'I think you're trying to get to the point here, Mr Gannon,' I suggested, taking a sip of my Scotch. I noticed that Kate Ebdon had no trouble drinking it.

'One name kept coming up, Mr Brock. It seems that this man is so confident that no one will dare to grass on him that he doesn't care. That's how powerful he is.'

'Or thinks he is,' I said.

'Maybe so, maybe so.'

'And is he one of the men who came to see you?'

'No,' said Gannon, 'but they mentioned his name. They made threats, like this man would be very annoyed if I didn't want to take up his offer. That was the way they put it.'

'Well,' I said. 'Are you going to tell me who he is, this mysterious character?'

There was a long pause during which Gannon was clearly struggling with concern for his own welfare, tempered by his doubt that the police would be able adequately to protect him, but secure in the knowledge that if he did not assist them, his troubles could only worsen. 'All right,' he said. 'His name's Charles Simpson.'

The enquiries took several months. Several months of frenetic activity that involved not only Homicide and Serious Crime Command, and the Flying Squad, but the Fraud Squad, and Revenue and Customs too.

To begin with, a highly qualified team of Fraud Squad officers, aided by Revenue and Customs, spent days unravelling the complex labyrinth of companies that Simpson owned, and which he used to hide the proceeds of his various rackets. They also followed the tortuous money trail that led to where Simpson had placed those proceeds, some of which were in offshore accounts. The Fraud Squad even managed to uncover details of substantial payments made to Kevin Fagan, Barry Todd and Geoffrey Strang.

The results were fascinating, and conclusive. It seemed that Simpson had been conducting his nefarious activities for years. Even before he met and married Anne Blakemore, or Anne Croucher as she had been at the time.

There was always a possibility that Simpson's highly tuned intelligence network might have alerted him to police interest, covert though those enquiries had been. Just to make sure that he didn't escape, a team of surveillance officers kept a round-the-clock watch on him.

Then, at last, I was ready to strike.

Assured that on the Monday morning in January that I'd selected for my raid, Simpson was in his office at his public relations company, I took Dave, Kate Ebdon and Tom Challis with me to effect the arrest.

'Good morning.' Simpson's unsuspecting secretary greeted us with a pleasant smile. But the smile turned to one of concern when Kate, Dave and Tom followed me into the reception area.

'We've come to see Mr Simpson,' I said.

'I'm afraid he's with a client at the moment, and he has a busy day scheduled. Would you care to make an appointment?'

'No, thanks,' I said, and made for the door of Simpson's office.

'You really can't go in.' The secretary rose from her chair, clearly agitated at my high-handed approach.

'Sit down, mate,' said Kate. 'We're police officers.'

'Yes, but—'

'I said sit down,' repeated Kate.

I flung open Simpson's door. He was indeed with a client. A youngish man in an expensive suit was seated in one of the armchairs in the corner of the large office. Facing him, in the other chair, was the man we'd come to arrest.

'What the hell?' Charles Simpson stood up. 'I'm conducting an important meeting.'

The secretary appeared in the doorway behind us. 'I'm sorry, Mr Simpson,' she said. 'I told them you had a client with you.'

'It's all right, Vanessa,' said Simpson. 'I'll deal with it.'

As his secretary left, Simpson turned to me. 'Just because you're police officers doesn't mean you can come barging in here any time you like,' he said. He was very angry, but I detected a hint of apprehension in his expression.

'Charles Simpson, I have a warrant for your arrest on charges of murder, extortion, malicious wounding, grievous bodily harm, and money laundering. I have to tell you that other charges may follow, including conspiracy.' I turned to Dave. 'Caution Mr Simpson, Sergeant.'

Before Dave had finished, the client stood up. 'I think I'd better leave you, Charlie,' he said, and made for the door.

'Not so fast, mate,' said Kate, stepping in front of the man.

The client then made a mistake. He pushed Kate violently in the chest in an effort to escape.

But as he passed her, Kate seized his right arm, and in a flurry of skilful movements, placed him in a crippling thumb lock. 'I'm arresting you for assaulting a police officer,' she said mildly.

Generally speaking, Kate would not have bothered too much about being pushed but, like me, she had sensed that a man who called Simpson 'Charlie' might be a co-conspirator rather than a client.

'This is outrageous,' Simpson yelled. 'I demand to get in touch with my lawyer.'

'You'll have an opportunity to do that at the police station,' I said.

It was then that Simpson made a futile attempt at escape. Swerving round me, he suddenly ran towards the door, but police officers are always ready for such a manoeuvre. Tom Challis, who was playing 'goalkeeper' in the doorway of the office, seized Simpson and promptly handcuffed him.

'Naughty, naughty,' he said.

By the time the custody sergeant had charged Simpson, provided him with a meal, and awaited the arrival of his lawyer, it was half past two.

But at last Dave and I sat face to face with Simpson and his solicitor.

'My client is a respectable businessman,' the lawyer began, 'and never in my entire professional career have I seen such a set of fabricated allegations. I have advised my client not to answer any questions. And I warn you, Chief Inspector, that I shall challenge each and every one of them.'

It was the usual legal trumpery to which CID officers were accustomed.

'I don't intend to ask him any questions,' I said.

That seemed to throw the solicitor off balance. 'You don't?'

'No. Now that he's been charged, I'm not permitted to ask him any questions, as I'm sure you're aware.'

'Then, what, may I ask, is the purpose of this interview?'

'Mr Simpson has had the charges explained to him,' I said, 'and I'm merely giving him the opportunity to make a statement under caution, if he wishes to do so. But he need not say anything unless he wants to.'

The solicitor held a brief whispered conversation with his client, and then turned to me. 'My client has nothing to say, and I wish to have him bailed.'

'I'm not prepared to bail him,' I said. 'But you may, of course, apply for bail at the hearing before the Westminster magistrates tomorrow morning.'

And the best of luck, I thought. And I was right. At the hearing the following morning, Simpson was remanded in custody.

At my second interview with Anne Blakemore at Belgravia police station, I went straight to the point. I cautioned her again, and invited her to have her solicitor present, but clearly she had done with him.

'I'm going to put a name to you, Mrs Blakemore,' I said, 'and I would suggest that he told you of his intention to have your husband murdered.'

'This is ridiculous,' said Anne Blakemore haughtily. 'I've told you all I know.'

'I don't think so,' I said. 'The man I'm talking about is your former husband, Charles Simpson.'

'I don't believe it,' said Anne dismissively, but the expression on her face belied her disbelief.

'I want you to listen carefully to what we have learned about him and his activities, Mrs Blakemore,' I said, and for the next ten minutes, I told her what the police knew of the plot to kill Blakemore.

During my detailed exposition, Anne Blakemore became paler and paler, and her hands, lying loosely in her lap to begin with, increasingly tightened their grip on each other. 'It's true,' she whispered, when I'd finished. 'Everything you say is true, but I was terrified.'

'In that case, are you prepared to make a further statement, Mrs Blakemore?' I asked.

'Yes.'

For the next two hours, Dave took down Anne Blakemore's statement. At times, she was clearly distressed, and we had to break off to provide her with a cup of tea and a glass of water. But eventually we had on paper everything that she knew about the plot.

It was that statement that formed the mainstay of the brief of prosecuting counsel.

A week or two later, the client who had attempted to escape when Simpson was arrested, appeared before the West London district judge.

He pleaded not guilty to the charge of assaulting a police officer.

Kate Ebdon, who always contrived to look small and helpless on such occasions, gave evidence of the man hitting her violently in the chest.

The client, who turned out to be a real client seeking to place a public relations contract, said that he didn't know Kate was a police officer, and thought that she and the men with her were intent on abducting Charles Simpson.

Barely able to conceal his mirth, the district judge found him guilty, and sentenced him to two hundred hours' community service. He expressed the hope that that service would entail cleaning a police station so that, in the future, he would know what police officers looked like.

TWENTY-ONE

The clerk of Number Two Court at the Old Bailey stood up and fixed his gaze on the prisoner in the dock. He read out Simpson's name, asked him to confirm his identity, and began to list the counts upon which he stood indicted. It took a long time.

'How do you plead?' asked the clerk, after each count.

'Not guilty,' said Simpson every time.

'You may sit down.' The judge, a senior member of the Queen's Bench Division, adjusted his half-moon spectacles and peered at the prisoner.

The Queen's Counsel, an attractive blonde in her forties, who had been briefed to appear for the prosecution, rose from the front bench, hitched her gown back on to her left shoulder, and opened the case for the Crown.

'My Lord and members of the jury,' she began, in pleasant and mellifluous tones, 'during the course of this trial, I shall seek to prove to you that this case arises out of the naked greed and unfettered criminality of the accused. Although amassing a great deal of wealth by legitimate means, it was never enough for him. I shall call witnesses who will testify that the accused went on to use that licit money to intimidate and suborn innocent persons. Nor was murder ruled out in order to achieve his ends, and although not committing those murders personally, the accused was the force behind those killings.

'On the face of it, he ran a successful business. But a closer examination of his activities presented a different picture altogether. For several years now, he has been operating a number of criminal enterprises, not the least of which is extortion. Several West End club owners will be called who will testify that the accused employed several persons of bad character to act as enforcers, if I may use that term. By the use of threats and physical violence, by committing arson, rape and murder, these undesirables terrorized vulnerable business people into parting with sums of money for what was laughingly called protection. It was, ladies and gentlemen of the jury, the exact opposite.

Far from being protected, these people were terrified into parting with even more money. But so great was the influence that the accused wielded that their victims were too frightened to go to the police. It is readily admitted that, in some cases, the activities of the victims were illegal, but that is not, nor has it ever been, an excuse for blackmail, extortion and violence.'

With a nonchalant flick of her forefinger the barrister turned over a page in her brief. 'Let us now turn to Hugh Blakemore, until his death the Member of Parliament for the constituency of Millingham.' Once more, she pulled her gown back on to her shoulder, and levelled an unwavering gaze at the jury of four women and eight men. 'Although a backbencher, he decided that part of his job was to investigate organized crime. In the course of those investigations, Mr Blakemore discovered that Charles Simpson was, to coin an apt phrase, the root of much of the evil pervading the West End. And the accused found that Mr Blakemore was getting a little too close for comfort.'

The barrister paused to take a sip of water.

'When Mr Blakemore threatened the accused that he would have the police take certain action against his activities,' the QC continued, 'the accused countered at first by circulating falsehoods about him. He started a rumour that Mr Blakemore was accepting bribes; he suborned other businessmen into believing it to the extent that they passed it on to the police during the course of their enquiries into Mr Blakemore's murder. The accused even circulated the story to Fleet Street newspapers. But, ladies and gentlemen, there was no foundation in that at all.

'It is not denied that Mr Blakemore was short of money, but there is not a shred of evidence that he ever accepted a bribe in his life.

'The threat to the accused's livelihood – nay, his very freedom – had now become so great, so dangerous, that Hugh Blakemore had to be removed.' The QC paused to give dramatic effect to her next statement. 'Quite simply, ladies and gentlemen of the jury, the accused had Mr Blakemore killed.

'During this trial you will hear testimony from four men, namely Michael Lever, Peter Crowley, Barry Todd and Kevin Fagan. I have to tell you that all four have criminal records, but that must not, in this case, influence your judgement of what they will say. The man Lever, ladies and gentlemen, has already pleaded guilty to inciting Todd and Fagan to commit the murder of Hugh Blakemore. Todd and Fagan have been convicted of that crime, and also of the murders of Geoffrey Strang and Solly Goldman. On that basis, therefore, you will see that none of these men has anything to gain by lying.'

The QC paused to take another sip of water. 'It is the Crown's contention that the man on trial here today was directly responsible for those murders, and you may think that the only crime more despicable than murder itself is the crime of inciting another to commit it.

'It is the Crown's further contention that the accused, through contacts within the prison system, first conspired with Lever and a certain Peter Crowley to incite a man called Kenneth Johnson to attack Mr Blakemore on his visit to Melbury prison. Unfortunately for the conspirators, Mr Blakemore was a man well able to defend himself. It is a matter of record, ladies and gentlemen, that Mr Blakemore rebuffed that attack to the extent that the man Johnson fell down a flight of stairs at the prison and was killed. It is necessary to point out that the coroner attributed no blame to Mr Blakemore, and the Crown Prosecution Service concluded that he had acted in self-defence and therefore had no case to answer.'

Counsel adjusted her glasses and glanced down at her brief. 'And so, alternative measures had to be taken. It is now that a certain Geoffrey Strang appears on the scene. Ostensibly a friend of Mrs Blakemore, and later of Mrs Blakemore's daughter, Strang was a weak character, and paid for that weakness with his life. A rather unsuccessful maker of cine-matograph films, Strang was persuaded by the accused, using an intermediary called Paul Tyler, to go to America to make a documentary about the New York harbour master; a docu-mentary, let me say, ladies and gentlemen, that had no chance of being made. It was a device; a device to lay a false trail. Strang was given the names of three American criminals with Mafia connections, and was bribed to offer them a substan-tial fee to murder Mr Blakemore. Whether such a contact was made is not known. But it did not matter. The trail had been laid, the red herring set, so to speak.'

An outburst of coughing from the public gallery caused the silk to stop, and she turned a censorious gaze on the unfortunate sufferer. Waiting until, in an embarrassing silence, the coughing man had sidled out of the court, she turned once more to face the jury.

'Following the failure of this transatlantic mission – if, in fact, it was ever meant to succeed – and in a devious attempt further to mislead, the man Strang was now given a large sum of money and instructed to contact Michael Lever with a view to his putting out what the criminal fraternity calls a contract. A contract on the life of a Member of Parliament.' The barrister's voice rose slightly to lay emphasis on what she clearly believed to be a most un-English crime.

'Lever, who had already been involved in the conspiracy, was under instructions to commission Todd and Fagan to commit the murder. It will be shown that the accused already knew Todd and Fagan, knew of their propensity for violent crime, and you may wonder why he went to this trouble, but as I said earlier, it was a device to put as great a distance as possible between himself and the actual murderers. Following a period of surveillance on the part of Todd and Fagan, we come to Tuesday the second of July, ladies and gentlemen. It was then that, mounted upon a stolen motorcycle, they rode along Fulham Road and, in a cowardly attack in broad daylight, mercilessly gunned down Mr Blakemore. Thus was the confidence, and the contempt for law and order, of the accused.'

The QC stooped and, with a frown on her face, whispered to her junior. There was brief shuffling of papers and the junior handed his leader another document.

'Detective Chief Inspector Brock of New Scotland Yard was appointed to oversee the investigation, and pursued his enquiries with doggedness. It was not very long, therefore, before certain information came to him which, coupled with the results of scientific analysis, led him to question certain suspects. Among those suspects was Geoffrey Strang. So concerned was Strang that he was about to be arrested that he telephoned the accused and threatened to go to the police, make a confession and seek to turn Queen's Evidence. Unfortunately for the accused, that call was itemized on Strang's telephone bill. But, ladies and gentlemen of the jury, it proved to be Strang's death warrant. Two days later, Strang was shot dead while sitting in his car in Golden Square in the West End of London. The murderer was Barry Todd.

'Now that the dual threats, in the shape of Blakemore and Strang, were out of the way, the accused, believing himself to be safe from detection once more, carried on business as usual. Those in what is best described as the vice trade were threatened, and monies extorted from them. One of the men who resisted, Solly Goldman, was murdered. Again, Todd and Fagan were the killers.'

The barrister paused, gave a dry cough and took another sip of water. Plucking a lacy handkerchief from her sleeve, she dabbed at her mouth before continuing. 'Officers of the Metropolitan and City Police Fraud Squad, and Her Majesty's Revenue and Customs began to examine the accused's financial affairs, and they discovered that he had bank accounts in Australia, New York and Amsterdam, and others in the Cayman Islands. Through intermediaries, he lodged monies in those accounts, showing them as payments to agents abroad for the apparently legitimate business of his companies. But this was a device with a dual purpose: to cover his nefarious activities, and to avoid the payment of tax. When he needed that money back here in the United Kingdom, he just showed it as the importation of capital: a computer transaction. You may ask how he could do this without the knowledge of Her Majesty's Treasury, ladies and gentlemen of the jury, but the truth is that they don't mind how much "foreign" money is brought into the country. But having been alerted by the police, Her Majesty's Revenue and Customs undertook extensive enquiries and the evidence of their findings will be laid before you.'

The QC glanced at the clock and then turned to the judge. 'I call Detective Chief Inspector Brock, My Lord,' she said.

Over the next six weeks, witness after witness testified. They were examined, cross-examined and re-examined.

As his task demanded, the QC who appeared for the defence, along with his two juniors, did their best to undermine the prosecution evidence, but it was to no avail.

On the Thursday of the seventh week, after retiring for three and a half days, the jury brought in a verdict of guilty on all the counts on the indictment.

In a dry, penetrating voice, the judge addressed the prisoner.

At some length, he lectured him on the enormity of his crimes and told him that, in his view, he had been rightly convicted.

Then came the sentence.

'Charles Simpson, you will go to prison for life. And I shall recommend that you serve at least forty years before you are considered for parole.'

I was surprised at the severity of the sentence, but I was sufficiently cynical to believe that if one of the victims had not been an MP, the penalty would have been less.

Prior to Charles Simpson's trial, Barry Todd and Kevin Fagan had each been sentenced to three terms of life imprisonment for the murders of Hugh Blakemore, Geoffrey Strang and Solly Goldman, the judge drily pointing out that they would be concurrent. The other offences for which they had been indicted remained on the file. Mickey Lever received a sentence of fifteen years.

The Crown Prosecution Service decided that Anne Blakemore had no case to answer; although possessing guilty knowledge, she had played no active part in the conspiracy, and was too terrified to inform the police.

Paul Tyler was extradited to America where he was convicted of the 1995 murder, and sundry other crimes, and sentenced to life imprisonment without parole. In view of the uncertainty about the underlying reason for Tyler financing Strang's trip to America, the Crown Prosecution Service had decided that there was insufficient evidence to convict him of any direct involvement in the deaths of Hugh Blakemore and Geoffrey Strang, and they declined to prosecute him. In any case, the fact that he was being returned to the United States to face much more serious charges would make any such prosecution pointless.

Todd and Fagan later appealed against conviction; and Simpson and Lever against conviction and sentence. The three appeal court judges could find no flaw in the Old Bailey judge's conduct of their cases and, so far as Simpson and Lever were concerned, saw no reason to interfere with the sentences that had been passed upon them.

Although I was convinced that Gina Watson had been blackmailing Hugh Blakemore, the Crown Prosecution Service decided that there was insufficient evidence to mount a prosecution. But the police investigation had so unsettled her friend

Fiona Savage that she moved to a flat in Teddington, and never spoke to Gina again.

Caroline Simpson at last secured a role in a television serial. When she went to Chelsea to break the good news to her mother, she found Anne dead in bed. The coroner's jury's verdict was that she had died accidentally from a lethal cocktail of drugs and alcohol.

By the way, we never did solve the puzzle of the American passport in the name of Vincent Rosso of Delaware, Ohio, found in the motorcycle leathers used by Todd and Fagan when they murdered Hugh Blakemore. But that's police work for you.